THE MERMAN

Carl-Johan Vallgren

TRANSLATED
FROM THE SWEDISH
BY
ELLEN FLYNN

Published by Hesperus Nova
Hesperus Press Limited
28 Mortimer Street,
London, W1W 7RD

www.hesperuspress.com

This edition first published by Hesperus Press Limited, 2013
© Carl-Johan Vallgren 2013

Carl-Johan Vallgren asserts his moral right to be identified
as the author of this work under the Copyright,
Designs and Patents Act 1988.

Havmannen first published in Swedish by Albert Bonniers

English translation © Ellen Flynn, 2013
The translator's moral rights have been asserted.

Text designed and typeset by Madeline Meckiffe

Printed in Great Britain by CPI Group (UK) Ltd, Croydon, CR0 4YY

ISBN: 978-1-84391-473-0

There is no beginning and no ending. I know that now. For others, perhaps, there are stories that lead somewhere, but not for me. It's like they go round in circles, and sometimes not even that: they just stand still in one place. And I wonder: what are you supposed to do with a story that repeats itself?

In another world, in the stories I told my little brother, there was always a beginning to everything and an ending, and the ending was the most important thing. I used to tell my brother that the beginning might not always be very nice, but the main thing is that it leads up to a point where things get better.

'Once upon a time there was a boy called Robert. He grew up in Skogstorp, a little place outside Falkenberg, in a street that was named after a flower, just like all the other streets in Skogstorp. Together with his mum and dad and his big sister Nella, he lived in a maisonette that was actually an apartment with a garage and a patch of garden. No one had ever bothered to plant anything or sow grass seed in that garden. His mum wasn't the type to take an interest in that sort of thing, and neither was his dad. Robert and Nella's parents were not like other parents. They didn't work, they didn't have a car, they didn't go on holiday with their children in the summer, although there might have been one time they did, but it was so long ago that nobody could remember any more. But that's how things were: their parents were there in the beginning, but they would not be there at the end…'

So I could tell him the story, and he would listen, wide-eyed, as he scratched at the rash between his fingers and waited for the story to take him to a place where everything was far better.

But that was difficult. He had to get past some obstacles first. It's not easy to get from the darkness into the light. That's the point of stories.

'Robert wasn't like the other children in the neighbourhood where they lived. He was shy and clumsy and not that bright in school. He had poor eyesight, and probably had done ever since he was born, because he was forever injuring himself when he was little, walking into walls and sharp corners, stumbling on rocks and kerbs, or on the stone jetty down by the sea in the summertime. But because his mum and dad were the way they were, they never took him to the optician's. It wasn't until he was in Year Two that the school nurse began to suspect something and made an appointment for him with the optician. Then he got glasses that just kept getting stronger every year. The glasses were a whole story in and of themselves. They were almost always held together with tape because the lads at school would snatch them from Robert and break them, and because he was still so clumsy and would walk into things or trip over so they would break, and because his parents didn't care the slightest bit about it, just as they didn't care what their children were up to, what time they came home, how they were doing at school, if they were hungry or thirsty, what they looked like, if their clothes were dirty or torn, if they were happy or sad, healthy or ill. It was Nella who had to look after all that. She was the one who cleaned and tidied the house where they lived. She was the one who did the shopping if there was any money. She was the one who helped Robert with his homework, athough it wasn't particularly hard because he was in the remedial group and had only basic maths and basic English. Nella was the one who looked after him because nobody else did, and because in a way he didn't care what kind of person he was, as if his life were something that had been thrust upon him in passing, with a set of instructions written in a foreign language that he didn't really know how to follow. She was the one who made breakfast and made sure they went off to school. She was the one who washed their clothes. Nella was the one who cooked their meals, although she didn't know how to make that many things, but Robert never complained, he said her food was the best he'd ever eaten, that her boiled sausages were the tastiest, her black pudding was the most delicious, her fish fingers were the best, but he had nothing to compare them with: all he knew was the food from the school dining room.

'Nella was the one who forged the signatures for the sicknotes on the days Robert couldn't make it in to school; she was the one who concerned herself with all the little things that make life bearable, at least for a while. And she was the one who mended his glasses with ordinary tape, and she put a bit of a plaster on one of the lenses because her friend the Professor had told her it could fix his squint. Nella wanted to do more for him, but there wasn't enough time, or resources, or attention. There just wasn't enough of some things, no matter how they rationed them out.'

That's about how I might tell him the story – a story he could recognise himself in, even though it was not pleasant at all. And without his noticing, with little, little words, I continued: 'Nella's name was actually Petronella. She had given herself that nick-name because that was what the kids in Skogstorp called a stinging nettle, and she thought it was a fitting name for someone like her. When she was little, she actually believed that her skin could sting like a jellyfish or a nettle, and that was why people avoided her. She was two years older than Robert and in Year Nine. Besides her classmate Tommy and a guy she called the Professor, she had only her little brother. Maybe, if she thought about it, she really only had him. If she really searched deep in her heart, she would actually choose him ahead of the others. It was as if she'd been born for that reason, she used to think, born to protect him from the ones who called him retarded or idiot. To protect him from the ones who called him a freak. To protect him from the ones who picked on him more and more with every passing year. Because of his glasses, because of his squint, because he was poor at reading and writing but was really as clever as anybody else, because of the eczema on his hands, and because he couldn't hold in his pee when they ganged up on him. Because of all these things. But everything just got worse. More and more joined in, more and more persecuted him. And Nella didn't always manage to come to his defence. There are always places in a school that are out of sight. And she couldn't do anything from her classroom, not when they had a free period at different times, not when they dragged him off into the woods behind the gym.

There is a beginning and there is an ending. And everything has to get worse before it gets better. That's how it always is in stories. It's as if they invite it, as if nature itself invites the pain to intensify before it can ebb away. But one day the pain would disappear. One day, something would happen to change history, to transform it into a new, better story. Something would whisk them away from that time and that place; namely, autumn 1983 in Skogstorp, a small community outside Falkenberg in Sweden; something would put a stop to the story, bring it to a conclusion, and transport them away from there so a new story could begin.'

'Who?' asked my little brother. 'Who's going to come and save us?'

And I didn't know what I was supposed to say. *Someone*, I said.

'Did you really mean what you said about me being just as smart as anybody else?'

'Sure. If only they had discovered your vision problems sooner, you wouldn't have fallen behind.'

'When I was little, I thought I was stupid when I didn't get what the teacher was talking about. But it was just that I couldn't see the letters… Who do you think is going to come and save us?'

'I don't know.'

'Maybe a policeman? Somebody who's really strong. A real hero. Or maybe a big animal. Nella, imagine we had a tame lion. Then nobody would dare do anything to us, would they? Imagine we had one, and we went to school every morning with a lion or a monster, or else it could be a wolf, you know, like the Phantom has, and then we'd tie its lead to the bike racks. Do you think they'd dare do anything then?'

And I could hardly bring myself to look at him out of shame.

'Robert, I promise, one day they'll stop, one day everything will be different, we'll get through it! There's always a beginning, and there's always an ending.'

'Or is it Dad who'll come and save us? When he comes home, I mean. Maybe he's changed. He said he would, he said he'd change everything.'

I shook my head. It was so childish of him to place his hope in Dad.

'No, we can't count on Dad. He's never going to change. But something else will happen that changes everything – I just know it.'

That was what I kept telling him. And he believed me, for a little while at least, because I was the only person in the world he trusted, because I was his big sister and two years older, and there was nothing else that could help him.

FALKENBERG, OCTOBER 1983

It's strange, the things you manage to notice even when you're running for all you're worth: the reddish-brown berries that had rotted on a bush next to the climbing frame; the shadow in front of me; my own shadow, which was dashing ahead like a leviathan with its underside in a shallow inlet. Puddles in the long-jump pit with autumn leaves floating in them. A red cap somebody had lost on the running track – the same colour as the gravel, just a shade deeper, not dissimilar to blood. Gerard was standing in the smoking area, trying to light a fag. He was fifty metres away. I still knew it was him, though: I could see his hands cupped round the lighter. He had gloves on, leather gloves. At any rate, he wasn't with the others down in the woods.

I managed to think that: at any rate, Gerard wasn't with the others down in the woods. The boy had something seriously wrong in his mind. It was as if the parts of his brain were connected up the wrong way. And all of this was connected with Gerard: the reason I was running like a madman was down to him and what had happened eight months before.

It had been in February, behind the newsagent's kiosk by the main E6 road, maybe around eight in the evening. I was there to buy some fags for Mum. Gerard and his gang were standing a little way off, over by the crazy golf course that was boarded up for the winter.

'My fingers are bloody freezing in this cold,' he said. 'We can warm ourselves up on the damned cat.'

And then he laughed that Gerard laugh that sounds almost kind-hearted, even though you know it's exactly the opposite.

I couldn't understand anything. Warm yourself on a cat? The

others laughed as well, Peder and Ola, and a few younger lads that people usually call the trailers, because they follow Gerard around wherever he goes and carry out his orders without batting an eyelid: clearing up after him in the school dining room, carrying his stuff around, running errands, nicking fags and sweets, stealing booze from their parents' drinks cabinets, getting petrol for his scooter – anything their leader might require.

It was a kitten. He had it in a plastic carrier bag hanging from the handlebar of his scooter. As I stood in the queue at the kiosk I watched him pick it up and cuddle it, stroking it against his cheek like a living cuddly toy and scratching it behind the ears as he gave meaningful glances to the others. It was no bigger than a small rabbit, black with a white patch on its chest. I heard him say that it was purring like an engine, and it did not protest when he held it up by the scruff of the neck. Maybe it belonged to one of the trailer lads, or maybe one of their younger siblings. It wouldn't surprise me: Gerard could very well have asked one of them to bring it along from home. Or perhaps it had just been unlucky enough to turn up in the wrong place at the wrong time.

'I'm freezing,' said Gerard. 'Is there somebody who can give us a bit of juice?'

The lads in the scooter gang would often siphon off petrol for him when he ran out. Peder, Gerard's right-hand man, took out a length of plastic hose, stuck one end into the tank on his Dakota and started siphoning petrol into an empty soft drink bottle.

'Can you hold the bag?' said Gerard, handing over the carrier bag the kitten was in. 'Open it,' he said.

Peder opened it.

'And now the petrol, please.'

Gerard was handed the bottle, took a sniff, wrinkled up his nose and then poured its contents into the carrier bag. The kitten let out a little shriek inside. 'Now give it a bloody good shake, Peder. I want that damn cat to be completely fucking marinated in petrol. Otherwise it'll go out in five seconds.'

Peder gave a little giggle, uncertain of what was going to happen. 'You're not going to do it, are you?' he asked. 'Gerard, for fuck's sake, you can't set fire to a kitten in a carrier bag. There'll be an explosion.'

Gerard giggled back. The trailers giggled. That was what they were expected to do.

'Of course I'm going to fucking do it. I said I was freezing, didn't I?'

'Okay, then let's move,' said Ola to the others. 'Move further away, lads. A definite risk of explosion here…'

There was not a person in sight. The woman in the kiosk couldn't see anything from her angle. It was a Saturday night in February, and a couple of inches of snow had fallen that afternoon. Then the rain had come and transformed everything into slush. People were staying indoors, watching light entertainment programmes or the feature film on TV. Robert was with Mum. Dad had recently disappeared again and would be away for nearly a year.

I went over to the cycle rack to fetch my bike. I did not want to become a witness to something I would be sorry for. I saw Gerard tie up the carrier bag and I remember thinking, he's not going to do it. Not even Gerard is that sick.

He placed the bag down on the asphalt, took the soft drink bottle that was still a quarter full of petrol, and carefully poured out a thin fuse line over towards the fence. The trailers were worried now; you could see it in their movements, as if they were itching.

'So you're gonna do it?' asked Peder. He had pulled up his top lip to expose his teeth in a wolf's grin. He was enjoying this almost as much as Gerard, but he would never dare to do it himself.

'I fucking said so already. I'm freezing, innit.'

The kitten was stirring around in the bag. Perhaps it was starting to get low on air, perhaps it was starting to panic. A slender paw was sticking out of the plastic. She was trying to claw her way out.

'And just what the hell are you staring at, you fucking bitch?' asked Ola.

It took a few seconds before I realised he was referring to me. I couldn't tear my eyes away from the bag on the ground, the way it was writhing and pulsating, like something being born from a soft egg.

'Nothing,' I said as I inserted my key into the lock and started to walk towards the road.

'That fucking slimy cunt,' I heard Peder continue. 'Her and her fucking retard brother in the class for mongs. You can't even tell whether she's a boy or a girl. No tits, not even any hair on her cunt. And she bloody stinks. I don't think they've got a washing machine at home. Maybe not even a shower.'

'Will you shut up?' said Gerard. 'Give me the lighter.'

He didn't care about me. As far as he was concerned, I could have been made out of thin air. He had hardly ever seen me, even though we had been in the same class together since primary school.

I carried on towards the pedestrian crossing. The smell of petrol stung my nose. They were going to kill it, I thought, and there was nothing I could do.

They're going to kill him and there's nothing I can do. They're going to kill him and there's nothing I can do. That was a new earworm now, going round and round as if a radio had got stuck in my head. My lungs were about to explode. The shouting from the woods rose and fell, sometimes louder, sometimes softer. I didn't see any teachers. Not even the caretaker, who went round with his rake and wheelbarrow with a grouchy expression. Where were all the adults? L.G., the playground supervisor, the security guy? Then I remembered: it was a teacher's birthday. They were having cake in the staff room.

Faces looked up at me in surprise as I ran like a madman, as if I was fleeing from a murderer or a wild animal that had escaped from a circus. Pupils on their way back to their classrooms, mostly Year Sevens and Year Eights in their jackets and down-filled body-warmers. Had they come from the woods, had they seen what they did to him, and sneaked off because they didn't want to be witnesses?

I could taste blood in my mouth now. Someone was laughing at me: a girl from Morup, who was also called Ironing Board, just like me. Everywhere fallen leaves on the asphalt. The colours were

almost soaking up into my eyes. A week ago there had been a
storm and the trees had dropped the remains of their autumn
apparel. Red leaves. Yellow. Like blood and tattered entrails. More
faces ran past like water, some from my brother's year, the ones
who usually were nasty to him, calling him a mong and a retard,
or 'pissypants' because he could not control his bladder out of
pure fear, but now doing something else, on their way up to the
common rooms to hang up their coats and head off to the next
lesson. Further away, by the car park, a teacher stood talking to
a parent. But I didn't even have time to call over to them, and
anyway the distance was too great, they wouldn't have heard.

Past the gym and the plants. Two Year Nines came along, each
with a lolly in their mouth, avoiding eye contact with me. I could
hear my brother's voice now, very clearly, he was really screaming,
like an animal being slaughtered. I had never heard him so terrified before. I wondered where Tommy was keeping himself. Why
wasn't he running up to me? Then I remembered: he hadn't been
at school since last Wednesday. Presumably he was ill or maybe he
was helping his brothers with their boat. I had rung him every day,
but no one answered...

They were going to kill it, and there was nothing I could do. I don't know
why the cat was on my mind again. It had been last winter, shortly
after Dad had disappeared again. Yes, I did know why. I didn't
want to deceive myself; didn't want to be like Mum and just stick
my head in the sand. I knew why I was running. I knew why they
had singled out my brother. Gerard had figured out that I had
blabbed. That morning there was a note in my locker. It said that
L.G. had found out what had happened last winter, that Gerard
had to go up to the headmaster's office, that it must have been me
who had blabbed and that they would take it out on Robert.

I remember how I had walked away from the kiosk with my bike,
very leisurely so as not to get Peder and Gerard het up. They're
like animals, I had thought; if I started to run it could trigger their
hunting instinct.

'Oi, Ironing Board, come here a minute.' It was clear who Gerard was talking to. For some reason he had decided to notice my presence. 'Or whatever the hell your name is. I said stop.'

I halted mid-step. He might be serious, I thought: after nine years in the same class together, after thousands of hours of lessons in the same classroom, despite having posed in all those class photos together, maybe he never had learnt my name. It was entirely possible, and would explain an awful lot.

'I want you to pay attention to this,' he said. 'And if I want anyone to have it confirmed, like somebody who isn't here, who might be doubtful, who claims I would never do it, then I'll tell them they can ask you. You get me? Ask Ironing Board, I'll say. She was there. Like a witness, you get me?'

He smiled at me, all friendly, as if this was any run-of-the-mill matter of confidence.

'I can't rely on Peder and Ola. They just say what I tell them to say. Everybody knows that. So that's why I want you to watch. Stand over here.'

I put down the kickstand on my bike and went over towards him.

'That's enough,' Gerard said matter-of-factly. 'Don't come any closer, you really do reek, just like everybody says.'

I was maybe five metres from them. There was another paw sticking out of the carrier bag, scratching at the ground. The mewing was a bit quieter now.

'Are you really gonna do it?' asked Peder again. 'You're fucking nuts.'

'What do you think, faggot? That I'm some kind of animal torturer? No way.'

Gerard suddenly no longer seemed to care about the cat. He took a few steps to the side, took a piss out into the evening darkness, tapped out a cigarette from a packet of Prince, put it in the corner of his mouth and started flicking his lighter. Only a few feeble sparks came out, like those from a damp sparkler.

'You thought I'd do it, didn't you?' he asked.

Peder laughed. 'Well, yeah, what the hell was I supposed to think? You poured petrol over it.'

'Honestly, do I look like a guy who tortures defenceless animals? Do I? Ola, what have you got to say?'

Gerard looked almost concerned. You could sense uncertainty spreading among the trailers.

'Dunno, really.'

'*Dunno*? So you have no opinion?'

'Same opinion as you.'

'And what opinion do I have, exactly?'

'Like I said: dunno.'

Gerard shook his head, disappointed.

'Shit, I'm freezing,' he said quietly. And then he turned to me as he managed to produce a flame with his lighter: 'What are you looking at, you fucking bitch? Did I say you could look at me, huh? Who the hell gave you permission to do that?'

I was down in the woods now, the cat memory had vanished. I followed the path among the birch trees, stumbled over fallen branches, over a root that was sticking up, carried on past the mound of stones where Robert would play on his own when he was in his upper years of primary school and I couldn't protect him because I had started Year Seven and was in a different part of the school complex. I remembered how I used to search for him there in the afternoons. He was only ten and was always on his own. The other kids had gone home or else were having fun with their mates in the playground. He used to sit on a big rock in his worn discount jeans and look at me as if I were a messenger from a distant planet. His wispy hair that fell over his forehead. The eczema on his hands that kept getting worse, even though I helped him to rub cream into them every day. His glasses, almost always broken and held together with tape. I had to cajole him to get him to come away from there. That was when things were at their worst at home, and if it had been up to my brother he would have slept in the woods overnight – maybe even lived there for the rest of his life…

I carried on up the little hill and stood at the top. It was completely silent now. I could no longer hear the shrieks. In the distance behind me, the schoolyard stood deserted. The ceiling lights were on in the classrooms; I saw silhouettes of people sitting down at their desks. *There is always a beginning and an ending. They've killed him. It's not what they wanted to do, but that's what happened, the stakes were raised. And I wasn't able to protect him, I wasn't there when he needed me.* My heart was pounding as if it were an animal trying to escape from my chest, to claw its way out, like the cat had wanted to claw its way out of the carrier bag last winter… Gerard's face had looked almost resigned as he crouched down and set fire to the invisible fuse of petrol. It must have gone very fast, and yet I remember it as if it had lasted several minutes. The fire must have reached the bag in just a few seconds, but in my memory it wended its way over the asphalt like a long, luminescent snake, over towards the wriggling, mewling bag. There was an explosion, but it wasn't particularly loud, more like a banger, sort of like a miniature firecracker.

'Bloody hell,' said Peder. 'I didn't think you would do it.'

'I said I would. I'm freezing… Take a look at the fucker!'

I hadn't known until then that it was trussed up. Each pair of legs was bound together with wire. And it was still trying to run, limping round in a little circle as if it were chasing its tail. It looked like a little burning carousel. The noise it emitted was reminiscent of a whimpering infant. Flames rose up from its fur, as if it were electric. You could hear the plastic melting, it sort of fizzled around the cat's fur. Its ears were like two pointed wicks on lit candles. The cat opened its jaws, and it looked like it wanted to say something. And for a moment that's what I actually thought: that it wanted, to say *stop*, or *what are you doing, have you gone completely mad?* in plainly comprehensible language. But instead its mouth and tongue began to burn, and then it grew silent. It did not emit any more sounds, just ran after its own tail, in an ever-decreasing circle, like a small, fiery swivel chair, and you could hear how the plastic was melting into its skin, how its nose and eyelids were melting, and then came the smell of summer, of barbecues in the garden, of charred meat from the back garden, that scent of food and smoke that hangs over Falkenberg long into August after the last holidaymakers have gone home. Finally it simply lay down. Collapsed under its own weight. Its nose had fused with the plastic somehow, it was lying with its mouth open and panting. Staring straight ahead, wild-eyed, because its eyelids had been burnt off. Loud wheezes came from its windpipe, like those from mine as I stood on the brow of the hill looking down over the woods. Staring and blinking away tears, staring again, alert to the slightest movement among the trees.

I went down the slope. Not a single movement anywhere. Had they let him go? Was he in his classroom right now, reading aloud from the remedial maths book, where everything was far too easy and so difficult for him for precisely that reason? Had they suddenly let him go when the bell rang? I knew that wasn't what it was, yet I couldn't help hoping, wishing, just as I had done my whole life, trying to wish and hope away everything terrible, like trying to change the course of events by sheer will.

There was a small clump of trees over to the left. His cap was hanging in a fork in the branches.

'Robert?'

No reply. Just the sound of the wind that had started to blow, bringing with it the smells from the sea.

I continued through a thicket of juniper bushes. For the first time I noticed how cold it was. I had left my jacket in the common room. Through the window I had seen them dragging him off, towards the gym: Peder, Ola and the trailers; I'd seen how he was trying to resist in absolute terror, I dropped my books on the floor right then and there and raced towards the doors. Someone grabbed hold of me by the exit, I couldn't remember who it was, somebody who wanted to stop me helping him, but somehow I broke free, ran in the opposite direction down the corridor and got out through the Year Eight door. By that time I couldn't see him anywhere.

'Robert? Where are you?'

A slow movement just behind me. But when I turned round, there was no one there. Only a lone crow flying off between the trees.

'Robert!' I shouted. 'Can you hear me?'

Thirty metres away was the fence that marked the western boundary of the school grounds. There were only fields and gravel tracks on the other side, leading down to the sea. I leaned against a tree trunk, shut my eyes and listened.

You're a witness to this, Ironing Board, if any of my mates ask. Gerard did it, you'll say. Nobody believed he'd dare, but he actually did it. He's crazy!

The plastic had melted into the flesh. Its stomach had burst, guts had come out – intestines, I think. Peder had looked away in disgust. There was a strange glow coming from its hindquarters. Gerard, that sick bastard, tried to light his cigarette on the body. 'Can you feel it?' he asked, 'it's warmer now. I was fucking freezing before. It's better now.'

Eight months had passed since then, and suddenly, today, they had got it into their heads that I had blabbed and decided to take their revenge out on my brother. I didn't understand any of it. Somebody else must have seen them by the newsagent's kiosk that night. That was the only explanation. The question was, why hadn't they come forward until now?

'Here he is, Ironing Board!'

The voice came from the other direction, beyond some juniper bushes… Robert was squatting with his face turned towards the ground. Blood was dripping from his nose. His eyes were shut and he looked like he was sleeping. His trousers had been pulled down and they were wet; he had wet himself out of fear. They had stuffed things into his pants: pine cones, twigs, pages ripped out of his maths book. There were pine needles and grass sticking out of his nostrils and mouth, and a cigarette in one ear. Four lads from the trailer were standing round him in a semicircle. Behind were Ola and Peder.

'What the hell have you done?' I asked. It must have sounded ridiculous, because at the same time I was relieved they hadn't had a chance to do anything worse. It was nothing personal. It was me they wanted to get at, and the easiest way to get at me was through Robert.

'Does it feel better now, you fucking mong?' someone asked, nudging him with their trainers. 'Get up! God, he's disgusting. Totally pissed himself.'

'This is because you snitched on Gerard. Hope you get this into your head, Ironing Board. It's your fault your brother's pissed his pants.'

I recognised him from the games room, where Gerard would hold court during free periods. A big lad in Year Seven. Robert had pointed him out once, he was one of the ones who was always nasty to him. I wondered where he had been when they burnt the cat alive. I couldn't recall.

When we started secondary school we were given a leaflet about what to do in situations like this: *When pupils are treated badly by others: contact the school welfare officer, teachers or head of year.* I remember how I'd just laughed at that. That would have just made everything ten times worse. *Tell your parents if you are unable to contact the school administration yourself.* Some words bear no relation to reality. And it doesn't enter other people's realm of consciousness that someone could have a mother and father like mine.

I put a hand under Robert's chin and gingerly raised his head. They had drawn things in ink on his cheeks. A cock on one, a swastika on the other. They'd written 'mong boy' on his forehead. He still had his eyes shut, and I could understand. Why should he look out onto such a vile world?

'It's my fault,' I whispered. 'Forgive me, Robert. It's me they wanted to get at.'

'Doesn't he look nice?' One of the lads gave him a scratch behind the ear as if he were an animal, maybe a dog. He was still wearing his glasses. The plaster on the left side that I had stuck on there was black with dirt. One of the arms was loose, but it could be mended. That's what I was thinking about: practical things. How it was better in any case than if the lenses were broken or if they had chucked them into the woods. It could take several weeks f or the school nurse to get hold of new ones, and during that time he wouldn't be able to see and would get even further behind in his lessons.

'*If there's a beginning then there is an ending,*' I whispered, '*and the ending is always better.*'

I crouched down and put my arms round him, exactly the way I used to do when he was little. He shivered slightly, as if he were cold. I could hear his heart fluttering in his chest, like a terrified little bird. '*There is a beginning, but you don't need to worry about that. It's the end that counts, because that's where a new, better story begins.*'

Maybe it was stupid of me to whisper to him. In the animal kingdom, a simple sound or movement from the prey is sufficient for the slaughter to begin.

'Move it, Ironing Board. He hasn't finished eating his lunch.'

That was Peder. I'd sort of tried to forget he and Ola were there. And that Gerard was probably pulling the strings behind the scenes. He didn't even need to be there in person; he issued orders to the others, who carried them out to the letter. Or maybe it was Peder's own idea – something he was doing to get on his boss's good side?

'That's what happens when people blab, Ironing Board.'

'I didn't blab!'

'Sure. But how many people were actually there? Us and Gerard and then the old lady in the newsagent's, but she couldn't see anything from where she was.'

He turned to Robert and tried to imitate Gerard's friendly psychopath voice:

'We told your sister to be a witness and say what she'd seen if somebody didn't believe us. And of course what we meant was if one of the lads at school doubted us, not some fucking teacher or a cop. But your stupid cow of a sister must have misunderstood everything.'

The trailers appeared unsure what they should do. Their energy was in the process of ebbing away. Someone needed to act to make things start to happen again. Ola tore up a handful of grass and started stuffing it into my brother's mouth. I tried to cover his face, but someone grabbed me by the hair and dragged me off along the woodland path.

'Have you seen his disgusting scaly fingers, it looks like he's got fucking leprosy. Eat up some more hay, you goddamned donkey. This is because your sister blabbed…' They prised open his face and shoved more grass into his mouth and nose, I could hear him spluttering, heard his gag reflex, and knew I couldn't leave him in the lurch again. I screamed, or at any rate I heard something distantly reminiscent of my own voice, I scratched at the hands that were tearing at my hair, turned round so I ended up on my belly. Now there were several hands pulling at my hair. Someone must have come over to help out. I didn't say anything; dirt and pine needles were poking into my eyes, I shut my eyes and lashed out until someone caught hold of my arms and pinned them up against my back.

'Lie still now, you little cunt.' And then there were hands tearing off my trousers and knickers, ripping them off as if pain had no meaning, as if I were something to which they could do whatever they wanted because I wasn't really alive, hands trying to stuff something into my arse without even bothering to spread my bum cheeks apart, just shoving something sharp and spiny, and I hoped it wouldn't break apart in there.

My vision was starting to turn black. When I could see again, they had turned me round a hundred and eighty degrees so I could see my brother where he was sitting hunched up on the path, five metres behind me, with grass sticking out of his mouth, nose and ears, like a strange scarecrow.

'Now go and feed your sister. Give her some fresh straw. She needs to have a reward so she won't blab any more in the future. Then she can go. But we're keeping you. It feels like we're not finished with you yet…'

It was the commander who had turned up at last: Gerard had sort of materialised among the trees in an unbuttoned leather jacket, trainers with the laces undone, gloves on and his friendly psychopath's smile. The trailers led my brother over to me, where I lay on my front with my arms pinned against my back. He screwed up his eyes for all he was worth as he knelt down in front of me.

'It doesn't matter,' I said. 'I promise. Do what they say, Robert.'

And then I turned to the boss:

'There must be some way to solve this, mustn't there?'

'I can't really hear what you're saying.'

'I said, there must be some way to solve… for you to let him go.'

'Still can't hear. Can you speak up?'

'How much do you want to leave us alone? I can get hold of some money.'

He lit a cigarette and exhaled smoke through his nostrils, like two grey tusks.

'That depends. How much do you value your brother? What do you reckon is a fair price? Fifteen hundred?'

'You can have as much as you want. Just so long as you leave him alone.'

'To be honest, I don't think he's worth fifteen hundred. You can haggle him down a bit. Let's say nine hundred… or a thousand kronor. Then we'll leave him alone for the rest of term. So the next question is, when can you pay?'

I could no longer speak and just stared down at the ground, the green moss and the fallen leaves.

'Did I hear one week? Then we have an agreement. Next Friday. Otherwise, he'll basically be mine, your little brother. Sort of like a security deposit.'

'Here, have a little feed,' I heard Peder hiss to my brother, 'and go and feed your cow of a sister until she's right full up. She wants to, she said so herself. Come on, you fucking spacker!'

Tears ran down his cheeks as they placed a fistful of grass in his hand. He held it out towards me, keeping his eyes shut. But I did not flinch. There was one way to get out of this, for them to leave us alone, at least for the time being. And so, like a confused animal, I began to eat grass and pine needles out of my brother's outstretched hand.

The sun was lower in the sky now; in a few hours it would be dark. Nothing would separate the sea from the sky. Trawl nets lay spread out to dry on the grassy slope behind us. Hawsers and anchor chains rolled up like skeletons of gigantic sea serpents. Music was coming from one of the fisherman's huts. A truck drove past on Glumstensvägen, beeped at someone, and disappeared in a cloud of exhaust fumes. The smell of fish permeated the sea air. It was constantly there in the background, like the main ingredient in all the other smells.

We each sat on our own bench and looked out over the dock. Herring gulls crouched in an endless row along the pier. On the quayside there were small piles of ice that had fallen out of the fish crates when they had been offloaded from the boats that morning. A wild mink slid into the water over by the boat launch.

'How are things?' I asked my brother.

'All right. How are you doing?'

'Okay.'

He blushed. Removed his glasses and then put them back on; a nervous gesture I'd seen him perform thousands of times before.

'I saw what they tried to do to you. Stuff a pine cone up there... how sick can people be?'

'It's all right. It didn't start bleeding, at any rate. Did you see the mink over there?'

He watched it without much interest as it swam some way beyond the quay, with its head above the surface like a little periscope, much more graceful in the water than you could have imagined.

'So what have we actually done to them, Gerard and those guys?'

'I happened to see when they set fire to a cat last winter. And now they've got it into their heads that I snitched on them.'

'Well, did you?'

'Nah.'

'And what has it got to do with me?'

'Not a thing. Other than the fact you happen to be my brother.'

The waves struck against the breakers in front of the outer dock. If I turned to face south I could see the old lighthouse, which whisked its light over the harbour at night. Other than the mink and the gulls, there was not another living soul to be seen. The music from the hut had stopped. Oddly, there was no wind.

'That's not your fault, Nella. If they didn't have a reason they would have made one up. If you're sick enough to set fire to a cat, you can come up with anything. Do you think Dad would have been able to do something if he'd been here?'

My little brother has a load of over-inflated hopes concerning our father. Maybe because he doesn't know him as well as I do. It would soon be a year since the last time we'd seen him. And when you're twelve, going on thirteen in December, that's long enough to start to forget certain things and remember others that do not completely correspond to reality.

'I'm sorry to disappoint you, but no.'

'Well, I'm sure he could do something. When he's back home I'll tell him everything, I'll tell him their names and where they live, and I promise you, he'll sort them out. He'll bash them so hard they won't dare to breathe a word again.'

He sort of nodded to himself, as if he were watching everything on an internal cinema screen, and I wondered how sick the situation had seemed in my brother's eyes as I lay there in the woods on my front with my knickers pulled down, a pine cone between my buttocks, eating grass out of his hands.

'Actually, that's not a wild mink,' I said in order to change the subject. 'Its fur is too nice. It's probably escaped from one of the mink farms.'

'I didn't know they could swim.'

'Dad told me once. Remember, he worked on a mink farm when you were little. Anyway, sometimes they manage to escape from their cages, and then they usually head for the sea to hunt for fish.'

I kept my gaze fixed on the surface of the water, but the mink was gone. It had probably swum back to the dock underwater.

'Are you going to pay a thousand kronor?'

'I don't have any choice.'

'But how are you going to get hold of that much money?'

'It'll work out somehow…'

My brother picked up a stone and chucked it out into the water. The eczema between his fingers was about to split open. The cream had run out. I had forgotten to buy another tube. I mustn't forget the next time I was in town.

'What do you want to do?' I asked. 'Head home or stay here a while?'

'Home to what?'

'No, of course. You're right…'

Maybe, I thought, it had been a mistake to offer money to Gerard so he would leave us alone. How was I going to get hold of a thousand kronor within a week? And what made me believe that he would be satisfied with that much?

I looked over towards the houses that were huddled behind fences and dense hedges above the harbour. I could see the roof of the detached house where Tommy lived. I ought to ask him for advice. Maybe go over and visit him, even though he was ill, and ask to speak to him, or ring him up later that evening. Or make another attempt to get hold of the Professor.

After everything that had happened, there was no question of going back to school that day. When Gerard and his gang had disappeared, I took my brother by the hand and went over to the cycle racks. Somewhere inside the school building, some teachers had just recorded us as absent. Perhaps they had asked our classmates if they knew anything. I could see in my mind's eye how everyone in the class shook their heads and tried to look innocent, except for Gerard, Ola and Peder, who just giggled, totally cool and calm. A report would be sent to the school welfare officer. A letter would be sent to Mum, which she would not even endeavour to open. I myself would be summoned to a meeting with L.G., our head of year, and as usual I would deny that there was any particular reason that I had gone off with my brother and played truant that afternoon; oh, no, nothing in particular had happened, we just felt a bit out of sorts, I'd say. And it was Friday and there were only three lessons left.

'Let's go down to the sea,' I had told my brother. 'We'll get a new pair of trousers for you first, though, and wash off what they wrote on your forehead.'

So we took our cycles to Glommen, my ladies' bike which I had found in a skip last spring, and Robert's little bike, which I had managed to scavenge from the Professor so he'd have something to get around on.

We would cycle to Glommen quite often in the summer, to meet up with Tommy or to look at the boats when they returned with their catch. But it felt strange to be there on an ordinary school day in October. Desolate, somehow. No kids running around. No tourists. No fish vans arriving from the wholesalers. Maybe it was the silence that caused me to peer out towards the fisherman's hut where somebody had been playing music. Two silhouettes moved about behind the dirty window, bent down, tried to lift something heavy, gave up, straightened up and caught their breath.

'Where do you think Lazlo is keeping himself?' asked my brother. He had taken his glasses off and was looking at them indecisively.

'I don't know. Maybe in town. Or maybe he didn't want to have any visitors and was hiding under his bed. He's like that sometimes.'

We had cycled past the Professor's farmhouse on our way to Glommen. I had got it into my head that we ought to tell him what had happened. Not because I expected he'd be able to help us, but there are some things you just have to let out. We had peeked in through the kitchen windows. It looked the same as usual inside: a load of books and notebooks where he wrote down things he'd read somewhere and thought were interesting. Medicine bottles scattered around on shelves and tables. And then all the stuff he collects: stuffed birds, fossils, old coins and stamps… We had gone round the house and peeked into the barn: the Amazon was still there, which indicated that he wasn't far away. We called out for him a few times, but if he was in the vicinity he didn't reply. And so we cycled on to Glommen.

That was what I was thinking as we sat there on the quayside: not even the Professor had been any help, and there were two whole days to go until Monday. Two days of an all-too-brief chance to catch our breath before the school week started up again…

'I hate these glasses,' my brother said. 'I look like a nutter in them. Like a monster in a pair of cyclops glasses. That's why everybody's out to get me. People can't stand being around a freak.'

I took them from him, adjusted the earpiece that was bent, polished the lenses with the sleeve of my jumper and handed them back.

'I'll buy you new ones,' I said. 'I'll get a job this summer. And the first thing I'll do when I get paid is find you a nicer pair.'

'You serious?'

'A hundred per cent! If you pay extra, you can get the lenses ground so they're not even half as thick.'

Robert smiled slightly. Then he grew serious again.

'Where are you going to get a job?'

'At Torsåsen. They always need people. You earn twenty-five kronor an hour packing chicken. And if I don't get a job there, I'll look for something else. I'll be sixteen next year. Then I can work anywhere.'

He chucked a new stone into the water.

'You can't just leave me at home with Mum. You can't move out.'

'What makes you think I'm going to do that?'

'You'll be an adult soon, and then you can do whatever you want.'

He was on the verge of crying again, but he tried to hide it by turning his face away.

We sat in silence for a while. The door of the hut opened. Two men stepped out into the sunlight, noticed us, froze and went back into the dark again. The door was shut quickly. They looked like Tommy's brothers, but I wasn't sure. Their boat was usually moored on the southern quay, but I couldn't recall its name. The boats down here all had the same combination of letters, but with different numbers: FG 31 Lyngskär, FG 40 Tuna…

'If I move out, you can come along.'

'What if Mum says no?'

'She won't even notice anything. And if she does, we'll go so far away that nobody will find us…'

That was a game we'd been carrying on for as long as I could remember. When things were at their worst at home, we would lock ourselves into my room, get under the bed with a torch and then Robert would start asking questions and I would answer. Like a happy story about the future.

I looked at him as he sat beside me on the quay. He had grown nearly four inches over the summer, but he was still small for his age. He looked so brittle, like he was made of glass or something, and I suddenly remembered him through all his ages up to now. From when I had helped him learn to walk, even though I was just little myself; the years in town and then in Skogstorp, where I had protected him from the other children; how I reassured him, helped him with his homework, tried to cheer him up and make his life as pain-free as possible, given the circumstances. But there is always an ending and a beginning. That's how it is with every story.

'We can't just run away,' he said now. 'How would we get by?'

'We'll find jobs somewhere.'

'I'm not even thirteen. You're not allowed to hire underage children.'

'We'll have to make you older.'

'With a false beard and a fake ID?'

'Something like that.'

'And where will we live?'

'In a city, far away from here.'

'I don't like cities. I want to live in the countryside.'

'Then that's what we'll do. In a place where nobody knows who we are. Where nobody will find us. Not even Mum or Dad, if – against all the odds – they should decide to look for us. We can make up a whole new history. We can say that we came there with a circus, but it was so badly paid that we ran away. We can make up new names for ourselves.'

'Will we live in a house or a flat?'

'We can live in an old farmhouse, like the Professor.'

'No. I want to live in a new house. And there has to be nice furniture. And a video player and a stereo. Not like the ones we have at home, or like at the Professor's.'

'We'll get all those things.'

'And new glasses, of course?'

'That's the first thing we'll get.'

'And nice clothes. No rubbish from the Red Cross or oversized kecks from the discount store that people laugh at. We'll have proper jeans, brand-name ones. We'll buy everything new.'

And perhaps that was exactly what we would do someday, if only an opportunity would present itself. But not as soon as my little brother dreamt it. We were forced to be patient. Until the spring, when I would leave school, and then nobody would be able to force me to do anything. I'd be able to get a job and my own place to live. Mum wouldn't even notice if I moved out. And then Robert could stay there as much as he wanted.

The only problem was that he had to attend school for another two years, and I wouldn't be able to be there and look out for him. He had to make it on his own, otherwise social services might get involved and place him with a foster family somewhere, and that was the worst thing that could happen in my world.

'Anyway, I think things will get better when Dad comes home.'

'Why do you think that?'

'I just do.' He was lost in thought now. I noticed it in his eyes: it was as if a lamp had been switched off inside, and he had disappeared into a place where the world was exactly as he wished it would be.

'I'll bring him along to school, and we'll go down the corridors and I'll point out everybody who's been nasty to you and me – no, maybe not everybody, because there wouldn't be enough time for that, but I'd point out the worst ones, and then Dad will sort them out.'

'What do you think he'll do to them?'

'Nobody will dare to put up a fight when he gets as furious as he can get. Come here you bastards, he'll say to them, and then they'll obey because they won't dare to do anything else. And then we'll walk through the school together, and Dad will clear everybody out of the way.'

'What if some teachers come and tell him not to?'

'He'll just laugh at them. "My son isn't going to be in any damn remedial class any more", he'll say. "You can all go to hell. We're never coming back!" Then we'll go out to the car park, and Dad will have a car there, and everybody will have to get in his car and we'll drive off with them.'

'Where to?'

'To some place where nobody will come looking. Like a hideout. And then we'll lock them inside, in a cellar maybe. Or we'll throw them down an old well or something. We'll keep them captive there, chained and tied up, and every day I'll go there with Dad and do the same things to them they've done to me…'

He stopped talking and smiled to himself. I didn't say anything. This was something completely new to me. I had never heard him fantasise about revenge before.

The mink had turned up again. It was sitting on the boat launch, drying itself in the sun. It seemed to be keeping us under surveillance, at least that's what it felt like. Over by the fisherman's hut things were silent, but the men were still in there. It was Tommy's brothers, I was almost certain now. I could see their silhouettes through the window. They were moving things around, dragging something back and forth across the floor.

I don't know what it was, but something in the atmosphere had changed subtly, like in a film when the background music you hadn't really noticed suddenly stops. Maybe it was just the day that caught up with me, the thought that Gerard had got it into his head that I had snitched and he had threatened to do even nastier things to my brother if I didn't come up with a thousand kronor; and that it was all my own fault, that I was the one who had planted the idea in his head.

The rumble of the school bus came from over on Glumstensvägen. Soon the Glommen kids would get off by the bus shelter. Maybe someone would come down to the quays and the huts. I didn't want that to happen. I didn't want to encounter anybody from school right now, so I stood up.

'Come on,' I said to my brother. 'We're going...'

Two overflowing bin bags were sitting on the floor in the hall. A third one had fallen over and spilled out its contents over the floor. There was a puddle of vomit in front of the door to the loo: red wine, I assumed, mixed with food remnants. The apartment was silent. Presumably she was lying asleep upstairs. She wouldn't wake up if you chucked a hand grenade in through the window.

'God, it stinks,' said Robert.

'I'll sort it. Meanwhile, you can watch TV.'

He hung up his jacket, took a detour round the accident scene and disappeared into the living room.

In the kitchen, two empty bottles of Parador, that cheap Spanish wine, stuck out from the mess on the worktop. On the table there was a half-full wine glass with a dozen fag ends in the bottom. Old dishes were spread out on every available surface.

I took a jar of white pepper from the spice rack and rubbed a bit in my nose. Then I fetched the cleaning stuff from the cupboard.

I'd lost count of how many times I had done this. I might have been six or seven years old the first time I cleared up an adult's vomit. I think it was Dad's that time, after a party that had got out of hand. The vomit had lain on the bathroom floor for an entire day, nobody was bothered about it, people just walked around it, maybe swore a bit about the smell while they had a piss or did their make-up in the mirror before returning to the drunken party in the next room to dance, stagger around, sing, fight and fall asleep, until I couldn't stand it any longer and rinsed it away with the shower head. But I never got used to it. The smell almost made me pass out. I had invented that thing with the white pepper myself. You sneezed a bit at first, but then you got a burning sensation in your nostrils, like your sense of smell was numbed, and you didn't notice the smell so strongly…

When I had finished I put the cleaning things back and washed my hands in the kitchen sink. Strangely enough, I felt hungry. If Mum had received her benefits cheque or child benefit today, which strongly appeared to be the case, there must be food in the house.

I opened the door to the pantry, but there were only empty bottles in there – dozens of them on every shelf. The fridge was bare as well, with the exception of a few cans of beer and a bottle of gin, which, amazingly, lay untouched in the freezer compartment.

I found half a loaf of white bread in the bread bin; there was always something. There was a tin of tuna in a drawer. I made two sandwiches for Robert and one for me and took them into the living room.

Robert was sitting curled up in a corner of the sofa, smiling at something on TV.

'What are you watching?' I asked.

'A nature programme. About unusual sea animals. Giant squid and stuff. And some species that people thought were extinct until some fishermen caught them in a net near Australia… Is Mum asleep?'

'I guess so. Looks like she was partying pretty hard.'

'Nice. That means we don't have to see her.'

The TV room was just as desolate as usual. We didn't have any pictures on the walls, not even any potted plants in the window. Just an old sofa and a coffee table that had been there as long as I could remember, and then the TV and the stereo, each standing on a soft-drink crate on the floor.

There was another Parador bottle by the radiator. There were fresh burn marks on the lino; she had put out her fag ends right on the floor. Two days earlier I had cleaned and tidied the whole apartment, apart from the kitchen. And that morning, when we left for school, it had still looked habitable. I wondered how she was capable of trashing the place so much in a single day, and still having time to take care of her errands in town, cash her cheque and go to the off-licence.

When I went upstairs, the bedroom door was shut. I could hear her snoring inside; a rattling sound like from a dentist's suction tube.

She had been in my room. If only I had realised what was going on that morning I would have locked the door and taken the key with me. She had gone through everything. The desk drawers had been pulled out. The chair was overturned. Books were lying every which way in the bookcase. The basket of old scavenged toys had been emptied onto the floor; a few dolls with their hair cut off, a Barbie doll, my collection of Smurfs. She had even pawed through my knicker drawer. Then, when she hadn't found anything, or had maybe heard the postman coming with the cheque from the social, she had left without even closing the door behind her. I felt around behind the radiator: the envelope was still there, securely taped to the wall. My life savings were in there: three hundred kronor. I was going to need it in the near future.

I went into the bedroom. Mum lay curled up at the foot of the bed, fully dressed. Her lipstick was smeared across her cheek. An extinguished cigarette was gripped between two fingers. She was wearing her red coat from the discount superstore. That was where we bought our clothes. A couple of times a year she managed to save up enough to take the bus out to Ullared and go shopping. Jeans of unknown origin. Winter clothes. A few sweaters and jumpers; hardly what you could call stylish. That required her to stay sober for a while and to set aside a little money. Otherwise another six months could pass before the next shopping trip, and in that time we would have grown out of the clothes we had and would have to go round in trousers and sweaters that were too short, looking ridiculous.

There was a framed portrait of me and my brother on the bedside table. It had been taken shortly after we moved here. I was six and Robert was four. We actually looked quite happy at that moment. We were standing in the street outside the house, me in a denim skirt and T-shirt, Robert in a pair of shorts and a light blue shirt. I can't remember who took the photo. Maybe it was Mum? But if it was her, with whose camera? As far as I knew, we had never owned one. Other families have photo albums and movies where you can follow the children's lives through birthdays, holidays and confirmations. But not ours. It's as if they've always been uninterested in their memories. As if life has been too dirty, too sad, and that's why they chose to rub out the past.

There was an envelope sticking out from underneath the picture on the bedside table. I could see what it was: a letter from Dad.

When I came down into the kitchen, Robert was sitting in a chair, leafing through a comic book.

'Finished watching TV?' I asked.

'Nothing interesting on. Only kids' shows. I'm too old for that stuff. How's she doing?'

'Sleeping like a log, with her clothes on.'

'She could at least have tidied up a bit after herself. Look at the state of this place.'

He looked over to the sink in disgust and then out of the window.

'That was so weird in that TV show,' he said. 'There's loads of fish and animals that live way down in the ocean. I mean really, really far down, a few kilometres down, where there's hardly any light.'

'In deep-sea trenches.'

'Yeah, that's what they're called. And humans don't even know they exist. There might be hundreds of species we haven't discovered yet. And then I thought if we don't even know what's in our own seas, it might be the same everywhere.'

It felt best to let him carry on. I began cleaning up as he went on, emptying the ashtray, clearing away the bottles, running water into the sink.

'I mean, there might be a whole load of other creatures out there we haven't discovered yet. Even invisible ones. Or maybe I'm the only one who can see them. Just imagine, Nella… Imagine if one of them tapped on my window at night. And then I'd bring him along to school, even though I was the only one who could see him, and he'd protect me even though nobody noticed.'

'Maybe,' I said. 'But that might be a while off. So pay attention in your lessons for now. And put some cream on if there's anything left in the tube. You've got some new cracks in your hands.'

He got up from his chair. And I was filled with that love for him again – that special love that I feel only for Robert: my little brother with the skinny body, the ugly clothes no normal human would wear if they had a choice, with eczema fingers, taped-up glasses and behind them, those nice grey eyes that seem to have seen things no one else has seen.

Last spring when Robert was in Year Six, his class was supposed to go on a field trip. They would go to Denmark, it was decided. Visit Legoland and Copenhagen, go to museums, and last of all spend a whole day at Tivoli. They had been raising funds for the trip throughout their upper primary years: selling May Day flowers and raffle tickets, and holding jumble sales in the gym. Some of the mums had made baked goods for the raffles, and some of the dads who worked at the Falken bottling plant had got hold of free soft drinks, which the kids sold along with the cakes and buns.

The plan was to leave around the Whitsun bank holiday in May and to be away for four days, but my brother had started dreaming about the trip long before then. In the spring term they had done a load of group projects about Denmark, learning things about Danish geography and history, and the names of the members of the Danish royal family. They had read *The Little Mermaid* in Danish, drawn maps and given presentations. They were really excited. Robert chattered constantly about how much he was looking forward to Legoland, where everything – even the streets – was made from Lego bricks, and especially about how they were going to stay in a hotel, a proper hotel, where everything was so nice and you didn't have to make your own bed in the mornings, where people came and tidied up for you, and there was soap wrapped up like little presents on the toilet. It was as if he had forgotten that he would have to sit on his own in the bus during the entire journey, and that the other kids would tease him and nobody would include him in their gang.

Then it suddenly emerged that they had not raised enough money. Their teacher sent a letter to the parents saying the trip might not happen. It was decided to hold a meeting to discuss it, and all the parents declared that they were prepared to club together to contribute what was needed for their children – minus our mum and dad, of course. They weren't even there, and maybe that's why nobody bothered to ask what to do about the people who couldn't afford it. And thus what I think my brother had feared deep down came to pass: the class went on their field trip without him.

Throughout the Whitsun holiday I could hear him through the wall between our rooms. He was completely heartbroken. I suffered nearly as much as Robert, but there was nothing I could do to console him. The worst thing was that Mum had initially given him a vague promise that he would be able to go. But after a visit to Dad, she changed her mind. He had got in debt to some people, and things would be difficult for him if he couldn't pay.

That was basically the end of the discussion. My brother simply could not go along. The money, if there actually was any, was needed for other things.

That was what I was thinking about as I removed the letter from the envelope. About how we were all sort of tangled up with each other: me, my brother, Mum and Dad, and that whatever happened in their lives immediately contaminated ours.

The letter was written on prison paper, with the correctional facility's stamp at the top. It looked like it had already been opened and read by people at the prison. The glue on the envelope had come apart a little at the sides. The handwriting was childish and spidery, as if the letters were ashamed of how ugly they were and were trying to escape from the paper.

He wrote that he was going to be released three months early, said what date and time it would be, and asked whether Mum could meet him outside the prison in Halmstad. Then there was a paragraph where he was more personal and asked how she was doing, and whether she had any money because he was flat broke himself and wouldn't get his pay from the prison workshop until close to Christmas. He wrote that he had applied for jobs, at the chrome-plating plant and the fibreglass plant in Falkenberg, but that he didn't have any great hopes of getting any work.

I could see him in my mind's eye as I read the letter. How he sat in his cell, dressed in the usual prison uniform: a singlet, tracksuit and bathroom slippers. A packet of John Silver cigarettes lay on the table fixed to the wall. There were pages from girlie magazines hanging on the walls, photos of girls with names like Annette or Susie who resembled younger versions of Mum. I could see how he struggled with the pencil, chewing on the middle while he pondered his next sentence, the effort it took him to form lines and curves into letters, and letters into words, spiky and ugly, written under the greatest possible resistance. And then the noise from the corridor, a prison guard rattling his keys, some inmate listening to the radio or just screaming.

If I had counted the days correctly, he would be out in three weeks' time.

Late that evening, Mum woke up. Robert was already in bed asleep. I was sitting in the kitchen, trying to come up with a plan for the next few days.

'Morning,' I said as she came in and held out a glass of water.

'Keep your voice down, please. I feel like crap.'

'Obviously. You haven't even taken off your coat.'

She sighed as she searched the cupboard for some fizzy headache tablets.

'Dad's getting out in a few weeks. I was happy about that. Celebrated a little, if that's what you mean. He'll be home sooner than expected.'

'I know. I read the letter.'

She lit a cigarette. Her eyes flitted back and forth, like a butterfly. Then she noticed the envelope on the kitchen worktop and stuffed it into her coat pocket.

'Is Robert in his room?'

'He's asleep.'

'That's good.'

'They were nasty to him at school again today.'

'So why doesn't he defend himself? He can hit back, can't he?'

She sat down at the table and poured a sachet of the headache powder into her glass. She looked terrible: big bags under her eyes, hair sticking out everywhere. I didn't actually think badly of her, but it was about as hard to judge her as it was to understand her. That was something I sometimes thought about: if I tried to understand who she was, there was basically no room for judging her, and if I judged her, that reduced the chances of understanding her. She hadn't always been the apathetic woman I saw before me now. There were small islets of light in my memory where I sat on her lap as she painted my fingernails, afternoons where she could still bring herself to play with Robert and me, playing cards with us or football out in the street… Now, when she put out her hand to give me a pat, I flinched so strongly I nearly lost my balance.

'You shouldn't read other people's letters, you know,' she said. 'That's not nice.'

'And you shouldn't have been in my room looking for money. I had to spend half an hour tidying up in there.'

A long cylinder of ash fell from her cigarette. It landed in her lap without her noticing.

'And it looked like a pigsty down here. Sorry to mention it, but you'd puked in the hall…'

I could hear how that sounded: crazy. And yet it was true.

She got up and went over to the wall calendar. She was incapable of taking in what I had said, or else she didn't remember anything. I was happy about that, because I couldn't bear her guilty conscience.

'What day is it today?' she asked.

'Friday.'

'Dad will come home in three weeks' time. I want you to move in with Robert then. You'll have to share a room for a while.'

'How come?'

'We're short of money. Dad and I have decided to let out the ground floor, so we'll have to make your room into the TV room. We need to be able to watch TV, don't we?'

She opened the fridge door and took out a beer, then looked out of the window. It had started to rain – a heavy, steady Halland rain.

'Who's going to move in?'

'A mate of Dad's. They're getting released at the same time, and he has nowhere to live. He'll pay half the rent.'

'Do you know him?'

'No, but Dad does.'

'So he could just be any lunatic.'

'Please, there's nothing to discuss.'

It didn't matter what arguments I came up with, because never in her life would she question Dad's decision. I didn't want to start crying in front of her. There is nothing I hate about myself more than when I start to blubber. I cannot afford tears. They are precious, and you can't waste them if you're in my situation. The mere thought of one of Dad's jailbird mates in the apartment made me feel ill. And my room was pretty much the only thing I had. If I locked the door around me, any kind of storm could blow up outside and I wouldn't care.

'Come here, let me comfort you,' Mum said.

And once again, I viewed the situation as if from outside: a woman with greasy, straggly hair, with her lipstick smeared halfway across her cheek, reeking like a sick old dog, a mother who lifts up the tab on a can of strong beer, downs half of it in one gulp as she extends her hand to her fifteen-year-old daughter to *comfort her*.

I did start to bawl, even though I didn't want to. Like a little child. Bawled and bawled until my body felt completely exhausted, drained of all liquid, like a dry old loaf of bread.

It's not easy to piece together the bits of Mum and Dad's lives because they don't like to talk about themselves. Dad comes from a village near Umeå, as far as I know. He got kicked out of the house when he turned sixteen. He had ended up falling in with a bad crowd, he once told me, and his parents wouldn't put up with it. Grandad worked in forestry up there, and both he and Grandma were teetotallers and very religious. They fell out, and after Dad left they never saw each other again.

For a few years he roamed around with no fixed address. He lived in a boarding house for single men in Stockholm for a while, then spent time in Borås and Norrköping, and a while down in Karlskrona, where he worked at a boatyard. Then he headed to Gothenburg to look for a job.

He found employment at a small factory that made trawler nets for the fishing industry and camouflage nets for the army. He travelled all over the west coast of Sweden to deliver them: small crayfish nets and big mackerel nets, and even bigger cod nets with panels that let the by-catch out before the net is raised. That's how he ended up in Falkenberg a couple of times a year. The factory had customers in Glommen and Träslövsläge, and he met a load of people around here, including the crowd that Mum hung around with.

Mum had just turned eighteen when Dad showed up at a party in town, and she fell head over heels in love. She was training to become a seamstress in those days and was living as a lodger with a family in Falkenberg. At weekends she would go back to Okome, the village where my gran lived. The weekend she met Dad she was actually supposed to be there, but there was a snowstorm, and the bus that went to Ätradalen had been cancelled. So instead she went to a party with some friends from school, and a few of them had boyfriends who were fishermen. One of them brought Dad along, and that's how they met. That same evening they went out dancing. Dad paid for everything; he was dressed like a gangster, Mum had told me, in a suit and hat, and he must have stood out from everyone else. It's amazing to think, but she was only three years older than I am now.

They continued to meet up whenever Dad's route brought him to the area, and within a year she was pregnant. I don't think they really wanted to become parents. Dad liked going round the west coast as a free man, selling nets and trawls, and conducting shady deals on the side. And Mum was really too young.

When she got knocked up, she quit school and took a job at the same factory where Gran worked. She moved back into her old room at home and lived there until Dad quit his job and moved down here. They rented a ramshackle house in the village. Dad got a job at a timber yard. Then I entered the world.

After a few years the removal van headed to Vinberg, much closer to town. They had had a feud with Gran, who thought that Dad was going to ruin Mum's life. They were already drinking quite a lot in those days; social services came round and investigated; there was talk of my going to live with Gran or to stay with a foster family, but ultimately it came to nothing. Dad had also made himself unwelcome at work, got into fights and served a stretch for possession of narcotics. When he came out, he had no desire to take a regular job. He had contacts down at the docks, would buy vodka and diet pills from the Polish ships and sell them to shady characters throughout Halland. I know all this because I happened to find a box containing old court judgments and appeals in his wardrobe.

Robert was born just after I turned two. It was around Christmas, several months early. He had to stay in an incubator in the hospital in Varberg. Mum and I would go there to look after him. I have vague memories of a little doll asleep in an oxygen tent, a doll with loads of tubes and drips in his arms that you wanted to stroke, even though it was prohibited. You weren't allowed to touch him, and you could hardly talk when you were in the vicinity. Nobody knew if he was going to make it. The doctors couldn't say anything for certain, so we had to take it one day at a time. Dad never came along. By that time his criminal career had taken off.

I have clear memories of events from the time I was four. I remember the week when we got evicted from our flat in Vinberg and had to move into a council flat in town. And the night when the police entered the flat and turned everything upside down in their hunt for stolen goods, and how strange it felt because in everyone else's world the police are nice, helpful people. Another time I watched as Dad got beaten up by two blokes he owed money to. It was a summer evening when they rang the doorbell, and when Mum opened the door they chucked her aside like an old rag and headed straight for the sofa, where Dad sat watching TV with Robert and me on his lap. They hit him with a bottle and kicked him as he lay there. I don't know what possessed me, but I tried to protect my brother by grabbing hold of one of the men's legs. They didn't even notice me, just carried on punching and kicking until Mum came rushing in with her purse and they emptied it of all the banknotes and disappeared.

I have a load of sick memories like that. Of parties where total strangers turn up and stay for several days and engage in marathon drinking sessions, and when one passes out the next takes over, so it's basically never quiet at home. There's always someone left to carry on while the others rest up for the next shift. People whose names nobody knows, because they're only there once and then disappear, never to resurface, or ones whose names you do know, perversely enough, because they're sort of regulars at the end of the month when the benefits are paid. People who don't give a damn about your existence, who attempt to appear interested or concerned with a wine bottle in their hand, who knock on the door to your room and say, 'How ya doing in there little girl, hope we're not disturbing you.' They're actually worse than the ones who are complete bastards, because with bastards you at least know what you're dealing with: disgusting blokes who try to touch you up or undress you with their eyes. One time I heard my mum when some guy suggested we should have a shower together. She went completely mental and chased him out with a bread knife. Even so, the nice ones are almost worse – the ones who say they feel sorry for you, even though they're trashing the place just like the rest of them. And the sick thing is that you end up believing that's how things have to be, that it's normal to have a load of drunks in your house who try to come in and make small talk with you as if it were the most natural thing in the world: *How old are you, little girl? How are things at school?* Or with a trembling voice, they'll say they think it's disgusting that we have to put up with people like themselves.

Shortly after I turned six we moved out of our flat in Falkenberg. The house constituted a health hazard. There was mould in the bathroom and kitchen. The wallpaper had started to come off the walls, and the lino was curling up in the corners. It smelled musty, and the smell of mould even permeated our clothes. Mum complained to social services until out of pure pity they sorted out a place in the newly built maisonettes in Skogstorp. That's how we ended up here. I was going to start school that autumn, and I remember I was happy about it. Even though I was just little, I went round hoping that our circumstances would change for the better.

And they actually did, at first. It was nice here then. Everything was brand new. There was a playground nearby, and the street was surrounded by trees and flowers. It was as if Mum and Dad had been given a new opportunity, and they realised and were prepared to seize it. Mum made some curtains and bought furniture from the charity shop. My brother and I each got our own room. I'll never forget the day when they showed me where we were going to live. A whole room of my own with a fitted wardrobe and a view out over the street. It didn't really matter that the walls were paper-thin, that everything was built from the cheapest materials and that when somebody went to the toilet downstairs you could hear it throughout the whole apartment. Mum and I hung up a Bamse Bear poster together, and I got a new bed and new sheets with a Pippi Longstocking design on them. Dad happened to have some money. He had made a few deals and had also got a job at a mink farm in Olofsbo. That was in the summer, and sometimes my brother and I got to go there along with him. I don't know why I have such strong memories of that. Maybe because normally he hardly ever talked to us, kept himself to himself and looked at us as if we were strangers who just happened to end up under the same roof. And then suddenly he was transformed: open, almost happy. He had got a job he wanted to show us: the long mink sheds with no walls, with a saddle roof to keep the rain out; the silky animals who looked so friendly, almost like cuddly toys, five to a cage. Lovely animals, but dangerous. You mustn't stick your fingers into the cages because they could easily bite off a child's finger. You mustn't forget they are wild animals, Dad said. One of his tasks was to prepare the feed. He fetched fish silage from the boats down in Glommen and chicken innards from Torsåsen and mixed them with flour and water and ground it all down into mink feed. He stayed sober during that time, except during skinning. Then they all drank at the mink farm, to endure the blood and the smell of flayed animal carcasses.

That first year in Skogstorp I hardly ever needed to look after my brother. Mum was at home. Dad was working and avoided his old acquaintances. Four days a week Robert went to nursery, and that autumn I started at school.

I've saved that first class photo, and it's strange to see everyone there, just six or seven years old, like little prototypes of themselves.

Peder and Gerard are standing in the back row, showing the gaps in their milk teeth, already best friends back then, both wearing Lee jeans and denim jackets. They are about half their current size but still to scale; shrunken in time. I am crouching at the bottom over to the left, attempting to smile, as if I don't really know how.

It may not be evident from this school photo, but the fact is that I was an outsider from the very first day. Nobody teased me or did anything in particular, but it was just as if I didn't exist. Perhaps Mum and Dad's reputation had accompanied me all the way into the classroom? Perhaps the other parents had asked their kids to stay away from my brother and me? Or maybe it was because we lived in the new maisonettes on Liljevägen, which were viewed as a sort of slum where social services cases lived, and everyone else lived in detached houses or proper terraced houses with well-kept gardens; or the fact that I constantly went round in hideous clothes and my hair was straggly because my mum had forgotten to buy shampoo. As I remember it, I didn't care. Life had actually got much easier since we'd moved here.

When I was in Year Four, Dad owed somebody some money and stole in order to pay the debt. He ended up inside again, only for three months that time, but it was enough to put us back to square one. I remember when we visited him that autumn in Halmstad. That was the first time I'd been in a prison, and people were very nice to us. A female prison guard took Robert and me to a playroom where we would have to wait. We were given cheese sandwiches and squash, and while Mum was with Dad in the visiting room, the woman explained what a prison is. I didn't listen too closely because there were loads of toys in there, and then we got crayons and paper to draw on while we were waiting. I still have one of the drawings. It shows Dad in what I imagined was a prison uniform: black and white striped, the way they look in comics. Later, when he came down to us accompanied by a screw, I realised it wasn't like that. He was wearing the same tracksuit as at home, with a T-shirt underneath, sockless in a pair of brown sandals.

Children weren't actually allowed up in the wing, but they made an exception for us. Dad showed us his cell, which had real bars behind the window pane, and there was a bed and a table which were fastened to the floor. Robert was absolutely thrilled, as if he were in the midst of the plot of an exciting movie.

I don't know how the kids at school got wind that Dad was inside. Maybe it was the teacher who told them, or maybe the rumour just spread spontaneously. At any rate, everything changed. The others in the class started to call me names, they hid my clothes, put dog shit in my wellies and were generally nasty. And yet my brother's fate was many times worse. The kids in his class didn't even care about shunning him; they went after him physically right from the start. I dedicated the majority of my upper primary years to attempting to protect him, but no matter how hard I tried, I couldn't always be there. His problems just kept growing, with difficulties paying attention and truanting: he might vanish from school at any time, just disappear during recess and head down to the sea and stay there until evening. And then he started pissing his pants…

He got educational support and special teachers who helped him, but all this made him stick out that much more in the eyes of the others. Finally, people could do anything at all to him with no shame. Spit on him, kick his bike apart, pelt him with snowballs so hard that his glasses broke. And the words they spat at him, even though they were just young children: pig, puke, spazz, pissypants. Things like that.

The autumn when Robert started in Year Seven was initially a relief for me. I hadn't been able to be there for him the previous two years. As for me, I'd sort of fallen by the wayside as far as the others were concerned since Tommy joined our class. Apart from certain insults, like Ironing Board, nobody was particularly nasty to me any more. Gerard and his gang didn't give a damn about us.

At the very most, Tommy and I were a sort of vacuum in their world. And now my brother and I would suddenly be in the same building and sharing the playground. I would be able to keep a closer eye on the situation. And Tommy had also promised to help out, so if we both kept our eyes peeled we'd increase the chances of rescuing him.

That's what I had hoped. But instead everything just got worse. Murphy's Law, as the lads at school would say.

Early on Saturday morning I finally got hold of Tommy. It was one of his brothers who answered. I was just about to say that I'd seen him at the fisherman's huts the day before, but stopped myself at the last second. It took a while before Tommy came to the phone. The radio was on in the background. Somebody was clattering around with the crockery in the kitchen.

'I heard what happened at school,' was the first thing he said when he picked up. 'You should report them.'

'How do you know that? You weren't even there.'

'One of the lads from next door came here and told me. He said Gerard and his gang fed you grass.'

I told him about the kitten and all the rest, but I spared him certain details of what had happened in the woods.

'So now they think you blabbed?'

'It seems that way.'

I could hear him inhaling and exhaling, out of breath, as if he had run over to the phone.

'Or else he just made that up in order to give somebody a hard time. It happened to be you this time, it could just as well have been me or anybody else.'

'They wouldn't try it on with you. You've got your brothers.'

It struck me that Tommy didn't sound the slightest bit ill. Maybe he'd just been playing truant the past week.

'And they're saying they're going to take it all out on Robert.'

'What's he got to do with it?'

'Nothing, as far as I know.'

He was silent for a moment. Someone turned up the radio in the background.

'So what are you going to do now?'

'Pay Gerard a grand so he'll leave us alone. And to cap it all, my dad's on his way home with a mate of his to ruin the rest of our autumn.'

'Bloody hell… But how does Gerard know somebody blabbed?'

'Peder said he had to go up to the headmaster's office, and L.G. knew about what had happened. And since he hadn't reported it himself, it must have been somebody else.'

'Who else is there to choose from?'

'The lads in the gang, maybe one of the younger ones.'

'But wouldn't Gerard have checked that out? They practically shit themselves whenever he so much as looks at them. They would spontaneously confess without him needing to ask them.'

'It could be Peder or Ola,' I said. 'Didn't Peder have a cat at home when we were in Year Seven? She might have had kittens. It might have been one of them. A kitten his little sister got or something. And then Gerard just took it for himself, even though Peder didn't want him to.'

'I don't get it.'

'Well, somebody blabbed, and it wasn't me. Somebody who thinks he's gone too far.'

I heard a rustling on the line and the outlines of a voice whispering in the background.

'Are you still there?' I asked.

'Yeah… I'm here. How are you going to get hold of a thousand kronor?'

'It'll work out somehow. I was thinking of going into town later today… I've got some plans.'

'It might be best if you stayed off school for a while. Until things calm down.'

'Gerard would just view that as proof that it was me who blabbed.

I'm going to go in as if nothing happened. The hard part will be persuading my brother. Normally it's the Year Sevens who go after him. Now it's the Year Nines.'

'You've got to speak to someone… a grown-up, I mean.'

'Who with? My mum? You must be joking.'

Neither of us said anything. I considered the option of asking Tommy's brothers to do something. They had been known as fighters when they were younger. For a brief period they had even hung around a bit in Dad's circle, in the days when he worked at the mink farm. But since they had taken on the boat a few years ago, they had calmed down. They might be able to scare Gerard, but only for a short while. He was too messed up to go round being frightened for very long. And besides, I realised, it would only add to his rage.

'I saw your brothers yesterday,' I said. 'Robert and I headed down to Glommen after it happened. If you hadn't been ill we would have knocked for you.'

'What did you see?'

'Nothing in particular. They were just there…'

'Where was that?'

'By the hut. Shall we meet up this weekend? You sound like you're better now.'

'I can't. I've got some stuff to do.'

'What stuff?'

'Nothing in particular.'

His voice sounded odd again. I couldn't say exactly how, but something was not right.

'Have you had your phone switched off at home?' I asked.

'Eh?'

'I've been ringing every day since Wednesday, but nobody answered.'

'I had a temperature. Over 39 degrees. The phone is downstairs. I couldn't get up and answer it.'

'What about your mum and dad then? Or your brothers?'

'I've really got to go now,' said Tommy. 'I'll see you on Monday.'
'Can't we keep talking a little longer? I need some help to think.'
'Some other time, Nella, I'll see you around…'
There was a click on the line. I was utterly confused.

It had stopped raining when my brother and I rode our bikes down Solrosvägen that morning. There were a few lads playing hockey in front of the shop. A bunch of teenagers came roller-skating down from the E6. Early-rising fathers were out washing their cars. They stood in their driveways with their hoses and sponges, with cigarettes in the corner of their mouths and impenetrable expressions. Behind the curtains in the detached houses, families sat eating breakfast and children looked forward to the day – games, trips into town and crisps in front of the TV that evening. It could have been us sitting there, I thought, in a parallel universe our physics teacher told us about, where everything looked exactly the same as in this one, only with tiny differences, like all right-handed people would be left-handed, or everyone who had brown eyes would have blue eyes instead. But something had gone wrong, and Robert and I had drawn the short straw as usual.

My plan was to start at Junior Centre, a clothing shop in Nygatan. People's child benefit had just been paid for the month, so it would be packed in there. Girls and boys around my age, with parents bringing up the rear with their wallets wide open. People from nice families who would never set foot in discount stores. Besides, they had stuff that would be easy to convert into cash. A reversible Mickey Mouse sweatshirt would sell for thirty kronor at school, and a pair of brand-name jeans for double that. Pricier clothes brought better returns, but they were also monitored more closely. I would start there and then continue on to the shops closer to the centre of town.

'We'll start with JC,' I told my brother. 'I'll tell you exactly what you need to do…'

Nobody paid us any notice as we went in through the door. There was a guy in his twenties standing behind the counter, bagging up purchases at the till. Two other shop assistants were helping people over by the changing rooms. There was a queue; kids were waiting with jeans and sweaters in their arms. My brother stayed by the entrance while I went round and did a recce.

JC was quite small inside. There were no mirrors on the ceiling for the simple reason that they were not needed; the entire shop was in plain view, with no concealed angles or dark corners. Light entered en masse via the display windows facing Köpmansgatan. In the middle of the shop was the jeans display, with piles of Dobbers and Levi's. There were sweaters and T-shirts on a shelf behind them. I went back over to my brother.

'I want you to take a pair of Dobber jeans and roll them up so the label doesn't show. And then pick up some T-shirts and join the queue for the changing rooms. Can you manage that?'

'What do I do when I get there?'

'Just go in, close the door behind you and stay in there until I get there and go in the next cubicle. When I knock on the wall, you hand the jeans to me, I'll give you a pair of reduced-price jeans which you then take out and put back on the pile. It's foolproof – they can't nab you for anything because you won't have anything on you.'

'What about you?'

'Don't worry about me. See you out by the bikes afterwards.'

I watched him slink off towards the jeans display. A shop assistant watched him with a beady eye.

They had the last of the summer clothes on a clearance table. I found a pair of cheap jeans and took them over to the area where the brand-name trousers were. Next I picked up a pair of medium-size Dobbers and a couple of sweatshirts that were hanging on an adjacent rack. Then I went over to the winter coats and pretended to look at the price tags. As far as I could tell, no one was watching us. Store detectives generally attempted to look like ordinary customers, maybe holding a pair of socks in their hand while they discreetly observed people. And they were always dressed in plain clothes. I knew all that even though I'd never been caught myself. I knew about that sort of stuff – who were the thieves and who were the cops out there.

Ten minutes later we were in the changing rooms, in adjacent cubicles. It smelled like the school changing room after PE class: a peculiar mix of sweat and deodorant. I tapped lightly on the divider wall. My brother obediently handed over his jeans and got a pair of cheap ones from the clearance table in return. I pulled on the Dobbers and then my own kecks from the discount store over them. I heard him open the door and knew that the shop assistants would be eyeing him suspiciously, even though he emerged with the same number of items he had gone in with, and that they would continue to observe him as he put them back in their places, the odd little guy with the taped-together glasses, and while that was happening I just had to open my door and walk out as if nothing had happened – they would barely even notice me…

A minute later I was back out on the street. My brother was waiting for me by the cycle racks, just as we had agreed.

'Where've you got the jeans?' he asked.

'Under my other ones.'

He gave a whistle.

'What a pro. So what do we do now?'

'We carry on until we're done.'

As we cycled off towards the Kronan shopping centre, I pondered my next move. Cheap or expensive stuff? There were pros and cons with each. Something like bottles of Date perfume, for example, I'd be able to sell with no effort at all. Almost all the girls at school used that. Most mornings in the common room you could hardly breathe for all the Date Anna or Date Natalie the girls had been spraying over themselves. They were in the department stores and were easy to nick. The problem was that they were cheap and wouldn't bring in more than a tenner for a bottle, which meant that I'd really have to make an effort to accumulate a sizable amount.

Brand-name clothes were a completely different matter. The school snobs were mad for Pringle and Lacoste. They had them at Johansson Brothers, but the shop assistants there kept a close eye on everything that cost over a hundred kronor. Maybe, I thought, it might be worth the risk if my brother went in first and attracted their attention, asked some stupid question about autumn fashions or if he could please use the customer toilet. If I was lucky, nobody would notice me, I could hide behind an older customer, sneak over to the Lacoste sweaters in the corner and get hold of one before they could react.

Actually, I didn't like nicking stuff. I only did it in emergencies. I could sort of see Dad in myself whenever I stole something, and I didn't like the idea that we might be similar; that we might feel the same things or think the same way.

There were other ways of getting cash that I found preferable. Like returning empty bottles to collect the deposit, or hunting for certain types of magazines in skips. There was a junk shop down by the docks that paid a krona apiece for old copies of girlie mags or worse stuff. Skips are full of that kind of thing. If people only knew what their old men read when nobody's looking. But if I spent a whole week going through all the skips in town looking for porn mags, I wouldn't get seven hundred kronor. It was quicker with clothes and gadgets.

'Where to now?' my brother asked.

I had made my choice:

'Kullens Shoes…'

Kullens was located in Schubertvägen on the other side of the railway line. They had brand names: pricey trainers and women's shoes, and a weak point in the building itself that could be exploited. I wondered which would be better: smart shoes or trainers? A pair of Stan Smiths would be easy to flog at school. The lads were mad for them, you could see loads in the schoolyard – ten, fifteen kids, all wearing identical white trainers. With smart shoes I was a bit less sure, especially about what was in fashion just then. The Dobber jeans might bring in fifty kronor, and a pair of shoes the same. The problem was that we didn't have time to get hold of much more before the shops closed, and we were nowhere near seven hundred kronor. I needed to get hold of more expensive stuff. Unfortunately Gerard wasn't particularly interested in fashion. It was hard to imagine him in a Lacoste shirt or a lambswool sweater from Lyle&Scott. He might be interested in gadgets, maybe a digital watch. But it was risky. If I got caught, life would be really terrible.

The customer rush at Kullens was over. I wandered among the shelves, trying to seem as if I wasn't looking for anything in particular. I picked up a pair of trainers in passing, pretended to look at the price tag and put them back. Finally one of the shop assistants came up, a young girl with a gap between her front teeth.

'Are you after something special?'

'Some wellies, actually. Preferably with a lining.'

'They're further back. Check on the shelves behind the children's shoes.'

I nodded in thanks.

'Is there a customer toilet here, by the way?'

'In the same direction, go out into the corridor by the emergency exit sign, that's where they are. And if you need help with the boots, just shout.'

She went back towards the till. I checked out the ceiling: no mirrors as far as I could see. I waited until she had her back turned to me, took a pair of Stan Smiths from the rack and headed off towards the toilet.

Right next to it was a staircase leading upstairs. I stuck a key in the notch in the toilet lock and turned it so it showed red. If she decided to come back here, it would look like I was inside having a pee…

The upper floor was nearly empty, except for a few mirrors fixed to the walls. There was a balcony door in one wall that led out onto a fire escape. I opened the door and placed the trainers on the landing. My brother was standing on the pavement opposite. I waved to him that the coast was clear.

Then I went back downstairs, unlocked the toilet and found the rack of wellies. I tried on a couple of pairs and placed them back on the rack.

'Didn't find anything?' the assistant asked as I walked past the till.

'No, not the right colour.'

'We'll get some new ones in at the end of the month. Red and light blue. You can come back then.'

My brother was waiting over by the railway bridge. He had the trainers strapped onto the parcel rack on the rear of his bike.

'That was smart with the stairs,' he said. 'How did you know about them?'

'I'd been and done a recce. In case there was an emergency situation.'

'These are really nice trainers.'

I nodded.

'Try them on. They're your size.'

He looked at me, taken aback, and then at the trainers.

'Mum will know we nicked them.'

'She won't notice a damn thing. She's on her way into one of her phases again.'

'But when she comes out of it?'

'By then they'll be so worn out, we can say we found them some-where. Anyway, you can start off wearing them at school. And then change out of them before you go home. You can keep your old shoes in your locker, and change in the mornings and the after-noons. Nobody will notice anything.'

Robert blushed slightly.

'They're really nice,' he said quietly. 'Thanks.'

'I didn't pay anything for them.'

'No. But you ought to sell them. Gerard is going to want his money.'

I reached out and stroked his head. His hair was starting to get long. I would have to give him a haircut again soon.

'Listen, Robert, I'd get maybe fifty kronor for them, at most. That's small fry. I'm just wasting my time with this.'

He looked both terrified and happy: terrified at the thought of what Gerard would do if he didn't get his money, and happy about the trainers, a pair of regular trainers that were in style for once.

'You look like one stylish dude,' I said. 'All you're missing is a pair of cool kecks and you'll be the king of Year Seven. And who cares if Mum finds out. What can she say?'

I watched as he put the trainers on. His hands were trembling, he was so excited. I took his old ones and put them on top of an electrical enclosure, a pair of brown canvas shoes from the discount store which he had outgrown several months ago.

'So what are you going to do instead?' he asked. 'We need to get the money.'

'We'll head to the electronics shop. They've got something there I think Gerard's interested in.'

A few weeks previously when I was in town, I had seen a personal cassette player in the display window of the electronics shop. Just as I had hoped, it was still there. It was the latest model from Sony, which was in a class of its own. No Panasonic or Philips or any of the other makes that were just trying to imitate a genuine Walkman. It was in an open box with the headphones plugged in. There was a price tag on the door of the cassette compartment: 1,199 kronor.

'Is that the one you're thinking of?' Robert asked as we stood outside the shop.

'Yeah.'

'Over a grand. Can you get sent to prison for that? If you can, I don't want you to do it.'

He looked properly scared.

'Don't worry. I'm not fifteen yet. That means they can't do anything.'

'How do you know that?'

'I just do. Come with me.'

In order to reach the cassette player, you had to bend over a metre-high screen without anyone noticing. There mustn't be anyone walking past in the street and no one could notice anything inside the shop. The good thing was that the small display window was in a fairly remote part of the shop, behind some shelves of electrical goods that shielded the view from the till.

We cautiously walked past along the outside of the shop. It was half full inside. I was going to need Robert's help to manage this, but I was no longer sure it was worth the risk. If I got caught, the police would get involved straight away. The thought of a foster home popped up in my mind again – the worst horror scenario: being split up from my brother.

We sat down on one of the park benches outside, and I explained the situation to him.

'I think we should do it,' he said. 'Think about Gerard.'

I was doing just that: thinking about Gerard and his sick mind, where anything at all could happen in a fraction of a second. Gerard on one side of the balance, the cops on the other. I really had no choice.

'Right, I'll go in first,' I said. 'And then you go in a little later. But don't wait too long, a minute maximum. And stay right by the door or by the tills. Check out the record players or something. Pretend you don't know me. Don't even look in my direction. And when it's time, you ask the guy at the till if he can help you.'

'With what?'

'Anything. A record needle. The price of a tape deck.'

He nodded earnestly.

'If they spot me, you run like hell. Don't think about me, just get out of there, as fast as you can. Then I'll see you at home.'

There was music playing over the loudspeakers as I stepped over the threshold. An assistant was bending over a cabinet, getting something out for a customer. Some kids were crowded round the ghetto blasters. There was an older man standing at the cash desk, talking on the phone. The manager, I thought. He looked like one anyway, dressed in a suit and tie, with a name badge on his chest.

Just behind him, in a glass display case, was where the portable cassette players were kept. The one in the window, I thought, was the only one in all of Falkenberg that it was possible to nick without having to break in.

I waited for him to hang up, and then I went up to the counter.

'Have you got any ordinary extension leads? I'm supposed to buy one for my dad...'

He nodded towards the smaller display window. Thick black strands of hair stuck out from his shirt cuffs: he was hairy all the way down to his fingers.

'Three-way plugs and cables are on the bottom shelf.'

There was a ding from the door as I went over towards the corner. Out of the corner of my eye I saw my brother come into the shop.

I was over in the electrical department now, right by the display window. The guy behind the counter could still see me. But he only had to move a metre and the coast would be clear – if he turned his attention to Robert, or if some other customer waved him over. I picked up an extension lead, pretended to look at it doubtfully, as if I were hoping to discover some defect that might make them reduce the price. The hairy bloke cast a glance in my direction.

Then I heard my brother say something, and the manager left his station and went over to him. Nobody would see me now, as long as no customer suddenly turned up by the shelves to pick up a cable. I went up to the window. The pavement outside was deserted. I bent over the screen, stretched my arm out as far as I could, got hold of the cassette player, straightened up and jammed it down inside my waistband.

It was over in a couple of moments. I stood completely still, like an animal that stops in its tracks to check for enemies, scents, spies. A single movement in the vicinity, a single hostile face and I would dash through the shop to the exit and vanish into the crowd. But nothing happened. I heard my brother ask something about the gadgets that were in the display case, and the manager hummed and hawed in reply. I took the extension lead and went over to the till. The fatty who rented out videos turned up and put it in a bag. I paid with money from my envelope: eight seventy-five.

The shops were about to shut. New rain clouds had scudded in from the coast, it was drizzling a bit, and if the temperature fell there would be fog. We cycled past the cinema and checked out the film posters. *Flashdance* would be coming in two weeks' time – six months after its premiere in the rest of the country. There was a notice for something called the 'Up With People Show' on the door of the theatre. You could go along on a journey round the world and dance and sing in a youth perform-ance, but the deadline for applications had expired a month ago. I didn't have anything to compare it with, but everything felt a bit delayed in this town, as if time lagged a bit just on our latitude, an hour or so a day, so that we unavoidably got a little further behind every year. 'A bright spark in Falkenberg.' That was the new slogan the tourist information office had come up with for the coming tourist season. That was the very last thing I felt like: a bright spark.

But my brother seemed happy as he rode round on his bike in his new trainers. I got a huge lump in my throat just looking at him, as if a piece of apple had got stuck in there. I had to swallow several times to get rid of it.

We stopped at the chemist's and bought some hand cream. Robert needs a special type that's really expensive. A cheaper one would have made him scratch his hands until they bled. I rubbed some into his hands on the pavement outside. The skin on the back of them was rough and covered in sores. His fingers were completely chapped, and a sort of white scaling had formed between them.

My envelope had been emptied of cash, slightly but cruelly. The hand cream cost thirty. Now I needed 738 kronor to make Gerard happy. I hadn't a clue what the cassette player would fetch. The best thing would be if he accepted it instead of the money.

'I'm not going to go back to school,' said Robert. 'Not as long as Peder and those guys are there.'

'You mean until the end of spring term?'

'Yeah. And I don't care what they say.'

'If we don't go, we'll just get them even more het up. And anyway, I'm going to get the money together. I promise.'

My brother looked at his hands as if they were some kind of strange creatures that had attached themselves onto the ends of his arms and refused to let go.

'Do you think my eczema will ever go away?'

'One morning you'll wake up and it'll be gone. You've got really nice hands…'

'They're disgusting. Ola and Peder are right: I look like a leper.'

'I don't think so.'

'You're only saying that because you're my sister.'

'Well, maybe…'

'But I'm happy you are. Otherwise everything would feel even more worthless. Like it's not worth the effort. School. Mum and Dad. All that crap.'

My brother gave a guilty smile. A black Peugeot with 'Stop Union Bullying Tactics' stickers in the rear window was parked right in front of us. There was a handbag on the passenger seat. The door was not locked; someone had dashed into the chemist's a minute before closing time and left their handbag there. A woman stood at the till and was about to pay. Soon, at any moment, she would realise she had forgotten her money.

I did it virtually without thinking: opened the door, stuck my hand in and got hold of the purse. I didn't touch the cards, just opened the section where the banknotes were and took what was in there, shoved the money in my pocket and shut the door. We had managed to walk about ten metres when the woman came out running, fetched her handbag and disappeared into the chemist's again.

'We shouldn't start riding, right?' asked my brother. 'It might look suspicious. Better to stroll along as if nothing happened.'

'You're a fast learner,' I said with a sour tone. 'Soon you'll be ready to start working with Dad.'

'Thanks!'

'I meant it ironically. By the way, did you know he's coming home soon? In two weeks and six days' time, to be precise.'

'Everything will work out okay, Nella. As long as Dad's out.'

I did not bother to contradict him. This was his day. New trainers. News about Dad. Reality would soon catch up with him. Dad would turn up with a jailbird mate, chaos would ensue, and my brother and I would be forced to share a room while a storm engulfed the entire sea outside.

Tommy wasn't at school on Monday morning either. It wasn't like him to be away for so long, at least not without saying why. I wondered whether something had happened. Maybe he had had to help his brothers with their fishing? Sometimes when they returned with big catches he would stay at home without asking permission.

Large cliques sat at the tables in the common room, telling each other what they had done at the weekend. Some lads were playing cards, gin rummy or twenty-one, shouting over each other's heads and generally whingeing that there were five whole days left until Friday. A couple of Glommen kids disappeared out into the corridor, so it was clear the school bus had arrived. I put my PE bag in my locker, as well as the plastic carrier bag with the Walkman wrapped inside.

'Did you have a good weekend?' someone behind me asked.

It was Ola. He had snuck up without my noticing.

'It was okay.'

'That's nice to hear. Hung out with your retarded brother, maybe? Or with Tommy? Or that cripple you're mates with?'

'I was at home.'

'Okay. Just wanted to know if you've started scraping together some cash yet. Gerard needs it by Friday at the latest. Otherwise there'll be interest payable. Lots of interest.'

Cripple, I thought. He must mean the Professor.

'He'll get it, you can tell him that.'

I looked over towards the doors. People were still coming in from the schoolyard. Perhaps Tommy would turn up there anyway, reassurance that I didn't have anything to worry about.

'I hope so… Oh, and Ironing Board, I hope you're not going to blab about what happened in the woods last Friday. Like you blabbed about the cat, I mean. Because that story is getting bigger. Gerard had to go up to the headmaster's office again. And L.G. rang my dad at home last Friday. It's making me pretty upset, as a matter of fact.'

His ID tag around his neck was moving in time with his Adam's apple as he spoke. He had a 'Non-Smoking Generation' sweat-shirt on under his denim jacket. I presumed it was a joke, because he smoked.

'A whole load of shit has blown up, and in my opinion it never needed to happen. It's a tragedy, in fact.'

He noticed something on his thumbnail and bit it cautiously. Looked at it. Bit it again.

'Whose cat was it?' I asked.

I don't know where that question came from; it just popped into my head from nowhere and came out of my mouth. Ola looked away towards the corridor, where people had started to shuffle off to their classrooms. A tiny piece of his thumbnail had got stuck on his bottom lip.

'How the hell should I know? It just happened to be there… a little farm cat, they're a penny a pound. Who cares?'

'Wasn't it Peder's? Doesn't he have cats at home?'

'I dunno anything about it, Ironing Board. And if I did know anything about it, I'd make sure I forgot it, and that's what you should do too.'

I already regretted getting into a conversation with him, but it was too late now. That's how it is with words, I thought: they're always on their way somewhere, like tiny invisible missiles. They could strike anyone, and the damage was impossible to calculate.

Ola took a packet of cigarettes out of his pocket, tapped one out and placed it behind his ear.

'I don't think you should talk about that cat any more. We just won't mention it again. That'll be better for everyone.'

It was as if our conversation wiped out an old picture of him and replaced it with a newer one: his nails were chewed down to the quick, leaving only narrow strips that were embedded in his fingertips like pillows made of meat; his strong thighs and muscular arms. The face he had started shaving in Year Six, with a downy moustache and hints of a beard... the fleshy nose, the tracksuit jacket that was straining at the shoulders. He sometimes lifted scrap iron in Peder's basement. I had heard them bragging about how much they could lift on the bench press. And yet I got the sense that he was scared of me.

'Social Studies test,' he said, nodding in the direction of the classroom. 'I'm aiming for straight Fs again this year. But Social Studies is like the fly in my ointment. No matter how hard I try, I always get a D. I think the teacher's a queer. He gives me better marks because he hopes I'll wank him off.'

I finished the test in twenty minutes. The questions weren't particularly hard. We were doing foreign policy, learning about NATO and the Warsaw Pact, the forms of government in different countries, and the names of presidents and prime ministers: Andropov in Russia, Thatcher in Britain, Kohl and Mitterrand in West Germany and France. Even though I hadn't had a chance to revise I had a decent grasp of all that. And there were more important things to worry about than my mark in Social Studies.

I handed in my test paper and went over to the door. Gerard looked at me with his creepy smirk, Peder waved, and when I glanced over my shoulder I realised that the entire class was following me with their eyes.

Out in the corridor, I slunk into the first decent toilet. I felt like I needed to have some peace for a while.

I just sat there with the door locked and looked at the graffiti on the walls, cocks that people had drawn and phone numbers you were supposed to call if you wanted to have a shag or get a blow job. Sometimes there would be things about me and my brother as well, but I didn't see anything this time. Maybe the caretaker had come by with his tin of paint?

I wondered whether the Tommy situation had anything to do with me, and all the other stuff that had happened. But I didn't think so. In his case, it was about other things. It was strange that he wasn't back. He'd said he was healthy and was going to come today. The more I thought about it, the stranger I thought he'd sounded on the phone.

The toilet was located opposite the staff room. When I opened the door, I ran straight into L.G. There was no chance of getting away. He stood there like a huge roadblock, dressed in his worn-out corduroy jacket and jeans which he hoped would make him look youthful, and he did not appear to be in any sort of hurry.

'Ah, I'm glad I've got hold of you,' he said. 'You were absent all afternoon last Friday. Have you got an explanation?'

'I was ill.'

'You have to report that. Those are the rules. You could have rung from home.'

'I forgot. I caught something during recess. Suddenly felt sick.'

L.G. stood with the door open, as if he were considering whether to bring me in for a longer interrogation. I could see the staff room behind him: people sitting smoking and reading newspapers as they waited for the next lesson.

'You know what, Petronella? I don't believe you. But I won't bother with it this time. I won't send a letter home to your parents…'

There were coats and bags hanging in the cloakroom in a corner that was not visible from the front desk. I thought: if you can get in there without anyone noticing, there's a small fortune there for the taking.

'I think you had other reasons for being absent. And you should know one thing: you can always come and talk to me if there's something worrying you. It's part of my job, you know.'

It would have been so easy, I thought, to let my guard down for a moment, to just open up, tell him what had happened, get all the crap that had been building up off my chest, and when I was in full flow to remember to tell him that Dad was on his way home and that Mum was probably lying asleep in her own vomit while we were standing there killing time. But I just didn't feel like it.

'I've got an issue right now that has to do with some of your classmates. I can't reveal what it's about, but I wonder whether you've been having a tough time precisely because of it. If you have, you can certainly come and talk to me about it. And whatever you say, I promise I will not pass it along to anyone else.'

'It's no problem. I just got sick, something with my stomach, and forgot to ring. I'll remember next time. How is Tommy, by the way, is he still at home?'

L.G. gave me a strange look.

'Wasn't he in Social Studies today?'

'No.'

'It's the same thing there: absent without calling in sick. It sounds as though I'll have to bring this up at the next class assembly so everyone knows what the rules are.'

He sounded formal again, on the way back to his role masquerading as a teacher. He looked at his watch; I understood that my time was up.

When I reached my locker, Jessica, the class gossip, was standing there waiting. She was wearing her Takano jumpsuit with leg warmers and Peter Pan boots, and fingerless gloves in white lace. She embodied a sort of summary of all the girls in Year Nine, with Nivea Ultra lip gloss, home-permed curls and round white rings round her eyes from the goggles they wore on the sunbed. The only mismatch was her acne. Underneath her face powder she looked as if she'd been hit by a hail of buckshot.

'How'd the test go?' she asked.

'Okay. Why are you asking?'

'I thought the questions were hard. Like that one about the Pershing missiles, what countries they're in. And why do we have to memorise all the names? You should just ask someone who knows if you don't. A teacher or somebody.'

She looked at me like it was my fault there was something called Social Studies that existed in the world. She was a good pupil, almost as good as me, but she didn't think it was appropriate to admit it. Presumably she was convinced it would make her less attractive to boys.

'Did you know Gerard had to go to the headmaster's office last Friday?' she asked. 'Did you know about that before you ran off?'

'No.'

'He's been reported to the police for something… that's what it was about. He spent an hour in the office because of that. L.G. was there too. And the school welfare officer. Somebody said they saw a policeman up there too. I heard a rumour it was about a whole load of sick stuff they've done… a whole kettle of fish that's going to get blown wide open. Stuff they've been up to this past year. Everybody was talking about it at the weekend. The whole school, it seems like.'

I took my PE bag out of my locker and tried not to listen to her. The Walkman was right at the back of the shelf, along with an envelope containing five hundred kronor. Two hundred and seventy were my own, and the rest came from the old lady at the chemist's. Maybe the best thing was not to drag it out any longer, just go and find Gerard and tell him what I had to offer? But he didn't seem to be in any great hurry.

'Was that why they went after you and your brother?'

'Huh?'

'Because you guys knew something?'

'I have no idea what you're talking about.'

Jessica took her chewing gum out of her mouth and inspected it between two fingers.

'What exactly did they do to you? In the woods. I didn't want to listen when they were telling about it. It sounded so gross. Is it true they took your clothes off?'

'No. And why are you pretending you care?'

She chewed her gum like a cud again, and seemed to ponder seriously whether it was time to blow a bubble. I could smell the aroma of Juicy Fruit mingling with the smell of minestrone soup from the dining room.

'But I do, really. I thought they went too far. Peder said they pulled your trousers off and…' – she lowered her voice – '…stuffed something up back there. That's really disgusting! I wouldn't have been able to bear it. Did it hurt?'

It felt completely ridiculous to be having this conversation. And yet I couldn't resist answering.

'So why didn't you tell somebody? L.G. or the headmaster? If you're so concerned about me now, tell them you heard that Gerard had done disgusting things to me. Do me that favour and maybe some things will change around here. But you don't give a damn, Jessica, you're just pretending, and there is a hell of a difference.'

'Well, excuse me for living, but you're fucking mental. Always suffering soooo much. A real victim.'

She smacked her hand against the locker door and went on her way. I stood there in a cloud of Juicy Fruit and Date perfume. Date Natalie, it smelled like.

Communal PE on Mondays was one of the more annoying parts of the school week. I couldn't stand how the girls checked out each other's bodies in the changing room, commented on who was fat or thin, whose breasts had grown the most or how you deal with everything down there. I was badly off in those respects, with hardly a hint of breasts and nearly bare between my legs. I wasn't even anywhere close to having regular periods. At the end of primary school I usually didn't bother to shower because of all the glances and all the talk, but when we started Year Seven it became sort of an unwritten rule. And I'd rather be called Ironing Board than 'puke' or something along those lines. For the boys, it was pubic hair that mattered, all kinds of hair growth really, the more the better, and their voices breaking of course. The ones whose voices hadn't broken by Year Nine were classified as third-class citizens. There were some who tried to disguise it by lowering their voices. Like Petter Andrén, the smallest boy in our year, who valiantly attempted to seem mature by speaking way down in his throat, all mushy and muffled, like he had swallowed solid darkness. I might have preferred that if I'd had a choice, because in the girls' changing room it was all about the bodies, and how you smelled, if you were nice and clean or not…

The teacher had started bringing out the vault boxes from the equipment room when I entered the gym. Caroline Ljungman and her clique were passing a basketball back and forth. Jessica gave me an angry stare as I walked past. Jonas Bengtsson, the class football star, was dribbling a ball in front of an enthusiastic audience of lads. The smells made me feel ill as usual; the stench of ingrained sweat, of the fear of ball games and unpractised exercises, of old scornful laughter and floor burns, of rubber mats, leather, climbing ropes and greasy Roman rings.

Gerard and his gang were doing stretches by the wall bars. It seemed like they were waiting for me. I tried to ignore them, but it was like the terror had taken me over again. As if it had been visiting somebody else over the weekend, but now it was back, rested, fresh and ready for new challenges. When Gerard waved me over, I didn't dare do anything else.

'I heard from Ola that you've started scrabbling some money together,' he said. 'You're doing well, Ironing Board.'

He winked at me as he placed one foot on a bar, extended his leg and stretched his body forwards.

'I think I've got enough already.'

'How'd you manage that? Sucking off old blokes for money?'

Peder grinned.

'Do you know what the ideal girl looks like, Gerard? One metre tall, flat head and no teeth. So you've got somewhere to put your drink while she's sucking you off.'

'That sounds more like a description of your mum, to be honest.'
That shut him up. Gerard turned to me again:
'Did you have anything nice to talk about with L.G.?'
'What?'
'You two were standing there talking outside the teachers' lounge.
Like old mates there… Shooting the breeze.'
I didn't understand what he was fishing for, so I said nothing.
'Ola saw you when he came out of the test. He said you were
having a serious conversation, isn't that right, Ola?'
The henchman nodded decisively as he spoke:
'It fucking well looked like he was about to start pawing at her,
Gerard. L.G. might be a paedo, and Ironing Board looks like a
five-year-old.'
'I don't like this,' said Gerard, taking his foot off the bar. 'Come
on, you can tell us a little about your conversation… Oh, and move
back a bit, I'm not going to lie but there's something about the way
you smell, I can't take it.'
I noticed that people were staring at us. Jennifer, who had been
one of my worst irritants in primary school and who constantly goes
round slouching because she's ashamed of being so tall. Markus
Larsson, the class clown who's also known as 'The Vulture' or
'Filter Specialist' because he's always cadging fags off people in the
smoking area. Nicke Wester, the music freak in the Clash T-shirt and
a badge with a crossed-out picture of Eurovision songstress Carola
Häggkvist. It was as if I were suddenly seeing Gerard through their
eyes, in a totally new light. He was shorter than I usually imagined,
his cheeks rosier in a childish way, hardly any hair on his arms
and legs. Eyes light brown, hair blond. He did not have a sturdy
build like his minions, and his hands were like a girl's. I couldn't
help wondering what he had done. What was that kettle of fish that
Jessica was talking about, that was about to get blown open?
'Let me tell you one thing, Ironing Board. I actually started to believe
what you said last Friday, that you weren't the one who blabbed.
I started to think, okay, it's not her, it might be somebody else.

You sounded *plausible*, is that the word? So I thought: I'll let her pay so her brother will be left alone, she might actually be okay, that chick… but now, when Ola's seen you with L.G., I'm starting to doubt that.'

'I was asking him about Tommy… if he knew where Tommy is.'

Gerard started to do some more stretches, now his other leg. Out of the corner of my eye I could see Patrik Lagerberg circling round us with his gelled yuppie hair. It took only a single glance from Gerard to make him skedaddle over to the other side of the gym.

'That's what you claim, sure. But you might be lying. People do that sometimes. Make up things about other people. About me, for example. That I would burn kittens alive, for example. Somebody apparently told L.G. that. And also told him a whole load of other stuff while they were at it. Worse things. Which got me thinking.'

He put his foot on the floor, leaned his upper body towards the wall and started stretching his calf muscles.

'Things you can't know, Ironing Board. But I didn't realise that before late last Friday, after I'd been up in the headmaster's office. It was only then that I realised it couldn't have been you.'

I glanced at Peder. But he did not move a muscle. Ola did not betray anything either: the same ice-cold expression, as if they were carved out of stone.

'But you could have said that about the cat. And maybe some-body else told about all the rest? That's entirely possible. But when you're standing talking to L.G. during recess, it's like I get confused. I don't know what to believe. I don't know where I've got you.'

He sighed and pushed a strand of hair off his forehead. He had long eyelashes, like a girl.

'I don't know anything. But an agreement is an agreement. So I want my money. See you by your locker after our free period.'

He waved me off with the back of his hand, as if I were a fly, and carried on with his stretches.

I tried to avoid them for the rest of the lesson, tried to avoid thinking and planning altogether. Tried to avoid attracting the fear which had temporarily snuck into a corner behind the wall bars. I stuck close to the teacher, pretended to be interested as he explained how to improve my vaulting technique, queued obediently at the various stations, laughed when the others laughed, when somebody didn't make it up onto the vault or landed with their arse right on top and had to wriggle down the other side; I pretended to be impressed when Petter Bengtson did a back flip on the crash mat; pretended to commiserate with Mats Ingelstad who shied away like an unruly dressage horse when faced with an obstacle that was too high; cast critical glances at Lilian and Sandra, who constantly chattered about what they were going to wear to school and who had decided the previous night to wear identical leotards and who now resembled two little versions of a keep-fit instructor from TV; laughed at Markus the joker, who was another one whose voice hadn't broken and who attempted to conceal that fact by speaking in a low voice, unnaturally low in his throat. I became one of the crowd, basically, because it was so much easier to exist there.

Exactly as promised, Gerard turned up by my locker five minutes before the end of our free period.

He was on his own, and something told me Ola and Peder had been given orders to stay away.

'Show me what you've got,' he said.

I opened my locker and took the Walkman out. He looked at it briefly.

'Where'd you get hold of that?'

'Mum gave it to me on Saturday. It's brand new. The price tag is still on it. It's a genuine Walkman.'

'Do you think I'm blind? What else would it be, a toaster? And what am I supposed to do with it? I'm not even interested in music. Music is for faggots like Nicke Wester. How much money have you got together?'

'Five hundred. The tape player cost twelve hundred, so that makes seventeen hundred in all.'

'Give me that.'

I handed him the envelope. He didn't even open it, just stuffed it into his back pocket without counting the notes.

'How's your brother doing?'

'Fine.'

'Just wondering. It can't be easy being in the remedial class and stuff. A little retarded, hard to grasp things. And incontinent, is that what it's called, when you piss yourself?'

I didn't reply, and just felt round to find where the fear was. In my neck, it seemed; it was completely stiff.

'And your dad in the slammer. Isn't that right? Nobody to look after you, like, nobody to look up to. And your mum is round the off-licence pretty much every day, she's like a regular customer there, isn't she?'

He leaned against the lockers and stared at a spot on my left shoulder. Then the reached out and plucked something off: a single hair.

'Honestly, Ironing Board, who do you think you are? If we assume it wasn't you, I mean… There were only six of us by the newsagent's kiosk, after all.'

'It *wasn't* me…'

'You won't know that for sure until I've decided. And I haven't yet. Tell me, who seems more nervous, Peder or Ola?'

I was hoping the bell would ring; I didn't want to get drawn into anything else, didn't want to get any more tangled up in what Gerard and his gang had in mind. I didn't want him to touch me again, to remove any more strands of hair from my clothes. There were only two lessons left: Home Economics and English, and I wasn't going to be in either one. I had other plans.

'What did you think of lunch?'

'Huh?'

'Minestrone soup. Even though it's Monday. Peder hardly ate anything. I was shovelling it in. Five open-faced sandwiches with cheese as well. And salad. I didn't taste anything odd. Did you?'

'No.'

He took the Walkman out of my hand. He pressed Play, even though there was no tape in it, and then Stop.

'Peder wasn't hungry. He thought it tasted strange… Isn't that a sign of nervousness? I've changed my mind, by the way: I'll take care of this for you. You nicked it, right? Your stupid slag of a mother would never be able to afford a Walkman. And like I said: a thousand kronor by Friday.'

'You just got five hundred!'

'I don't remember that. My mind is just a blank.'

'You've got it in your pocket.'

'I've made a deduction. You were talking to L.G. That has a price. And tomorrow I've got to go up to the headmaster's office again. A big meeting with the school administration and the welfare officer. Even my dad has to go. Between you and me, Ironing Board, I'm just laughing at all this. What the hell are they going to do? Tell me how to live my life? What's right and wrong, what you can and can't do. I don't give a damn… I've never given a damn about any of it.'

He looked at me, completely emotionless, as if all this were just a sort of business arrangement, any old thing. And then I suddenly remembered his parents, from school prize days and events over the years: the nervous little couple who always drove up in posh cars, impeccably dressed, but seemingly terrified of their own existence – and Gerard's expression when he caught sight of them, a look of shame, almost of disgust.

'I'll get my money by the weekend,' he said in a friendly voice. 'If you want to quibble, we'll make it two thousand straight away. And it's not just about you and me, is it?'

He nodded towards the window that looked out onto the schoolyard. I followed his gaze. Several Year Sevens were standing in the smoking area, huddling against the wind. On a bench by the basketball hoop sat my brother, prodding a pile of leaves with his foot. He was on his own, as usual. He was wearing his Stan Smiths.

'Remember when we learned about the Second World War last term… what the Germans did with all the retards…' He placed a hand on my shoulder. 'Nobody else would be sad, Ironing Board, only you.'

I stood there facing the window as Gerard disappeared down the corridor. My brother looked awesome in his new trainers. I had given him the jeans, too; they were a little big for him, but at any rate they were a real brand name. He was beaming from ear to ear until he realised it was a bribe, that I really did want him to go to school as usual, despite what had happened. It took a great deal of persuasion to get him to come. I explained how important it was that we didn't stay away like scaredy-cats, because that would only sharpen their bloodlust.

Somebody went over to him outside and said something. A lad in his class who suffers from a load of strange tics and is basically unable to keep still. I saw my brother perk up and nod. Maybe he got a compliment on his clothes. I felt like going out to him and keeping him company for a while, and I might have done it too, if I hadn't had other things to think about.

Tommy's house stood behind a dense hedge that protected it from the winds off the sea. It was a two-storey detached house with fibre-cement cladding and a grey brick-built annexe, which the family let out to tourists in the summertime. To the left was a driveway leading to the garage and a shed, where they would tinker around with boat engines. There used to be another house on the plot, an old farmhouse, but Tommy's dad had it torn down when the family built their new house in the Sixties. He was part of the Celes family and was born in the village. Tommy's mum came from Träslöv, a fishing community some thirty or forty miles north. Through his father, Tommy was related to almost everyone in Glommen. The families had intermingled for generations, and everyone kept track of which branches they belonged to.

I parked my bike by the gate and went up the gravel path. People freely came and went in each other's houses down here. Nobody locked their doors, not even in the summer when the place was full of holidaymakers. Tommy had said there were never any break-ins in Glommen; there was no reason to break into an unlocked house.

I rang the doorbell. When no one opened the door, I went in.

The bed was made in his room upstairs. His schoolbooks lay on the desk. A pair of jeans hung over one arm of the chair. Dirty tube socks littered the floor. I spent a while looking at a picture hanging above his desk. It showed a fishing boat on its way into Glommen harbour. It was the family's previous boat. Tommy's dad had painted it. When he retired, he took up painting in his leisure time. I sat down on the bed and wondered what to do. Wait until he got home, or start searching?

It struck me that he might be in the basement. His brothers had built a games room down there, with a ping-pong table and a little bar with beer taps. Tommy would sit down there and play video games sometimes, but if his mum or dad suddenly came home it could be awkward if they found me somewhere other than in his room. To say nothing of how weird I would feel if his brothers found me in the basement. They didn't frighten me, but there was something that made you not want to end up alone with them.

I went over to the window. I could see the lighthouse a little way off. At night it shone into the room, but it never disturbed Tommy. It might be in his blood, I thought, that love of lighthouses. In every family down here there were tales of some ancestor who had run aground and drowned because of poor light from a lighthouse.

On the chest of drawers by the window was our school year-book, open to the page with our class photo. Gerard was sitting in front on the left in his usual uniform: leather jacket, patched jeans and a bandanna round his neck. His scooter helmet was on his lap, and the gloves, as if he had something to hide underneath. Peder, who was seated next to him, seemed to be most inclined to agree in the presence of his boss. He had placed his hands on his thighs; if you looked closely, you could see he was giving the photographer the finger. Furthest to the right in the top row, as if we wanted to get as far away from them as possible, were Tommy and me: Tommy in his Tintin top and me in my usual T-shirt with a picture of a cat on it and a pair of trousers that were too small. My hair was unwashed. No make-up, of course, and my T-shirt was dirty. I had my eyes closed.

The fact we were standing next to one another in our class photo was as much of a given as spring following winter or the sun coming up each morning. Tommy had arrived in our school in Year Five, together with an entire class from Glommen. The pupils had been divided up among the old Skogtorp classes. We were assigned desks next to each other in our first lesson. I still remember the feeling of change then: as if the cards had been reshuffled and

I was dealt a new hand. From that moment onwards it was like I no longer held any interest for the others; I was invisible to them. Actually, it was hard to explain why we were drawn together. We didn't have all that much in common. Tommy was a little brother and I was a big sister; he was a boy and I was a girl; he came from a fishing family in Glommen, where his relatives had been living forever and he knew absolutely everyone, whereas I had only my brother and my parents.

But ever since that day we'd stuck together. We revised together, played during recess, chatted, discussed anything and everything that interested us: books we were reading, teachers and the other kids in our class, what they were like, why they thought and acted the way they did. I would go home with him after school as often as I could, but only if I knew that Robert was all right on his own. We were usually in the room where I was now, where I recognised every object, the exact position of the furniture and the smell of the wallpaper and the rug. We would usually listen to his brothers' records, play games or play down by the docks. And if my brother wanted to, he could come along. Tommy never raised any objection about that. He knew that Robert was part of the deal if he wanted to be friends with me.

That was what I was thinking about as I stood by the window and looked out towards the docks; how meaningless everything would have been if I hadn't been friends with Tommy.

It was deserted down by the quay. Hardly any boats were in. I could see the roof of their hut. Smoke was coming from the chimney. Presumably, I thought, he was down there helping his brothers.

There was a van parked in front of the hut when I went down to the docks. Its back doors were open. A man sat in the cab, smoking. The door to the building was closed but there were people inside; I could hear someone talking. I don't know what caused me to turn round and go over towards the turning area for vehicles instead. Something about the man in the van, I think: the way he carried on smoking, kind of aggressively, a little like Dad.

I carried on past the old storage halls and went round the corner to an old covered mooring. There was a fence at the rear, and I could see out to the quay between the slats. The man had got out of the van now, as if he had just been waiting until I was out of sight. He took a crate out of the back of the van and called out to someone who was inside. The door opened. I saw Tommy looking out. The man handed him the crate. Then the door closed again, the man got into the van, started it up and vanished in the direction of Glumstensvägen.

The area around the docks was dead quiet; the only noise was the sea, which sounded a constant drone in the background. Just off to the left, at the edge of my field of vision, something moved. When I looked over I spotted the mink again, the same mink I'd seen three days before. It was sitting on a rubbish bin thirty metres away, observing me. Then it leapt down and disappeared from sight.

I had just made up my mind to leave when the door opened again and Tommy's brothers came out. One of them took a tin of chewing tobacco out of his pocket and began rolling a plug. The other crouched down and dried off his shoes with a hankie. I couldn't figure out what was up with me: why didn't I just go over and ask about Tommy, or call out to him as I approached? Instead, I stayed there, crouching behind the fence.

It started to rain, a light drizzle that made me shiver. They were discussing something over there, gesticulating to one another. One of them rapped his knuckle significantly against his temple. Then they all burst out laughing and put their arms round each other's shoulders as they walked up towards the village. But Tommy was still there. I saw him close the door after them.

I waited until his brothers were out of sight. Then I climbed over the fence and followed the asphalt path down to the fisherman's hut.

'Who is it?' he asked when I knocked.
'It's me, Nella.'

'What the hell are you doing here?'

He sounded angry and jittery at the same time.

'Trying to get hold of you.'

'Go away. Get lost!'

'How come? We need to talk.'

'Get away from the door, they can see you.'

'Who's "they"?'

'My brothers.'

'I'm staying here until you open up.'

It was quiet, as if he needed to think it over. Then the latch was raised and he let me into the darkness.

I couldn't see anything at first; there was a piece of tarpaulin hanging over the window.

'Did anybody see you?' he asked.

'I don't think so… why do you want to know?'

Tommy stood on a stool by the window, turned up a corner of the tarpaulin and looked out. Seemingly relieved, he climbed back down and switched on the light.

I hadn't been inside their hut for several months, but everything seemed the same. Nets hung on hooks on the wall. A broken barometer indicated a storm. Coiled-up ropes lay on the floor. Lobsterpots were piled up in one corner. Bailers and floats lay jumbled up in boxes. And in the middle of the floor stood Tommy, looking pale, as if he were still running a temperature.

'Why did you have the light off before?'

'I was just about to leave. It's important that nobody sees anything when I open the door… and it can barely tolerate any light.'

The lamp, I now noticed, was angled towards the wall. Most of the space was still in darkness. I heard a sort of panting coming from over by the end wall.

'Is there someone here?' I asked.

Tommy gave a laugh, a laugh I'd never heard from him before, not at all happy-sounding.

'I guess you could say that, someone – or rather, something.'

He looked at me as if I were a complete stranger, as if he had never seen me before in his life.

'There's way too much going on here, I don't even know where to start.'

The crate I had seen him take in earlier was right by my feet; it was full of fish guts, cod heads, roe sacs, fins and tails.

'Who was the guy in the van?'

'Jens, a bloke in the boat crew. He was with my brothers when it happened.'

Tommy bent down, picked up a cod head and looked at it in disgust.

'We're not sure what it eats yet. Not every kind of fish, anyway. But it seems to like rubbish… fish guts and fins. It doesn't care for shellfish.'

He tossed the head back into the crate and looked as confused as what he had just said. I didn't understand any of it.

'My family have brought up a load of weird things out of the sea,' he continued, 'basking sharks, moonfish, porpoises, old mines from the war… in the Fifties there were tuna out there. My dad told me you could see shoals of over a thousand fish, and the biggest ones weighed over two hundred kilos. They brought them up with a hook, baited with mackerel, with steel cables and hawsers. Dad's got photos at home…' Tommy gave another laugh, as if he were reassured by telling old fishing tales. '…where he's standing in the long side of the boat, hooking a tuna through its gills out by the Lilla Middelgrund bank. My Uncle John is standing by, ready to thread a line around its tail fin. Do you know how they located the shoal? With binoculars, a shoal a hundred and fifty metres across – the whole sea was churning. Then in the early Sixties, they just disappeared, the tuna, just as suddenly as they'd turned up.' He sat down on the stool beneath the window, but got up again straight away, as if he'd received an electric shock. 'Dad was on the *Zentora* too, the neighbour's boat, 1977. They caught eighteen tons of cod in a single trawler net. It was in the newspaper afterwards. Seven people worked flat-out for twenty-one hours outside Laesö to clean the fish. What I'm trying to say is that strange things happen some-times, people get strange catches, but this is something else.'

I heard the noise again: a low whimper, followed by a sort of wheezing sound, like air being forced through something moist.

'What on earth is that?'

'I don't know what the hell it is. They brought it up in the trawler net outside Anholt. They panicked and hit it over the head until they thought it was dead… but it survived.'

I wondered if he was still ill. If he had a fever and was delirious. Nothing he was saying made any sense.

There was another box on the floor, I now realised, filled with bottles of medicines. There was a label from a veterinary clinic on it. Tommy pushed it aside with his foot. A large dark patch was visible on the concrete floor underneath. Oil, I thought. Or blood? The same blood his brother had wiped off his shoes?

'Thank God it's asleep now,' he continued. 'Doped up. it's impossible to handle otherwise. It's incredibly strong, the bastard. That's what we've got the medicines for. Jens knows a vet. There are syringes there, too.'

I don't remember what I was thinking, only that something was wrong and Tommy was shaken in a way I'd never experienced before. He didn't say anything else. Just took me by the arm and pulled me further into the room.

Over by the end wall was a wooden crate, maybe three metres long, a metre wide and about as deep, the kind you use for trans-porting a boat engine. That's where the noise was coming from. And the smells… the strange smells… of fish and sea and blood.

I looked down into the crate. And even though I saw what it was, I didn't take any of it in.

'What is it?' I whispered.

'If it were a female and I'd read about it in a storybook, I know what I would answer. But this… I haven't got a clue.'

Whatever it was, it was big. It must have weighed several hundred kilos. Its arms resembled a human's or a large ape's. A sea-ape, if there is such a thing… long and slender, with small hands on the ends. But its joints faced the other way, and there was webbing between its fingers. There were sort of nails too, or rather claws, blue-black in colour. Its upper body was almost human: you could see a chest and an abdomen with something that resembled a navel. But its hide consisted of armour-like scales, like the skin of a large lizard. There was hair growing on its shoulders: long, bristly hairs, almost like horsehair. It's difficult to describe what I was seeing, so that's why my comparisons are strange. Its lower body was shaped like a hammer, a long cylindrical body that changed into a fin, almost a metre wide. It looked like the tail of a small whale. Its lower section was completely smooth, with no hair. But its scales were all black there, and appeared to be even thicker.

Its face was unlike anything I'd ever seen either: half fish, half mammal. Its forehead was low and pointy. It had no nose, instead a kind of nasal bone that stuck out in the middle of its face. Its eyelids were half closed, and behind them you could sense black irises and eyeballs as big as a horse's. It seemed to be asleep… or hibernating.

'What on earth is it?' I asked again.

'I dunno.' Tommy shook his head. 'I really haven't got a clue.'

I stared at the creature as if entranced. Its jawbones were huge, its mouth horribly broad. I knew that it could open its mouth almost as wide as its entire face. It sort of had lips, too, with horseshoe-shaped bones underneath; you could see them clearly because its lips were very thin. Its skull was pointy, as if it had grown skin over a curiously cone-shaped hat. Its head was covered in the same type of hair as its shoulders: like a cross between human hair and horsehair. On each side of its head was a narrow notch with flaps: like ears, I supposed. And then its neck: short, broad, and where the collarbones would have been on a person: two gills.

'It's got lungs and a windpipe just like us,' said Tommy. 'And gills as well. I don't get it.'

I couldn't get any words out. Just stared at whatever it was that I had never stared at before in my entire life. The puffing noise, I understood, was coming from its gills, but only when it breathed out. It seemed to be breathing in through its mouth.

Then, suddenly, it moved, a sort of shudder went through its body, and the movement resembled nothing I had ever seen either. There must have been bones and muscles involved that other animals do not have: simultaneously a light and heavy movement, incredibly clumsy and smooth at the same time. Its head turned towards us, the eyelids flickered and my instincts told me to back away and to run, but I stayed put, as if I no longer had the strength to move.

For several seconds, I thought it was going to open its eyes and look at me. But instead it sank back into hibernation, became almost motionless, except for its ribcage, which steadily rose and fell. There was an open flesh wound on one of its cheeks. You could see right inside the creature's mouth there. You could see its tongue that was big and pink like a cow's tongue, see its teeth – fish teeth, loads of them, relatively small, but razor-sharp. A little further up by its temple was a large bruise. There was blood clotted around it. Small bone chips were sticking out of its flesh.

'They used the boat hook,' Tommy said in a quiet voice. 'Its whole cheek was torn open. They didn't have a choice, it could have killed them.'

'But how... I don't get it.'

'With its tail. It's aggressive, I've seen it myself... and really strong. He must weigh two, three hundred kilos.'

He took a cigarette out of the packet his brother had left behind, and lit it. I had never seen him smoke before; it looked almost indecent. Like photos you might see of street children in impoverished countries. He took a deep drag without coughing. Then he bent over, fumbled over the creature's body down there and turned over a flap of skin on its tail fin.

'See for yourself,' he said. 'It's a male.'

Even though I didn't want to, I couldn't help looking. Its penis was the most human-like part of the whole creature. It looked like it could be on any grown man at all. It felt shameful to look at it, sort of like spying on someone in the shower or peeping through a keyhole at somebody doing something dirty.

'Leave it be,' I said. 'Don't do that.'

'It doesn't notice anything. You can touch it. The body, I mean. It's totally pumped up on this stuff.' Tommy picked up a syringe that lay in the bottom of the crate, and a brown bottle that had a little liquid sloshing around in it. 'Anaesthetic... the stuff they use at the zoo to put animals to sleep. He's had the same size dose a polar bear would get. He won't wake up for hours.'

It was only now that I realised the creature was tied down. A heavy rope was wound around its tail fin. Its arms, or what you might call its reverse-jointed limbs, were fastened to the bottom of the crate with steel cables. I felt confused in a way I'd never been before. My whole head was swimming with questions, a mishmash of questions, an entire landslide: what it was, where it came from, why it was still alive, and how long it would survive like this.

Tommy took my hand and placed it on the creature's body. It was cold and slimy. I felt how my hand sort of stuck to its hide. The whole thing just felt wrong: that it was here in the first place, that it had a gender, that it was bound and drugged up, and that Tommy wanted me to touch it.

'Let me go!' I said.

'Calm down. There's no danger. It can't hurt you.'

'It's not that… it just doesn't feel right. Tell me what happened instead.'

It was the Tuesday before when Tommy's brothers had gone out on their boat. It was perfect fishing weather. As I understood it, that had to do with the winds: they affected the surface temperature and made the cod shoals head towards the fishing banks. That was why they took an extra deckhand out on the boat: they might have needed another pair of strong arms if they got a big catch.

First they had gone to their usual reefs, the places where they knew the fish would normally be. But the echo sounder had shown only small shoals not worth trawling for. They had lain still just north of Marsten and discussed what to do: head back to the marina or head out further to the north-west. Finally they decided to go in the opposite direction, towards Anholt. In fact, those were Danish waters and, according to the rule book, they weren't allowed to fish there. But Anholt was special. Not that long ago people in Glommen had relations on the island, married into each other's families, fished together; the border only existed on the nautical charts.

It was around midday when everything happened. They were by a bank a few nautical miles inside Danish waters when the echo sounder showed a large shoal of fish. It was moving strangely, Tommy said, not at all like it should, sort of splitting up and then joining together again, suddenly diving and then immediately coming back up towards the surface. Nobody said anything, but they suspected it might be porpoises or whales that were hunting in the shoal. It was unusual for whales to come so far into the Kattegat, but it happened sometimes. Pilot whales, for example, had made it as far south as Öresund. After talking it over for a while, they decided to put the trawl net out. There were no Coast Guard boats in sight, and if any fishermen from the island turned up, they would turn a blind eye to their presence. With the eldest brother as the helmsman, they followed the shoal at a leisurely pace. Tommy's next older brother Olof and the lad, who was called Jens, were standing on the shelter deck, each with a pair of binoculars. They were hoping to catch a glimpse of a whale, or at worst a Danish Coast Guard vessel that they would have to get away from as fast as possible, hopefully without needing to let go of their net.

All that was significant in leading up to what happened next. The fact that they were there against the rules, that they were breaking certain laws. People from Glommen were known for their suspicion of authorities: customs, the police, the Board of Fisheries. And maybe there were other things on board the boat that made them unwilling to involve outsiders.

They had had the trawl net out for less than half an hour when they decided to bring it back in. Tommy seemed unsure exactly in what order events had occurred, but then he hadn't been there. Maybe it was the idea that there were whales in their path, that they might destroy their equipment; maybe they had seen something on the echo sounder or identified some strange movement in the hawsers. At any rate, they started to bring in the trawl net again.

They discovered it when they made the lift. It was tangled up in the net, struggling for its life. As I understood Tommy, they tried to let it out through the side panel, but the creature was too big. Finally there was no other option but to bring it in. It was incredibly aggressive, striking out with its tail, throwing itself this way and that all over the place, and it managed to make some large tears in the net. They had never seen anything like it. At first they thought it was moving like a small whale, Tommy said, and that in itself was a problem because you have to report a catch like that. Then they realised what it was, or in any case what it resembled.

But why didn't they just chuck it overboard, I wondered. They couldn't, he explained. They couldn't even get near it: as soon as they got too close, it tried to attack, and they couldn't stay out at sea all night. Finally they panicked and started hitting it with the boat hooks. I could see it in my mind's eye, how they kept hitting and hitting and how the creature tried to defend itself, how it threw itself upon them, biting with its jaws and lashing with its tail fin. I could hear how they struck it on the head, the low, blunt noise from the boat hooks when the gristle and hide split open, the blood that ran, all the chaos on that slippery deck, how the creature's cheek was sliced open when they tried to hook it, the men's screams, the terror in the creature as it fought for its life, and how at last, as the boat heaved, it slid through the hatch to the lower deck, struck its head and passed out.

They returned to Glommen with the creature in the cargo hold. They didn't know what they should do. The best thing, they said, would be to kill it, but that was easier said than done. To do that they needed a gun, but none of them had one. They discussed whether they should contact someone they knew: there were several people in the village who had a hunting licence, but the fewer people who got wind of what they had brought in, the better. Anyway, they would need a larger calibre weapon than an average shotgun.

The brothers had not told anyone what they had brought up that day. Presumably they were afraid of questions about what they were doing in Danish fishing waters, about the duty of notification, about fishing quotas that might already have been exceeded, and maybe because there were other things in the cargo hold that Tommy didn't mention. When they returned, the creature was still unconscious. Assisted by the dock crane, they lifted it up onto a trailer, rolled it into the hut and tied it down in an old machinery crate while they tried to figure out what to do.

Tommy had been dragged into the story against his will. He had noticed that something was not right. He had heard his brothers coming in and leaving the house at odd hours, heard them arguing downstairs in the games room. From the window in his room he had seen them in the hut, the tarpaulin they used to cover the windows, the strange sneaking around, and he wondered what was actually going on. On Thursday, even though he had a temperature, he went down there. His brothers had gone into town to sort something out; he opened the door with a spare key, went in and discovered the creature. That same evening he demanded an explanation from them. And because the story began to follow its own rules, he was suddenly involved in it.

'What are you going to do now?' I asked when he had finished telling his story.

'I have no idea.'

'Can't you phone the police or something? It has to go back where it came from. Or be handed in somewhere... I don't know.'

From the look he gave me, I understood that that was the very last thing that they wanted to do.

'I have no idea what they want to do,' he said. 'Leave it to die, maybe. But it's tough. It looks like it can survive a long time on land. A bloody amphibian... uses its gills to breathe underwater... and its windpipe and lungs on land.'

I looked over at the crate of fish guts that was over by the door.

'So why are they feeding it, if they want it to die?'

'Don't ask me. I'm not the one who's making the decisions here.'

Something didn't add up. Tommy's sentences that stumbled, skipped over certain words, went back to pick them up again, sentences that haltingly advanced over invisible obstacles, fell over them and got up again. And why didn't they throw it back into the sea now, when it was completely helpless?

I detected the smell of the creature again. The mermaid... although it was a man. The merman, merbull, mermonkey... the smell of sea, fish and blood. My eyes had adjusted to the darkness, and I noticed more wounds, flesh wounds and bruises between its scales, deep wounds where they stabbed it with the boat hooks the way bullfighters thrust and stab at bulls.

'Do your mum and dad know about this?' I asked.

'No. Since Dad retired from fishing they never come down here. Just me, Jens and my brothers... and now you.'

A *man*, a *male*, I thought as I looked down into the crate again; the words bore less and less relation to reality. It really was breathing through its mouth, and releasing the air from its gills; I saw the moisture there, the slime and the small air bubbles that formed. And then that horrible wheezing noise when the air was forced out. Tommy touched it, with exaggerated roughness I thought. And then the movement started again, that powerful trembling through the bound beast or fish or whatever it was. Smooth and clumsy at the same time.

'It's starting to wake up,' said Tommy. 'It can't tolerate the light. It probably lives down at the bottom of the sea and only comes up to the surface at night.'

And then I saw another thing I had never experienced before. The creature opened its eyelids, or rather the scales or flaps in front of its eyes. It looked straight at me. Its eyes were large, pitch-black and watery, as if it were suffering from an eye infection. But its gaze was completely human, and I noticed it was observing me and wondering who I was. It tried to lift one arm; its fingers scratched awkwardly in the air before its hand sank down again, restrained by a steel cable fastened to the bottom of the crate.

'It's suffering,' I told Tommy. 'Don't you understand that?'

But he was already heading for the door.

The Professor was sitting on a stool in his yard, busily doing something as I approached on my bike. On the ground next to his crutches there was a pile of boards and some rolls of chicken wire. He was holding a hammer in his hand.

'Hello there, Nella,' he said. 'What luck you're here. Can you give me a hand with this?' He pointed to the pile of boards with the handle of his hammer. 'Rabbit hutches. I got them from my neighbour. They need to be repaired before they can be used… for the summer, I was thinking. How come you're not in school, by the way?'

He looked at me, concerned.

'Has something happened? Come on, let's go inside.'

It felt safe sitting in the Professor's kitchen; it really did, among the usual jumble of things he'd found at flea markets or the rubbish tip, among broken radio sets and telephones he'd planned to fix, but had given up hope before he finished, among old books and stacks of articles he'd cut out of newspapers, about everything from UFO sightings to unsolved murders.

As we drank tea, I told him about Gerard and what had happened at school, that Dad was coming home and my room was going to be let out to a jailbird. And even though I told everything as accurately as I could, it felt like I was keeping certain key facts from him, such as the rules of the game underlying everything.

At one point, when he was hobbling over towards the stove to get his medicines, I was on the verge of telling him about what I'd just seen in the hut, only twenty minutes ago. What my brain was sort of refusing to grasp, the creature lying in the wooden crate, tied up and drugged, which made everything else seem unimportant. But at the same instant the words began to take shape in my mouth, I could see Tommy in my mind's eye, and even though he hadn't said so explicitly, I knew that I mustn't tell anyone. Not a single person. Not even the Professor.

'So what do you intend to do now?' he asked when I had finished.

'That's what everybody's asking me. And I'm hoping somebody else can tell me. Like maybe you.'

He opened a compartment in his pill case, took out three red tablets and two yellow ones, and weighed them in his hand.

'I think you need to divide everything up into smaller chunks,' he said. 'One problem at a time. Together they seem big, but not individually. And then you can try to solve them one at a time. That's what I usually do.'

He filled up a glass of water, placed the tablets on the tip of his tongue, swallowed and took a drink.

'And you need to have time to think. Stress makes everything worse… Are you listening to me, Nella? You seem as though you're miles away.'

I gave a start and looked at him.

'The worst thing is that Gerard doesn't seem to think I'm the one who blabbed.'

'Who does he think it was, then?'

'Somebody in his gang. He sort of feels it in his bones.'

'So why is he continuing to pick on you?'

'Because he thinks it's fun.'

'No human being is born evil. There are a thousand reasons why people turn out the way they do and do what they do.'

'But that doesn't help me. What might help me is a loan of a thousand kronor. So he doesn't take it out on my brother.'

'If I had the money you would get it, you know that.'

That was true, he would have given it to me on the spot. A million if that's what I needed. But he was completely uninterested in money, and that's why he never had any.

I dropped the subject and let my eyes wander round the kitchen. There was a box on the windowsill of oddly shaped stones: one of his many collections. His stamp albums were piled up on a table by the kitchen sink. A tall glass case next to the door to the hall contained his collection of taxidermy animals: small birds, a black grouse, a fox, a hare in its winter coat. I don't know how many times I had sat there admiring them, how the taxidermist had managed to capture them in mid-step. But now I couldn't. All that gruesomeness… the fact that somebody had killed them, split them open, cleaned out their flesh and organs and then stuffed them. Everything was leading my thoughts where I didn't want them to go.

'Isn't there a teacher you can talk to?'

'That would just make everything worse.'

'Your mum, then?'

'I may as well ask ask Father Christmas for help.'

'So you're hoping for a miracle, just like me.' He took a banknote out of his back pocket and folded it in half. 'Here. This is what I've got. Fifty kronor.'

I shook my head.

'I don't need it, now that I think about it. That was good, what you said about dividing up problems into smaller chunks. You can see the solutions better then. I'm going to forget about paying Gerard. It's no use. He'll still never get enough.'

The Professor smiled. As he must have done a lot more often before, I thought. Before the accident, where his leg was injured so badly he had to go on medication and use crutches for the rest of his life. Before he was transformed into that crow-like figure who hobbled his way through life on crutches paid for by the health service and read everything he could read and collected everything he could collect.

'Is there anything else I can do for you?' he asked.

'Yes… mermaids. Would you be able to find out what people actually know about them?'

'You mean the fairy-tale characters?'

'Anything that has to do with mermaids. Have people ever believed that they existed for real? Are there any male ones? Anything that might be related.'

'Is this something you're doing at school?'

'Maybe. Just see if you can find anything, and let me know. And then I was wondering if I could have a look through your keys.'

He put the fifty-kronor note back in his pocket.

'Sure. The box of keys! My collection. I keep it in the attic these days. Have you locked yourself out?'

'Sort of.'

'No problem. Just tell me what type of lock it is.'

The first time I ever met the Professor was at the library in Falkenberg. A year had passed since the bus crash, and while the authorities argued over whether or not he should be declared disabled, he got a temporary job there through the jobcentre. My brother and I had just discovered that the library was a good place to hang out when things were raging at home. They were open till seven, and if you were quiet and didn't make a nuisance of yourself you could stay there until closing time. We would read comic books or play games, and when I got tired of Tintin and Lucky Luke or of beating my brother at Chinese chequers I would ask Lazlo to find some interesting books for me. He just lit up when you asked him about astronomy or dinosaurs. And he would set off among the shelves and come back carrying huge piles of books. After a while, it felt like we were old friends. He knew what books I liked, and often he was just as interested himself. When there weren't many people around and he didn't have anything else to do, we would sit in the cafeteria and chat about all sorts of things.

One of the first things I did was ask why he walked with crutches. And without beating about the bush, he told me about the bus journey he went on to Germany, and about the accident on the autobahn where he had broken both his legs, and how the fractures were so severe that he would never be able to walk properly again. The ironic thing, he explained, was that it was the first time he'd been abroad, if you didn't count the two years in Hungary before he came to Falkenberg with his mother, and the accident had happened almost right after the bus drove off the ferry. All I got to see of Germany was a bit of motorway and a hospital, he said, and that was so depressing that I never intend to travel abroad again.

Soon after that he rented an old farmhouse just outside Skogstorp. When his temporary job at the library ended, he said I could come and visit. I was a little unsure at first due to my general suspicions about adults, but in the end I went. It seemed like he didn't have visitors very often, if you didn't count his mother, who usually came round twice a week with ready-prepared food, because he was almost overjoyed to see me. He offered me tea and showed me all his collections, and told me a load of weird things he'd read about in books.

And that's how it continued. I usually went to visit him a couple of times a month. Mostly just to chat a bit, and sometimes to ask about something I was wondering about or needed help with in school. Lazlo knew a lot about a lot of things, and if he didn't know he made sure he would find out.

I thought about that as I cycled back to Skogstorp. If there was anything written about mermaids, he would find it for me.

There was a car in the driveway when I got home: a black resprayed Ford Taunus that looked like it had been rescued from the scrap heap at the last minute. The windows were open for ventilation. My brother's little bike had been flung carelessly in the gravel next to the steps.

There were fresh tulips in a vase in the hall. I could smell Mum's perfume, the expensive stuff she hardly ever used. It took a few seconds before I realised what was going on: a rucksack on the floor, the worn-out cowboy boots, a leather jacket on the coat rack.

I hastily tidied my hair and rubbed out a spot of dirt on my trouser leg. I couldn't believe that I wanted to look nice for his sake.

The voice coming through the living room wall was so familiar, even though nearly a year had passed since I had last heard it.

He hardly ever phoned from prison. He didn't like to talk on the phone – he became monosyllabic and grumpy, and would sometimes could hang up in the middle of a sentence.

The radio was playing Swedish dance band music in there. A singer was crooning something unfeasibly sentimental, and Dad was humming along with the melody. Then his voice disappeared and was replaced by another one, a little squeakier. It wasn't Mum's or my brother's, but a man's voice that cracked a joke about something because Dad started laughing, that croaky laugh, like a fox with something caught in its throat.

Mum emerged from the living room carrying a tray. Her face lit up when she saw me.

'Hi, Nella. Guess what: Dad's home! It's crazy. He had misread the release papers. Almost three weeks out. You know he has a little trouble reading. And what do you know, an hour ago, he turned up. Aren't you happy? Go in and say hi to him.'

She had got dressed up in her bow-front blouse and a skirt, with a white scarf knotted round her neck. She looked like she was in love. Her cheeks were all rosy, and she had her best earrings on, silver hoops with red stones in them. Right under one ear was a fresh love bite. She had a real spring in her step; I couldn't remember the last time I had seen her so happy.

'Leif is here, too – Dad's friend. I'm just going to get some more glasses and cigarettes.'

I hardly recognised him at first. He had a shaved head and weighed at least twenty pounds more than he had the last time I had seen him. He was wearing jeans and a short-sleeved shirt. A new tattoo depicted a snake winding its way along one arm. When he went down, he had had sideburns and a ponytail that went down past his shoulders. Now he was completely bald. He must have shaved off his hair just recently, because his scalp looked rough, and in the middle of his head there was a little shaving cut with dried blood.

I couldn't tear my eyes away from his skull, dented and strange, with moles that reminded me of woodlice.

Next to him on the sofa sat a man I had never seen before, also shaven-headed, with a short but sturdy build.

'Hi, Dad,' I said.

He didn't see me at first, just turned his head slowly in the wrong direction as if he had heard a voice coming from inside the wall. Robert was sitting cross-legged on the floor opposite him, his face bright red from excitement.

'Nella, there you are. Come here and let me give you a hug.'

He held me so tightly it hurt, and the pain came together with his smells, the old familiar scents of the aftershave he always used, the sweetish smell of sweat that was his alone, the smell of alcohol and tobacco. He released me, then held me with his arms outstretched ,and I looked straight into his eyes. It was like there was no shine in them, you could only sense him at a distance, way down in the bottom of that gaze.

'Leffe. Say hello to my daughter, Petronella.'

Dad's mate gave a brief nod before looking down at his fist, where a can of beer was firmly clenched. He was also tattooed. A naked woman on one forearm; a heart pierced by an arrow on the other. Far down on his neck I could see another tattoo: a swastika, partially hidden by a thick silver chain.

'See how much she looks like her mum. Can you see it? Same colour eyes. Just as skinny. Bloody hell, Nella, how are you, girl?'

'Fine.'

'You've hardly grown since last time. I thought you'd have outgrown your folks by now. How are things at school?'

'Okay.'

'Just don't overexert yourself. It's not good to read too much. It can change you. Some people get so smart they turn stupid, if you follow me.'

He looked from Robert to me and back again, as if he were unable to decide which one of us needed his attention more.

'Christ knows if it isn't you kids I've missed most this year. I'm no good at phoning or writing letters, you know. That's how it is inside. Don't take it personally. You switch off, so to speak. So you don't go mad.'

He coughed and hawked up a gob of phlegm.

'Robert! Go out and fetch us a few more cans, they're in the boot of the car.'

My brother disappeared from the room, delighted to be honoured with this duty. The radio suddenly went silent. There was just a little rattling coming from the kitchen, where Mum was busy with something. Dad sort of peered to the side of me with his hazy eyes.

'Have you been looking after your little brother while I was away?'

'Yeah.'

'Helping him with his homework and things?'

'Sure.'

'That's good. He has a hard enough time as it is with all those damn learning difficulties… My daughter, on the other hand, is a genius,' he continued to his mate. 'Top marks in almost every subject. Fuck knows where she gets it from, not from me anyway. I didn't even learn my times tables in school. The old man could never live down the fact that he lived under the same roof as an idiot. My God, the number of beatings I got when I came home with those marks.'

He gestured towards the packet of cigarettes on the table, and his mate reached out and handed them to him.

'Have you got the car keys, by the way? I've got a few things to sort out. I've just got to tell the old lady.'

'Can't you call her something else?'

Dad gave a good laugh and crumpled the beer can in his hand.

'What? Lady? Listen to the word: lay-dee. It's a word that shows love and admiration. She appreciates it.'

'I just don't want any rows. Are you sure you can't stay here a bit? You haven't seen your kids in quite a while.'

'It's all right. They've managed for a year without me, why wouldn't they manage for another couple of hours?'

He stopped talking when Robert returned with his arms full of cans of beer. Something in my brother's posture, as he put the cans down on the table, made me see that they were similar; that someday he would look very much like Dad. Only a great deal softer, because he was completely different on the inside.

'Are you leaving already?' he asked.

'Just for a little while. Got to sort out a few things. And for Christ's sake, don't start bawling now.'

'Okay, Dad…'

'I mean it. I need some peace and quiet when I'm at home. You have no idea what kind of life it is in the place I've just come from. And it just keeps getting worse every year with all the foreigners inside. Turks and Yugos and all that shit. Isn't that right, Leffe?'

'It's worse than that. Pretty soon you won't even be able to speak Swedish inside any more. Now there's Vietnamese as well, and Kunta Kinte nig-nogs that you don't even know what bloody country they're from.'

'So no blubbing, if you please. You're a big lad now. They don't bawl.'

He took a can of beer, opened it, took a gulp and made a face.

'My God, I can't believe I read the papers wrong. Marika just about passed out when she opened the door. But it's the same with the little fellow here, he's got reading troubles too, isn't that right, Robbie? The exact opposite of your sister. It's like the letters all blend together. An *R* looks like a *P*, a little *s* looks like a little *a*… It took years before I realised it didn't mean I was thick.'

'Almost smarter than most people,' said his mate. 'How long can I stay here, by the way?'

'I'm the one who makes the decisions in this house, and because you've put me up in the past, I'll put you up. You can stay as long as you like, or until your supervisor comes up with something better. Have you thought of this, Leffe… we might celebrate Christmas together, but in a more homely place than Halmstad. What do you say to that, Robert? It'll be exciting with two grown-up blokes in the house, won't it?'

'Is he going to be here for my birthday as well?'

My brother was attempting to act as relaxed as possible, but he couldn't keep it up.

'Sure. You haven't got a problem with that, have you?'

'No.'

'Good. It just sounded like you might.'

That was the same old Dad, I thought as Robert looked away, as if he wished he were a hundred miles from there. I couldn't figure out what he was hoping for. That he had latched onto the wrong person, that this figure was some sort of doppelgänger, and that the right person would suddenly walk in through the door and chuck him out?

'And what have you done with your glasses?'

'They broke at school.'

'Mm-hm. But it looks bloody awful to go round with taped-up glasses like a fucking mental case. You need to learn to look after your things.'

Dad's voice was still calm, but to anyone who knew him, it took on a strange undertone. Mum heard it too when she returned with a tray of whisky glasses, a packet of Right cigarettes and the vase of tulips from the hall.

'Kids get into scrapes all the time,' said Leffe. 'I was the same when I was a kid. I had glasses for a while, too. They were constantly getting broken. I'd lose them when I was running or if there was a fight. If some bastard called me four-eyes, I'd punch him straight away.'

'I wasn't asking you now, I was asking the lad here!'

'Okay, okay, calm down!'

There was something reptilian about Dad when he got like this. Emotions and energy were transformed into their opposites, like when you flip a coin. He would go from impassive to full throttle before anybody had a chance to react.

'Aren't you ashamed of how you look, Robbie? Don't you under-stand that people will laugh at you if you go round looking like that?'

'We couldn't fix them any other way!'

'I don't give a damn if they can't be fixed. It's about respect. And a little fucking self-respect. Did somebody punch you? Is that why they broke?'

I shook my head as discreetly as I could, and my brother caught it out of the corner of his eye.

'No,' he said quietly. 'I just happened to lose them in the schoolyard.'

'Lose them? You need to learn to look after your things. Take them off!'

'Now?'

'Yes, now. I don't mean tomorrow.'

'But I can't see anything without them…'

'Do as I say!'

Nobody said a word. Leffe looked away, towards the TV, as if he hoped it would switch itself on and he could be swallowed up in the first decent programme. Mum was still standing there with some words on the tip of her tongue, things I knew she wanted to say, but didn't dare to, at least not right now when Dad had just come home. Robert took off his glasses, folded them up very care-fully and stood there with them in his hand.

'Bring them over here.'

Like an obedient dog, he went over to Dad. He was a millimetre away from bawling again, I could see it in his posture, in his walk, in the way he rubbed the back of his hand over the corners of his eyes. And as if I had telepathic powers, I tried to send thoughts in his direc-tion, that he needed to keep himself under control, not start to cry, not show any weakness, because that would make Dad even more furious.

'Give them to me.'

He held out the glasses and Dad took them, weighed them in his hand, looked at them as if they were some disgusting dead animal, before placing them in his shirt pocket with a grin.

'Good, I'll look after these for a while. Now make yourselves scarce for a while, kids. I need to talk to Leffe about something. And Marika, if you want to make me really happy you can wash my clothes. I didn't have time to before I was let out. They're in my rucksack.'

Late that night, Dad and his mate came back. They'd been away for a few hours, heading out in the car around nine and not getting back until around midnight. Not even Mum knew what they were up to. She was just happy Dad was home, was matching him drink for drink, judging by her sloshed laughter, and smoked scented cigarettes that we could smell all the way upstairs. But I knew things would be all right. This wasn't a night when everything would get out of control; I had a special radar for those sorts of situations.

I couldn't sleep, and neither could Robert. He would knock on the wall at regular intervals to check if I was awake. I didn't respond, even though I wanted to. He was worried about his glasses. He wouldn't be able to see anything without them.

As I lay in bed, it struck me that I couldn't remember what I'd done just a week before. I'd gone to school of course, oblivious to what Gerard had in mind and to the fact that Dad was on his way home. I'd done my homework and watched TV. I'd worried about my brother and how I was going to manage if Mum was heading into another one of her phases. But all the details were gone, as if they'd happened in someone else's life.

When I closed my eyes, the images from the hut came back. The creature that lay bound in the wooden crate; the syringes and blood spots on the floor. I saw the flesh wounds on its body, the cheek that had been sliced open, revealing its teeth and tongue. Some things were sort of lit up like close-up flash photos, as if my memory had secretly zoomed in on all the strange little details in order to store them better. There were auditory memories as well: the bellows

sound from the gills, the panting, the sticky sound of small air
bubbles forming and bursting. And then the eyes that looked at me
for a while. Something in that gaze unsettled me. It wasn't a human
being, but it wasn't an animal, either. But in a way I had understood
what it was thinking, that it was wondering what it was doing there,
wondering who we were and why people were mistreating it.

I'd set my alarm clock for three but woke up before it went off.
The house was silent. The only sound was the rain scraping against
the roof. I put my clothes on and crept down the stairs.

The living-room door was ajar. Dad was asleep on the couch.
Leif was lying on the floor with his jacket folded up into a pillow.
It smelled of tobacco and sweaty feet, with a hint of Mum's
perfume. They looked younger when they were asleep. Their
breathing was shallow, like that of two big kids. The glasses were
poking out of Dad's shirt pocket. I really should have fished
them out and given them to my brother. Dad probably wouldn't
remember anything in the morning, or else he wouldn't care about
them any more. But he was a light sleeper, and I didn't want to
risk waking him up.

I put my jacket on and sneaked out. My bag was still hanging
on my bike handlebars from the night before. In the pocket were
the lock picks I'd borrowed from Lazlo, a proper set of locksmith's
picks. I'd told him I needed them to open a locker at school.
He didn't look like he believed me. But if any of them worked, he
said, there must be something wrong with the lock.

The last scents of summer still lingered in the gardens. Fruit still
hung from the trees. Soon it would drop and get raked up with the
last piles of leaves.

As I cycled out on the gravel road that leads down to the sea,
the rain stopped. The lights of Falkenberg formed a hazy dome
on the horizon to the south. But in the other direction, towards
Glommen, towards the fields, farms and mink farms, the world
was quieter and darker.

I took the back route past the lighthouse to get down to the harbour. There were no lights on in town. I laid my bike in the grass behind the fisherman's huts. I had several hours to myself before the first people would turn up.

The area around the harbour was like a film set. A single street lamp cast its light on the quay, but the light did not reach as far as Tommy's hut. Nobody would be able to see me from a distance.

The lock opened with the third skeleton key. I lifted the hasp, opened the door and crept in. For a while I just stood still and listened. The only sound was the whoosh of the sea, and the wind that was on its way to bed, and then that noise… that strange panting noise, at first so faint that I barely noticed it, then stronger as I turned round. I tried not to think about it or even look over towards the wooden crate.

I put my book bag down on a folding chair. There was a back door some distance away. I opened it, went out again, put the hasp and the padlock back into place and used the back entrance. If anyone approached on foot, the place was locked from the outside. Everything would appear as usual.

I made sure the tarpaulin was securely covering the window. Then I switched on the light.

There was an empty syringe by my right foot. Blood spots formed a trail over to the crate. The box of fish guts was still by the door. The whole place smelled of the sea.

The light from the bulb was weak. Strange shadows stood stock-still in the corners. To my left, someone had covered part of the wall with a large cloth.

There was a faint thumping coming from the crate, rhythmic, three thumps followed by a brief pause and then another three thumps. It was awake now. It understood someone was in the hut, and that made it nervous.

'There,' I said. 'Don't worry, I'm not going to hurt you.'

It felt totally ridiculous. I took a step closer and stopped again.

I should leave, I thought, just leave through the back door, put everything back with the door and the lock and ride my bike back home. This was nothing to do with me. I'd just turned up at the wrong place at the wrong time, witnessed something I wasn't meant to see, just like with the kitten last winter. This was Tommy and his brothers' business, it wasn't even part of real life… it was part of the sea, the depths out there.

Then I took another step, and the rhythmic thumping started again: three thumps, then a pause and another three thumps. I went closer, closed my eyes as if part of me didn't want to see it, didn't want to see anything, just wanted to feel the presence of that alien, but not really be involved. When my hip bumped against the wooden crate, my entire body stiffened. It felt as if my eyelashes were stuck together, as if it was hard to open my eyes, as if I had to struggle with myself to be able to look again.

It lay in the darkness down there, hidden by my shadow. I took a step to the side so the light from the lamp could reach it better. Then I bent forward again, over the edge of what could have been a coffin… which perhaps already was a coffin for the thing that lay in there, a prison in which it would die and be buried.

The creature was awake. Its eyes were like two black marbles. As I moved, it raised its tail fin, beat three faint thumps against the base of the crate, paused, and repeated the same sequence.

'It's all right,' I whispered again. 'I'm not going to hurt you.'

Its gaze was sort of hypnotic, almost impossible to look away from. As if it was the one who decided when I would look in a different direction or finally get to blink. It was studying my face, my forehead, cheeks, mouth, chin, as if it wanted to imprint every single detail in its memory. The panting had stopped; it was calmer now, hardly frightened of me at all. It realised that I was not an enemy. So it lowered its eyes very slowly, as if letting go of my gaze, and instead glanced down at the cables that were wrapped around its wrists, the ropes it was bound with, and its scaly skin that looked dried-out and hard.

It was as if I hadn't managed to take in all the pain until now. The elongated wound that made its whole cheek gape, the bruises on its head, the small bone fragments sticking out of the skin at its temples. It was suffering; the pain was ever-present.

'I don't understand why they did this,' I whispered. 'Why they're hurting you... I'm sorry I can't help you.'

I looked around for some water to pour over it.

'Do you need something to drink?' I asked. 'Are you thirsty?'

Somehow, it answered. I can't explain how. It couldn't talk, didn't make any sign with its body, it didn't have any radio transmitter. And yet it understood my question. And somehow it answered, or it communicated with me. It was thirsty. It needed to drink, and it needed water on its body, on the skin that was made for being in the sea and was now drying out.

'Wait,' I said. 'I'll come back.'

Its tail fin beat nervously against the crate as I went round the hut, looking for a bucket. It grew worried when it couldn't see me: it no longer had the situation under control, couldn't anticipate what would happen. I mumbled some calming words as I searched through the cupboards. Finally I picked up a large bailer from the floor and filled it with water from the tap.

When I returned, it grew still again. Just looked at me, very calmly, with a sort of gleam in its eye, as if it appreciated my presence, and then past my shoulder, as if it was wondering whether more people were on their way in.

'It's just me here,' I said. 'You can relax. I've got some water for you.'

It was like when I talked to Robert, I thought, like when I'd try to calm my brother down when he was frightened and needed to hear my voice, and strangely enough, it helped.

I started pouring the water over its body. As the stream got closer to its face, it turned so I could rinse the wounds on its head and cheek. It opened its mouth a bit to drink, and I saw a row of dolphin's teeth and the jawbone behind. When the water was gone, I filled the ladle again and continued pouring water over it until I understood that it had had enough.

Outside it had started raining again. The raindrops sounded like a faint drumroll on the roof. It would be harder to hear if anyone was coming. The creature closed its eyes, and its body relaxed. Maybe it was going to go to sleep, maybe it had a special sleep rhythm that could not be altered. Its breathing was barely noticeable now; it was entering a dormant phase.

Its gills were closed and covered in congealed blood; it was breathing through its mouth now. The cables had worn through the skin on its wrists. Half-inch-deep wounds had filled with fluid; that's why it didn't move its arms. Without really thinking, I bent down and started to unwind the cables. I wanted to take away some of the pain, give it a little breathing room, help it the way I would have helped any person or any sort of animal. It was slow work: the steel cable was fastened to the floor with screws, but at last one wrist was free.

I immediately regretted it. When Tommy's brothers got here in the morning they would realise somebody had been here. I looked around for a swab or a rag. But before I spotted anything, the creature opened its eyes again. A piece of cable was bent over the edge. I tried to poke it back down.

It happened so fast I didn't have a chance to react. Its movements were incredibly quick, as if it broke the laws of nature. Its arm shot up out of the crate like a projectile and its fingers – or claws – grabbed hold of my hand and held it in a vice-like grip.

I thought my fingers were going to fall off or that the bones would break. That's how tight its grip was. Its claws were ice-cold and clammy. I let out a yelp of pain but stopped almost immediately. It looked at me again, very calmly, determined, as if it wanted to show who was in charge.

'Let me go,' I said. 'That hurts.'

Its eyes continued to bore into me. And I felt it again, sensed what it wanted and what it was thinking. It was asking for help. It was asking me to take it away from here, and it did not intend to let me go until it had got a promise.

'I promise,' I said. 'But I can't help you if you hurt me.'

It felt completely surreal. How could I know it understood? And how could I be so sure I understood it myself? Yet I knew that's how it was. I was absolutely certain. More certain than I'd ever been of anything in my life.

The pressure from its grip lessened, as if it was satisfied with my answer. Then it let go and let its arm drop. Its eyes darted nervously and its tail fin started thumping against the base of the crate again.

'Is somebody coming?' I whispered. 'Can you hear something I can't?'

Its fin beat faster. A faint sucking noise came from its gills. I looked straight into the creature's eyes; it looked terrified. And at the same instant I knew someone was approaching across the docks, towards the hut.

'I'll come back,' I whispered. 'I swear… as soon as I can.'

I just managed to turn off the light and get out through the back door before Tommy's brothers turned up. I recognised their voices in the darkness. They were standing in front of the hut arguing about something. One of them had a torch in his hand and was gesticulating wildly, making the beam point in all directions. I lay down in the grass behind the hut; it was tall enough to conceal both me and my bike.

After a while they stopped talking and unlocked the door. The lamp inside was switched on and a faint chink of light shone through a crack in one wall. Then I could hear their voices again, both agitated, and the back door burst open. I could see their silhouettes against the light. They looked round in every direction, talking agitatedly to each other, went back into the hut and came out again with another torch.

I wondered why I hadn't got out of there while they were unlocking the door. There was nothing stopping me, and they wouldn't have noticed anything until I was long gone. Instead I lay flat on the ground and felt the cold penetrating through my clothes.

One of them was searching by the dock, peering into the boats and checking behind the huts. The other one went down the asphalt path towards the covered moorings. I didn't dare move a muscle. From inside the hut came the rhythmic sound of the creature's tail fin, three thumps, pause, three thumps, but harder now, a sound filled with terror. I wondered whether they had noticed the steel cable was gone.

After a few minutes they returned to the hut. One of them shone his torch over towards the grass where I was hiding. 'They've got to be nearby!' said the other.

'Did you see if they took anything?'

'No, but there's a whole load of water on the floor.'

My heart was pounding. Why did they think there was more than one person? And what is there to steal inside a fisherman's hut? Soon they would look around more closely in there, checking that everything was in its proper place.

It felt like somebody had injected ice-cold water straight into my body when they went back into the hut. My school bag! I'd forgotten my bag with the keys in there. My name was written on the address label; the lock picks and my exercise books were inside. It was lying in plain view on a folding chair. But I didn't have any more time to think. A scream came from inside. Somebody was shrieking in pain.

Two days passed with no sign of Tommy. I went to school as usual, did my homework and tried to pay attention in lessons. It was no use. My mind was elsewhere. I was thinking about what had happened in the hut, the weird feeling I'd had of being able to communicate with the creature, that I had somehow known what it was feeling and thinking, and that it had understood what I said. I didn't dare phone Tommy. If he found out I'd broken in, he would go spare. And his brothers could hardly have failed to notice my bag, which was right there in plain sight.

I assumed that sooner or later one of them would turn up and put me on the spot. Give me back my bag and ask me to explain why it had been lying on a folding chair in their hut. And what would I tell them if they did?

Gerard wasn't at school either. People were saying he'd been suspended for the remainder of the term. Caroline Ljungman claimed she'd heard L.G. discussing it with the headmaster outside the front office. But nobody seemed to know anything for certain.

It was convenient for me. At least I didn't need to worry about Gerard for a while. I'd had enough on my plate coming to terms with what had happened in the hut and Dad's sudden return home.

On Wednesday after maths L.G. took me aside.

'You were absent on Monday as well,' he said. 'Two afternoon lessons. And you can't have been that ill because you were back yesterday.'

'My dad came home,' I said.

'That's no excuse.'

'Yes, it is. He got out of prison. I hadn't seen him for nearly a year.'

That line of reasoning worked. His eyes started to dart around. He cleared his throat nervously.

'I understand. But you still could have let me know. I treat that sort of thing as confidential.'

It was so easy to lie, I thought, the words just flowed out of me like water. I didn't even need to think in order to create a sort of logic in what I was saying.

'I went home in my free period and suddenly he turned up with a mate, with presents and everything. I was really happy to see him, I just forgot about the time. Put yourself in my place, if you hadn't seen each other in a year.'

L.G. hummed in agreement.

'What about Tommy?' I asked. 'Is he ill?'

'He's asked permission to have the rest of the week off. One of his brothers has been injured. They need Tommy to help out at home.'

The creature, I thought. So something had happened when they went back to the hut.

'We've lost a lot of men,' said L.G. with half a smile. 'By the way, have you thought about what I asked you the other day? If there's something that's happened to you involving your classmates? Or if there's something you want to talk about?'

'No,' I said.

'Are you sure about that?'

'Definitely.'

L.G. sighed and zipped his portfolio case shut.

'Well then,' he said, 'I'll just have to trust you, Petronella. But if anything changes, just get in touch with me. I promise to treat anything you say as confidential. Including that stuff about your dad. I suppose I should say congratulations. It must be nice to have him back home again.'

'Really nice.'

'And make sure you catch up on what you've missed. Especially maths.'

'I promise.'

He gave a little jump when the headmaster suddenly walked past in the corridor.

'Excuse me,' he said. 'I've just got to speak to that chap there about something.'

About Gerard, I thought. That's what everything was about these days.

On Thursday Gerard was suddenly back at school. When I arrived that morning, he was sitting on a table in the common room with an unlit fag in his mouth. The trailers had gathered round him: Ola, Peder and some lads from Year Eight. I took a detour so they wouldn't catch sight of me, sought refuge behind the coat racks and managed to make it to my locker without being noticed.

I'd just taken off my jacket when the caretaker turned up, stopped in his tracks and pointed at him.

'You have no permission to be here,' he said calmly. 'You know the rules. You're excluded until further notice, and that applies to the entire school grounds. I want you to leave. The rest of you can go off to your lessons and all!'

'Go fuck yourself!' was Gerard's brief reply.

'The door is over there,' bellowed the caretaker. 'You've got exactly thirty seconds.'

The common room fell silent. People stood rooted to the spot, watching the caretaker and the gang.

'You've got no right to ban him,' Ola said calmly. 'Education is compulsory in this country, isn't it?'

Gerard sneered in agreement.

'Exactly. It's not just my right to be here. It's also my duty.'

The caretaker looked at his watch and then at the gang. He was giving them an icy-cold stare that would have scared the shit out of anyone.

'Fifteen seconds! I'll pick you up and carry you out of here if you don't go willingly. I'm warning you, lad!'

'Go fuck yourself,' said Gerard again.

I couldn't believe he was still sitting there. The caretaker was close to six foot six with a big build. I'd seen him pick up rowdy pupils before, by the scruff of the neck like they were kittens.

'I don't give a damn what you or the headmaster say,' Gerard added, taking a lighter out of his jacket pocket. He lit his cigarette and blew two perfect smoke rings. 'I'll stay here as long as I feel like. So you can clear off. Go and rewire a plug somewhere, you fucking faggot!'

'Put that cigarette out before I give you a thump,' the caretaker said.

He was furious now; his whole body was shaking. But Gerard sat there as cool as a cucumber, blowing smoke in his direction and taking a swig from a bottle of pop somebody in the crew had handed him.

'Calm down. Here, want a puff, or are you thirsty? My treat!'

The situation seemed almost rehearsed, as if everybody knew exactly what they were going to do. When I looked round, I realised that more adults had turned up. The headmaster was standing at the foot of the stairs to the teachers' lounge. Several teachers had formed a semicircle behind the caretaker. Oddly enough, it was still completely silent. Or maybe I was the only one who perceived it that way.

'Okay laddie, I'm going to have to carry you out,' said the caretaker, now a bit calmer. 'And then I don't want you to show your face here again until we've decided you're allowed to come back.'

'Give me a break! Do you actually, seriously think I'm scared of you? That I'm gonna run away like a bloody Jew just because you're standing there trying to look all mean?'

'All right. That's it.'

It happened so fast, nobody had a chance to react. At the exact moment the caretaker took a step towards the table, Gerard was on him. There was not a single ounce of hesitation in his movements. It looked almost comical, like a scene from a cartoon, Tom and Jerry or something. Gerard smashed the drink bottle into the side of his head. You could hear the glass break and a dull thud from his skull. Something was switched off in the caretaker's eyes and he collapsed onto the floor.

He lay there on his side in an unnatural position with blood gushing straight out from his temple like a fountain. Gerard was standing over him, landing one kick after another on his head, really hard, with no concern about the consequences. The caretaker's head was bouncing all over on the floor. It was an unnaturally long time before somebody took action. And it wasn't any of the teachers; it was Ola who pulled him away. 'Come on, Gerard, bloody hell! Just leave the bastard... that's enough now!'

Like a school of fish, the trailers made for the door. Before they disappeared out into the schoolyard, Gerard turned towards me. Maybe he just mouthed the words, maybe it was impossible to hear his voice in all the commotion that had broken out, the girls' upset screams, somebody shouting to phone for an ambulance, the teachers and the headmaster crouching in a circle around the caretaker; maybe he said something else entirely, in which case it was just my imagination. But I thought I saw the words he was forming with his lips: 'This is all your fault.'

The school was buzzing with rumours for the rest of the day. Someone claimed to have seen the gang on their scooters up by the newsagent's kiosk, and when a police car approached they zoomed off into the woods on the path with the street lamps. Somebody else said they'd already been questioned at the police station and Gerard was being charged with grievous bodily harm.

Nicke Wester, dressed today in a ripped Ebba Grön T-shirt with a bandana knotted round his head, claimed to know why Gerard had been excluded: he'd threatened several of the teachers. Patrik Lagerberg, who had a different source, said the gang had brought back some hashish from Christiania at the end of the summer and sold it on to some older guys in town. But when someone asked why Gerard was the only one who'd been excluded, he had no reply.

Anyway, the caretaker seemed to have survived. When the ambulance came for him he was conscious, and one of the paramedics who was trying to calm down an upset teacher said that it looked a lot worse than it was, and there's always a lot of blood when someone is bleeding from a head wound.

I felt like I was going to be sick, the more I thought about it. If the caretaker, a fully grown man, easily weighing forty kilos more than Gerard and nearly two heads taller, didn't have a chance, what would happen to me or my brother if we happened to stand in his way?

During the last recess of the day I went over to the Year Seven wing to spend some time with Robert.

'Gerard isn't going to get away with this, is he?' he asked hopefully as he perched on the banister dangling his legs, on his own as usual. 'People must get sent to borstal at least, if they go after a caretaker?'

'Maybe,' I said. 'But you've got to be careful. If you see him, get out of there.'

'Are Ola and Peder still at school?'

'No. They cleared off with their boss this morning. Nobody knows where they're keeping themselves.'

'Maybe the police took them in? What's happening with the caretaker, anyway? Is he badly injured?'

'I hope not. But you've got to promise me: if you catch sight of Gerard, you have to get away as fast as you can.'

'Okay.'

My brother had removed the plaster from the lens of his glasses. His squint had returned.

'Fortunately, Dad was in a good mood,' he said when he noticed me looking at him, 'and gave me my glasses back. At first I thought he was going to keep them. And maybe buy me a new pair, cooler ones. But he didn't. At least I can see now.'

It was incredible that he was capable of refashioning reality in such a short time, like sweeping all the unpleasant stuff under the rug.

'Shall we walk home together after school, Nella?'

'Sure, if you want to.'

'Do you think Leif's going to stay over Christmas?'

'I really don't know.'

And that was the truth: I didn't know. I did still hope I'd be able to keep my room, because that was only the first night Leif had slept at ours. The following day he'd looked up an old girlfriend and asked if he could live there for a while. Dad was saying he should stay at ours. They had joint business, as he put it, loads of stuff that needed sorting out asap and it was better if they were living under the same roof. The previous night they'd disappeared with the car again without saying where they were going. I hoped they were involved in something illegal. And that they'd get caught before Christmas.

The house was empty when Robert and I got home. There was a note from Mum on the table in the hall. The Professor was looking for me. I phoned him while my brother went into the kitchen to see if there was anything to eat. He picked up straight away, as if he'd been waiting for the phone to ring.

'I was in Gothenburg yesterday,' he said, 'at the public library, checking into what you asked me about. I had a hospital appointment. My heart took a licking after my operations, as you know, and the doctors want to change my medication because the one I was on before had loads of side effects. But it went so well I could spend the rest of the day at the library afterwards. I've borrowed a few books that seem interesting. It would be good if you could pop by.'

I could hear my brother slamming cupboard doors and cursing under his breath.

'When should I come?'

'Now, if you've got time.'

'I'll be there as soon as I can.'

Out in the kitchen, my brother stood staring vacantly into the fridge.

'Nothing today, either,' he said. 'Not even a piece of crispbread.'

He went over to the sink and filled a glass with lukewarm water – the old trick to fool your stomach. I noticed I was hungry myself. After what had happened to the caretaker, I didn't manage to get anything down at lunch. And given the situation we were in, it could mean we'd have to go without food for an entire day, until the school canteen was open again.

'I'm sorry there's nothing here at home,' I said. 'I should've thought of that. Do you think you can manage on your own for a couple of hours? I've got to head over to the Professor's for a bit. I might be able to bring something back from there.'

With his back turned towards me, my brother nodded.

'I'll come back as soon as I can, I promise. By the way, you need a haircut. Your fringe is hanging down over your glasses, and there are tangled knots on the back of your neck. If you can find the scissors, I'll sort it out when I get back.'

The Professor was sitting in his reading room when I arrived. He was holding a teacup in his hand and had his glasses on.

'How nice you could come,' he said, pointing to one of the squashed-out armchairs. 'Have a seat and I'll show you what I've found.'

I could tell he'd done a thorough job. There was a stack of library books on the coffee table, with a notebook filled with jottings lying next to them.

'It'll be terrific to read your essay when it's finished. If I don't muddy things up for you with too many historical facts.'

With that, he picked up his notebook, looked inside and began to explain.

'The first time mermaids appeared in the sources was during classical antiquity. They were called Naiads then, or Nereids, and they were a sort of freshwater nymph that ruled over lakes and river channels. According to the descriptions, they had fish-like scales on their abdomen, but the upper body of a woman. They were related to the tritons and other gods of the sea in Greek mythology, but they didn't do a whole lot in comparison to those other figures... It would take another few hundred years, up until about AD 500 before the classic mermaid took shape. In a text called a "bestiarium" by one Physiologus, mermaids are described as a "fantastically shaped woman from the navel upwards, and like a fish from the navel downwards". The creatures, he writes, are happy during storms but sad during periods of calm, and they exert a strange attraction on seafarers: they lure sailors to sleep with them, and then they kill them…'

The Professor took a sip of tea and looked at me.

'Is the vocabulary I'm using too complicated?' he asked. 'Let me know if it is.'

'No, I'm getting the drift.'

'Okay. I'll carry on. In the fifteenth century the first more realistic reports of contacts between people and mermaids started to come in. In 1423 a Dutch monk by the name of John Gerbrandus wrote of a "wild sea-maid" that was washed ashore through a hole in a dyke in the Netherlands. The creature was found by some milkmaids and taken to a nearby farm. After they washed her and gave her some food and clothing, she remained on the farm where she learned to spin wool and perform simple kitchen tasks. After a while she was taken to a nunnery in Haarlem, where she lived until her death, without ever learning to speak.'

'So you think that actually happened?'

The Professor chuckled.

'No, I doubt it. Gerbrandus was not an eyewitness. He just wrote down a story he'd heard. That's how it was in those days: monks collected stories about strange occurrences. And when you think about all the wonders described in the Bible, it didn't seem unreasonable that the sea would be full of mermaids and other mystical creatures. God was the creator of everything, and nothing was impossible for God.'

He turned the page.

'Reported sightings of mermaids continued to turn up at regular intervals from voyages of exploration in the seventeenth and eighteenth centuries. This one's interesting…'

He paused at a bookmark in his notebook.

'In the summer of 1658 the explorer Henry Hudson led a convoy of ships along the Arctic coast of Russia. Near Novaya Zemlya on the 15th of June he recorded this entry in the ship's log:

"This morning one of our sailors on the lookout for icebergs sighted a mermaid off the port side. When he summoned me, another mermaid came to the surface. The first one was quite near the bow and looked up sternly towards the men who had gathered at the ship's rail. A great breaker took her, lifting her up and down. Her neck and back were those of a woman, her body of a size similar to ours, her skin very white. Her long hair, black in colour, hung down over her face. When she dived, we saw her tail, which resembled the fin of a large fish."'

'Is that made up as well?' I asked.

The Professor looked at me, touched.

'We'll never know. Even today, the Arctic Ocean is still fairly unexplored. And of course there are deep sea trenches with their strange marine fauna. Or else, which seems most likely, Hudson just saw what he wanted to see. Sea voyages could last for many months in the 1600s. They must have been incredibly boring. But he did actually make some sketches…'

He opened to a page in one of the books. In an old print there was a vague figure, half-seal, half-woman.

'Curiously, a famous English zoologist, P.H. Gosse, read about this and dismissed the theory that they might have been elephant seals, sea cows, walruses or anything like that.'

'What did he think they were instead?'

'An as-yet-undiscovered species of mammal. Hudson's experienced crew, he thought, would have been too familiar with large marine animals to err so greatly.'

That might be one possibility, I thought as I let my eyes wander round the Professor's cluttered reading room, to the bookshelves, newspapers and clippings that lay in piles on the floor. Maybe they existed at one time but then died out? Or else I was going up a dead end.

'Another episode that made headlines in European newspapers around that time involved some Dutch sailors who caught a "mermaid" off the coast of Borneo and kept her captive in a barrel of water. That was the famed Mermaid of Amboina, "five foot long, which from time to time let out small cries not unlike a cat's". Her body was examined after her death, and Dutch scientists of the era maintained with absolute certainty that it was a mermaid. Peter the Great, the Russian Tsar at that time, actually travelled to Amsterdam to obtain more information about the event. Afterwards, he was convinced that mermaids existed and sent an expedition to the Far East to try to capture one alive. Which of course didn't work out.'

The Professor made a dramatic pause before continuing.

'The scientific advances of the eighteenth and nineteenth centuries should have put an end to all the speculations about fantastical creatures. But that didn't happen. On the contrary, interest grew, and there were loads of reported sightings of mermaids. During the second half of the nineteenth century, for example, a great many mermaid skeletons were exhibited around Europe and the United States. The most famous one was part of P.T. Barnum's Cabinet of Curiosities. It's thought that the skeleton came from Japan, where fishermen produced them to order. Barnum's skeleton was examined by experts from the Royal Society and was judged to be a fake. Apparently it was made from the bones of an ape, skilfully joined to those of a dolphin.'

'So they never really existed?' I asked. 'Other than in people's imaginations?'

'Unless they just disappeared. In the twentieth century at any rate, all reports of mermaid sightings stopped.'

The Professor opened up the book from the bottom of the pile on the table. In a black-and-white photo was a little girl whose legs were joined together.

'Some researchers think the mermaid legend might have its origin in Sirenomelia, also known as Mermaid Syndrome. This is a rare genetic disorder. Affected people are born with their legs fused together and undeveloped genitals, and they usually die shortly after birth. Some of the preserved mermaid bodies that were exhibited to the public during the nineteenth century might have been children who died as a result of Sirenomelia.'

I had to take my eyes away from the photo. It looked so awful, that deformed little girl.

'And what about the males? There must have been some of them in the tales as well.'

The Professor looked at his pill case on the table, now with different-coloured tablets in it. He grimaced, and I understood he was in pain.

'The only thing I could find was a report in an English reference book. "Mermen" is what the males are called. And they seem to exist only as a logical consequence of the fact that there are descriptions of mermaids, so they would have someone to mate with.'

'Are there any pictures of them? Drawings or something?'

'None that I've found.'

I nodded. None of this helped me. I didn't even know what I'd been hoping for. That some of the stories might have been more plausible than others, that there might have been some extinct animal that resembled what I'd seen. But there was nothing.

The Professor got up and fumbled for his crutches, which were leaning against the table. I could smell food from downstairs in the kitchen. I'd smelled it the whole time, but sort of ignored it so the hunger pangs wouldn't get worse. I hated being hungry. Finally I couldn't think of anything other that nagging pain in my belly.

But the Professor wouldn't be the Professor if he hadn't been one step ahead.

'Is the fridge empty again?' he asked. 'Take as much as you like, Nella. This new medication seems to make me lose my appetite. There's enough for Robert as well.'

I'd cut my brother's hair so many times I could do it in my sleep. His hair that had to be dampened first and then combed out before it could be cut. The whorl above his right temple that I needed to be careful with, otherwise the hair wouldn't lie neatly. He sat stock-still on a stool next to the bathtub as big blond wisps fell onto the floor.

I sensed the smell of him, that special Robert smell that was sort of intensified when his hair was wet. It was like it had always been there, I thought, as if it was a part of me.

'Do you think the police have caught Gerard yet?' he asked, sizing himself up in the mirror.

'I dunno.'

'I hope so. And I hope the caretaker will be okay again. I like him. Just like I like the Professor. Be sure to thank him for the food.'

I felt ashamed, even though I didn't want to. Once when I was in Year Six I read an article in a magazine about children who were poor because their parents were unemployed. I could identify with every situation they described. Not having a packed lunch to take along on school outings and claiming to have forgotten it. Going round in clothes you'd outgrown, being hungry during the school holidays, not going to birthday parties because you couldn't afford to bring a present. It was the shame itself that was worst of all, feeling ashamed to tell the truth when teachers noticed you had holes in your trainers or when they got angry you didn't bring a pair of wellies for the outdoor day as they'd instructed. Or that everybody else had school bags while you came with your schoolbooks in a plastic carrier bag, which is what Robert and I had done through the later years of primary school. Or the shame I felt even though I didn't want to, when the Professor put the leftover vegetable casserole into a plastic tub and gave it to me.

'You know something, Nella?'

I ran my fingers through his hair. It was still so amazingly soft, just like when he was little.

'What's that?'

'I hope Dad ends up back inside. That he does something stupid so the police arrest him. Is it strange to think that?'

'No. That's what I think too.'

'Good. Then we think the same way.'

He grew silent and smiled at me tentatively in the mirror. But it was like I was somewhere else. Mermaids had never existed, I thought. And no mermen, either. Only in legends and people's imaginations. And yet he was there in Tommy's hut. Just as surely as my brother was sitting in front of me.

My school bag was hanging on my locker door handle on Friday morning, but no one was there. I'd overslept, and the corridor was deserted. My brother had left earlier. I'd asked him to wake me before he went, but apparently he forgot in his hurry.

Someone had put a note through the door: an invitation from Jessica and Lovisa to a party. Either they'd got the wrong locker, or else they wanted to play a trick on me. There was no name on the note. Presumably it was meant for Marcus Larsson, the minister of fun who had the locker to the left of mine. I folded it up and shoved it into the gap under his locker door.

To my surprise, everything was still in its place in my bag. My exercise books, pens, the lock picks I'd borrowed from the Professor. The diary where I'd marked my brother's lesson days and everything else he was too young to keep track of himself: dentist's appointments, appointments with the optician and the skin specialist.

'Pure luck I found it first…'

It was Tommy. He was perching in a niche behind the coat racks.

'It was underneath a chair that got knocked over. I don't know what might have happened if they'd found it.'

He hopped down onto the floor. The look he gave me was anything but friendly.

'What were you doing there, Nella?'

'I dunno.'

'Dunno. That's no answer. I've had to stay home all week and help out because of you. Olof's in hospital.'

He took hold of my arm and squeezed it. He'd never done

anything like that before, never been violent. That didn't exist in our world.

'Don't you get it? It could've killed him. God only knows how, but it had managed to work its way loose from the cable. And then it lay in wait, like a spider, for someone to get too close. And when my brother did, it broke his arm. Just snapped it, like a dry twig.'

It gradually dawned on me what had happened. When the brothers returned to the hut, Olof, the younger of the two, went over to see if the creature was awake. And before he knew what was going on, it had grabbed hold of his arm. The bone snapped up by his elbow. It also tore open a half-inch-deep wound along his whole forearm with its claws. Rickard, the elder brother, came to the rescue with a jack and beat the creature until it was unconscious. My bag fell off the chair in the melee.

They got in their van as fast as they could and drove to the hospital in Halmstad. Olof was still there because his arm was so badly injured the doctors had to operate several times. Rickard drove back to Glommen. Together with Jens, they moved the creature to a different place.

'Where did they take it?' I asked.

'I'm not allowed to tell.'

'What does it matter now?'

'It matters because of you, Nella. Somebody broke into the hut, and so that person might have seen what was in there. Things that shouldn't be seen. And now I'm not talking about a sea monster.'

He looked sort of doubtfully at me.

'So what are you talking about, then?'

'I said forget it!'

Tommy looked out of the window. The noise of tools could be heard faintly from the woodworking room. And the rattle of trolleys outside the dining hall.

'Is it hurt?' I asked, and heard my voice quivering. 'You said they beat it unconscious.'

'Yeah. And I don't know why I'm telling you about it.'

'Because you don't like what's going on either.'

'It was you who loosened the cable, wasn't it? You could've just stood there and looked at it. And given it some food or water or whatever you wanted to do. But did you have to try and release it?'

'But it's suffering.'

He was quiet again, just muttered something to himself, sort of forming his lips into words I couldn't catch.

'It understands what I say, Tommy. And I understand it. It thinks in a way I can understand… or in a way that makes me understand. I don't know if I can explain.'

I tried to tell him what I meant. It was precisely as I put it, yet different. The creature had sort of made me know what it was thinking, even though it thought in a way that was so different it couldn't be expressed in words. And in the same way, it understood me. Even I could hear how messed-up that sounded.

'You can believe what you want,' I said. 'But it's true.'

'I haven't got a clue what's true. It shouldn't even be there. It doesn't belong here. If there's anywhere it does belong, it's in the sea.'

'Well then, we should take it back there!'

Tommy gave me a look that seemed to say he hadn't quite decided whether or not I was crazy.

'We can't.'

'Of course we can. First it just needs some treatment. Otherwise it won't survive with those injuries.'

'The way you're talking, it's like we're talking about a person. But a real person is lying on an operating table in Halmstad right now, with injuries caused by that thing.'

'What would you have done if somebody had locked you up and tied you down? You'd try to defend yourself, wouldn't you?'

I thought about what Lazlo had told me. The legends about mermaids only described female creatures, but the one I saw in the hut was a male. 'Mermen' was the word the Professor had used – *a merman*. It still didn't matter. Whatever it was, I'd promised to help it. It was as if everything depended on that.

'There's even a name for them,' I said. 'Mermen.'

Tommy shrugged, as if he was giving up.

'Where did they move it to?'

'To the mink farm near Olofsbo. Where your dad used to work. Where Jens works now.'

'If I can prove it understands what I say, will you promise to help me?'

'I'm not promising anything. Come on. There's forty minutes left of art. The teacher's off sick. If we're lucky, the supply teacher won't record us as being absent.'

There was some sort of meeting going on in the art classroom. L.G. was standing in front at the lectern, looking out grimly over the class. The supply teacher was sitting in a chair behind him with a piece of chalk in her hand.

'... so if any of you know where Gerard is hiding, I want you to tell me. You can do it anonymously if you want. Write a letter. Or ring me at home after school. I will not reveal anyone's name. It's important that we get hold of him. His parents are worried. And as I said, the police would like to have a chat with him.'

'Is there a warrant out for him?' asked Sandra, appearing to relish the thought.

'No, he's a bit young for that. It's more like they're searching for him.'

'How's the caretaker doing? I heard it was serious.'

'Not too good, if I'm honest. He slipped into a coma last night.'

'Blood clots,' said a voice from the other side of the classroom. When I looked over, I noticed a policewoman who stood leaning against the wall. 'That can happen after severe trauma to the head... large accumulations of blood that put pressure on the brain.'

'And where are Peder and Ola?' someone asked.

'They're at home,' said L.G., wiping the sweat from his forehead with his shirt sleeve. 'Both of them have been suspended from school while the investigation is under way.'

'So they're not allowed to come here?'

'That's right.'

He was sweating under his armpits as well: two large patches were visible on his shirt. He looked really on edge.

'What investigation? About what happened to the caretaker?'

'Along with some other things,' said the policewoman by the wall. 'But it's nothing to do with you pupils. It's nothing to do with things that have happened here at school.'

'We just want to keep you informed,' said L.G. 'You're entitled to know what's going on. And as I said, you can come and speak to me if there's anything worrying you.'

When they left the classroom, I tried to piece together what I had heard. So the caretaker's condition had worsened during the night. When he was taken to hospital he'd been awake, but then he had begun vomiting and lost consciousness. Gerard had been in hiding since the attack, and according to the police Ola and Peder were refusing to say where he was. They were certain they knew, but they hadn't said a peep, not even during a lengthy interrogation at the police station. Their parents had tried to talk them round, but their loyalty to their boss clearly outweighed that.

'All three of them are gonna get locked up for this,' Tommy said as the class started to return to its usual routine.

'What else do you think they've done?'

'Haven't got a clue. But it must be some serious stuff. And anyway, you won't have to worry about the money for a while.'

But I was not nearly so sure about that.

The rest of the lesson continued in the usual fashion whenever a supply teacher tried to take command. Nobody cared about the assignment: a frame from a comic on the overhead projector that we were supposed to copy. Some people were sitting in groups around the tables, talking about what had happened. Petter Bengtsson and Markus Larsson were having fun drawing smutty pictures which they held up whenever the supply teacher looked away. Caroline Ljungman and her gang were discussing some lads from the upper school who they were going to meet up with that evening.

I wondered where Gerard could be. Maybe it was as I suspected, that Peder and Ola had squealed about what he'd done... and there were more – and worse – things than setting fire to a cat.

But now the external pressure had been cranked up, and they were standing behind Gerard. Out of fear, I thought. What else drives people?

Halfway between Olofsbo and the mink farm was the old abandoned cottage where Tommy and I used to play when we were younger. It was several years since we had been there last. The roof had caved in and the last few windowpanes had been smashed. Ragged curtains flapped in the wind. Long ago there had been an orchard round the house, but it was all overgrown now. It always used to feel creepy being there. You had a sensation that an earlier era was still in progress, with children still playing in the garden, dressed in old-fashioned clothes, just out of sight behind an invisible corner. When we were in Year Six we had a secret hideout in the old root cellar next to the barn. The entrance was overgrown with brush, but there was an opening at the rear if you dug out some of the earth. The groundwater had risen inside, forming a pool of stagnant water. There were tadpoles there in the spring; we used to catch them with nets, put them in jars and then try to raise them into adult frogs. But we never managed it.

I looked at Tommy walking ahead of me along the path. We'd met up in Olofsbo, parked our bikes behind the kiosk and cut across the fields. The mink farm was just a few hundred metres away, and no one would be there that day other than the guard dog. Tommy claimed he knew it because he went there regularly with his brothers to sell fish as feed for the mink. It was now or never, he explained. Skinning had just finished and the workers had been given the weekend off. The owners had gone off to the fur auction in Copenhagen. To be on the safe side, he phoned them up earlier that morning, and no one answered.

We went round the outside of the abandoned cottage and emerged on the other side of the fence. The mink farm loomed a hundred metres away. Like a picture of a prison camp, I thought, with its fence and the grey barracks beyond.

The site was large, maybe five hundred metres long and just as broad. The closer we got, the stronger the smell got. Of furry animals, fish and fertiliser. The mink houses were five abreast. There was a sixth one some way off, but it was not currently in use.

The house was over to the side. The windows were dark. The garage door was open, and there were no cars around. Twenty metres to our right the fence was concealed by some trees. That's where we would get in.

Warning signs were fixed to the wire fence. *Beware of the dog*, it said. Next to that were laminated photos of a German shepherd with a handwritten message underneath: *If dog attacks, lie still and wait for owner*.

The barking was louder now, but the dog must have caught the scent of something else, or heard a noise from a different direction, because it was on the other side of the property over by the main road.

It wasn't difficult to climb up into the tree and clamber out on the limbs. I felt butterflies in my stomach. Hanging ten feet above the ground, I could see every single building in the area. The long mink houses with open sides and curbed roofs, the cisterns where they collected urine and droppings to dry and sell as fertiliser. The barracks where the workers got changed, and the large building where the skinning was done and the pelts were dried. In the middle of the yard stood an old VW bus. A thick hose led from the exhaust pipe over to the building. Inside was the death box as they called it, where the animals were gassed to death.

The dog had stopped barking when we landed on the ground. All we could hear were the cries of the gulls and the roar of the sea. As far as I could see there was no chance of escape from there, at least not fast enough if the dog happened to come. But I was relieved on that score. When we turned the corner of the first barracks we discovered it chained to a post just inside the main gate. Maybe the mink farmer didn't want it to run around and terrorise the animals while they were away. Maybe the gate was the most important spot to watch because it was the only place where a burglar could get large quantities of pelts out. The dog didn't even notice us as we went over towards the farm less than a hundred metres behind it, because the wind was coming from the other direction.

The shortest way to the main building was straight through the first mink house. I got a flashback when we entered the space. I'd been there once with Dad a long time ago. Droppings on the floor. The dishes of animal feed standing next to the cages. The animals that watched us, curious, as we passed close by, pressing their noses against the mesh or standing up on their hind legs to get a better view. Normally there were five mink to a cage, but now the skinning was over and only the breeding animals were left, along with the ones with darker fur which would not be killed until later. Their little black button eyes looked urgently at us. Maybe they thought it was feeding time? Some of them were as fat as little pigs, and their colourings and patternings varied from one cage to the next.

The gulls' claws scraped across the flat roof. They usually scavenged for food at the mink farms: fish scraps, old bits of chicken, leftover mink meal that got chucked out when it went off. There were black-headed gulls out there as well; their creepy, irritating cries, as if they were mocking us. And soundless movements everywhere, sort of in the corner of your eye, as the mink scampered around to observe us as we went past.

The path ended at the door to the main building. It was locked.

'Wait here,' said Tommy. 'You can get in through the loading bay on the end.'

A minute later when he opened the door, the full blast of the smell hit me: the stench of blood and animal glands, of guts and flayed bodies, and something that might have been the animals' terror in the face of death.

We were in the actual killing room. Over by the loading bay was the steel box where the animals were gassed to death. Dad had told me that they would scream in there when the exhaust was pumped in. Most of the time mink don't make a peep – you might think they were mute, they're so silent. But when they were gassed, they would suddenly start squeaking like rats. It took a few minutes before they were dead, but afterwards you could see marks on the metal from their claws. In desperation they would try to claw their way out.

I suppressed an urge to be sick. The floor was covered in mink paws that had been cut off. Sawdust had soaked up the blood. In a large pile in the middle of the room lay hundreds of flayed animal corpses, stacked into a pyramid. The corpses were perfectly intact with yellowish membranes over bare flesh. The eyes were still in their sockets, teeth in the jaws; just the skin had been pulled off them like socks turned inside out. They resembled the Alien in that movie that came to the cinema when I was in Year Seven, only in miniature.

'People are gonna start turning up here soon,' I said. 'You can't leave animal bodies lying around like this. They'll start to rot.'

'Not for a while yet. Can't you feel how cold it is?'

He was right: the room was like a fridge. I hadn't even noticed I was starting to get cold.

'Come on,' said Tommy impatiently. 'We haven't got all day.'

There was a large workroom behind a door. It was warmer in there. The fans were on. Pelts were spread out on large tables, ready for dressing. Next door was a drying room, where the mink pelts were threaded up on racks. The finest ones could fetch several thousand kronor at fur auctions. There was a strange smell in here, too. I remember once Dad told me about the fat they scraped off the inside of the pelts which was then used in cosmetics and fine-quality shoe polish. Not just for anyone, but for really rich people. Could that be what the smell was?

A flight of stairs led up to a mezzanine level. We went down a corridor until we were standing in front of another door. We could hear the dog's barking louder from outside, as if the dog had scented us and was trying to reach the building.

'Stay here,' said Tommy.

He disappeared into a corridor that led off to the left, opened a cupboard and returned with a red painted box – the same box I'd seen in the hut that first night when he showed me the creature, the case containing veterinary medicines.

'You can play vet if you absolutely must. I have no intention of going near it again. No way.'

He opened the door and flicked a light switch on.

'Where are we?' I asked.

'In the feed preparation area.'

We were standing in a room lit by sterile fluorescent tubes. Leftover fish scraps littered the floor. Fins, tails and dried fish skins. In a coolbox there were chicken parts, heads, beaks, combs and feet. A gigantic meat grinder stood majestically atop a stand in the centre of the room. A funnel was fixed to the bottom, connected to a fat tube which in turn led to feed troughs. All around there were sacks of seed and fish meal.

'Have you been here before?' I asked.

'Loads of times. But not since they brought it here.'

'Where is it?'

'Over there, I think.'

Behind a screen was one more room, entered via swinging doors. There were glass panes in the doors so you could see in.

Tears filled my eyes when I saw the creature. It was lying on its side, chained to a pipe in the floor. Its arms were handcuffed, and just to make sure, someone had wrapped several rounds of fishing line around its claws. Its tail fin was also chained and fastened with a large shackle. A thin trickle of water ran from a suspended garden hose, positioned so it flowed over its body. It was not moving. Its eyes were closed, and dried pus and blood was visible around them. The webbing between its fingers was split. The gash in its mouth was still open, and the edges were black, like they were starting to go septic. It had more wounds on its body – dozens of them, fresh ones.

'What did they do?' I asked. But the question came out only as a whisper.

'I dunno…'

'Can't you see? It's got injuries everywhere.'

There was a Stanley knife lying on the floor. Was that what they'd used?

'Turn off the light. It can't stand it. There must be a switch here somewhere.'

Tommy found the light switch. Now only a faint light was coming in from the feed preparation area.

'You first,' said Tommy.

The creature lay dead still on its side when I went up to it. There was not a sound. For a moment I thought we'd come too late, that it was already dead, and I felt like I couldn't forgive myself. Then I felt the warmth of its body, and the moisture that sort of vaporised on its skin.

'Don't worry,' I said. 'No one's going to hurt you.'

I only realised now how big it was. If I stretched out alongside it, I'd only reach its waist. I placed my hand on its forehead, that strange dolphin-like forehead. It was hot. Maybe it had a temperature. Then there was a rattle from its throat and then a feeble movement of its tail fin that was restrained by the chain.

'Can you hear me?' I whispered. 'Do you remember me?'

It took a while. A sort of silence lingered within the silence. And then, very faintly, came an answer, an inaudible but completely comprehensible answer. It could hear me, it knew who I was, and it knew I was not alone.

'It's a friend,' I whispered. 'Don't be afraid of him. I told you I'd come back.'

Tommy was still standing in the doorway, as pale as if he'd seen a ghost.

'You're right,' he mumbled. 'I can hear him, Nella. He's talking to us...'

We'd never be able to explain this to anyone else, I thought, as I let my eyes pass over its body to see if it had any more injuries. Anyone who hadn't experienced it would not be able to understand what I meant by being able to talk without using words or even a voice. It was incredible, but that's how it was. The creature was communicating its thoughts to us. I wasn't imagining things; Tommy had heard it too, so there were two of us who knew now.

'This is an ointment for wounds,' Tommy said, taking a tube out of the medical case. 'Farmers use this stuff on cows when their udders get inflamed.'

He had ventured a little way into the room now.

'Good, let's start with that.'

'Maybe you should wash him first. The wounds, I mean. There's water here. We need some soap, too.'

He was still hesitating where he stood, a couple of metres away.

'He's not going to hurt you,' I said. 'He understands who's a friend and who's an enemy. And look at him!'

What could he possibly do? I thought. Injured, chained up, with a fever. And as if Tommy realised the same thing, he crouched down beside me.

We stayed for over an hour. Together we cleaned the creature's wounds and spread ointment over them. We found new gashes all over where somebody had cut or hacked at it with sharp instruments. There were fresh bruises on its head. From the night in the hut when Tommy's older brothers hit it with the jack, I supposed. A person would never have survived that sort of abuse, nor would most animals, but what we had in front of us was something else. It was in pain, that much we understood, but the pain didn't seem to concern it. The fever was worse; it knew it had to get over that if it was going to live.

We cleaned the wound in its mouth where the flesh had turned black, opened up the edges of the wound, rinsed them with surgical spirit and applied ointment there as well. Tommy said the gangrene would spread if we didn't put a stop to it.

It was really weird to touch its body. Its rough skin. The incredible hardness and the muscles underneath: animal and human at the same time. The fact that the creature let us touch it felt like a gift. All the time we were treating it, it was like the creature was accompanying us by means of a sort of melody, inaudible but still beautiful and calming, as if it was letting its inner being flow through us, out of gratitude for our help. It was speaking to us in its strange way, reassuring us that it recognised and trusted us. It wondered where it was, what sort of strange world it had been taken to, and if anyone could return it to where it belonged. These thoughts were interrupted only occasionally, when it lapsed into the fever and its body twitched as if it were dreaming.

When we gave it some water from the hose, it opened its mouth and stuck out its tongue tentatively to take a drink. But when Tommy tried to give it some fish from the crates in the feed room, it turned its head away, communicating that it was too weak to eat.

In the middle of all this I went off to have a pee. I had no idea what we were going to do now. Basically I hadn't thought beyond going to the mink farm and trying to help it. At some point we'd take it away from there, I thought, set it free, but we couldn't yet because it was too weak, and we'd need tools to undo the shackles, and I didn't know how we were going to transport it… or to where, for that matter.

The curtain had come down in the shower block by the toilets; there were hundreds of cartons of cigarettes stacked against the wall. Danish brands: Cecil and Prince. Goods that were easy to load, I thought, from one boat onto another out on the open sea…

When I came back, Tommy was washing the creature's arms. The nylon lines had rubbed right through the skin. He was carefully dabbing the areas with gauze.

'I don't get it,' he muttered. 'How come they're keeping it alive?'

'To mistreat it, seems like.'

'Or else they're just waiting for it to die on its own, but it isn't. It doesn't want to die. It's refusing.'

The creature had twisted slightly to one side. Its eyes were still closed. It hadn't looked at us even once, and now its temperature seemed to be climbing. It was sort of drifting in and out of consciousness, strange dreams we didn't understand, dreams of the sea perhaps – black, filled with water and currents, and then back to a shallow wakefulness where it sent thoughts to us, repeating to itself that it was not afraid of us, that it understood and appreciated what we were doing.

'There's a load of cigarette cartons in there by the showers,' I said. 'Danish brands.'

Tommy didn't answer.

'Your brother moved them here from the hut, didn't he, after I was in there? They had a boat full of fags when they came back from

Anholt. That's why they didn't get rid of him out there at sea. They didn't have time. They were in a hurry to get back home.'

'Forget you saw them, Nella.'

Tommy was right, I thought. The less I knew about things that were none of my business, the better.

I took a fresh gauze pad out of the medicine case and dampened it in the water. Carefully, I dabbed away the pus around the creature's eyes. It still had its eyes shut, was still drifting in and out of the fever, until we noticed a sort of increase in its concentration, how it kind of focused its senses.

It was like someone had flicked on a light switch; within an instant it was totally awake. Very calmly it fixed its gaze on us, one at a time, as if it wanted to imprint our faces in its memory. Its large dark eyes were filled with a sort of wonder. More clearly than before he asked if we could help him, back to the place where he belonged. To the world that was his, which he missed and feared he would never get to see again. To the sea… but not the sea as a word, because that's not how it worked. We just understood, without words, and we had begun to get used to it now, to this language that was not a language but rather a mystery. Then the connection was broken again, or however you want to put it, when the dog's barking got louder outside, and a vehicle pulled into the yard.

Just by the door to the feed preparation room was a staircase leading up to an open walkway. We hid there, crouching down behind the railings.

There were voices out in the yard. The dog was still barking. Strangely enough, I didn't feel particularly scared. We'd managed to switch off the lights and tidy up after ourselves. We stashed the medicine case far back in a cupboard.

'What do we do now?' Tommy whispered.

'We wait. It's probably one of the mink workers who left something behind. They'll leave again soon. It's Saturday, overtime and all that.'

The room looked like an old black-and-white photograph with

the lights off and just the light from the window openings coming in. I thought I could hear the creature moving, incredibly slowly from within its delirium, but the door to the space was shut and I couldn't see him from where we sat. Then there was the sound of another vehicle pulling into the yard, car doors opening and closing, and the dog's barking that kept getting more ferocious until someone yelled and it stopped.

There were people on the ground floor now, in the storage room it seemed like. They were talking down there, and someone gave a laugh. Then it was quiet again.

For a long while, nothing happened. All we could hear was a faint murmur of men's voices, and then the dog that was duty-bound to bark when it thought things had been quiet for too long.

Just when I'd started to think they were going to leave, some footsteps suddenly approached. The fluorescent lights were switched on. It felt like we were hovering above a big stage where the spotlights had just been lit and a performance was about to begin at any moment.

Two men came in through the door, wearing puffa jackets. One of them was smoking.

Then there was another, Tommy's eldest brother. And behind him, Dad and Leif.

I slumped down behind the railings. I didn't understand any of this.

'Wait here! And put out that bloody fag. There's half a million's worth of furs in here.'

Tommy's brother disappeared into the corridor. The others stayed there, looking around idly until he returned with armfuls of cigarette cartons.

'How many do you need?' he asked, turning to Dad.

'As many as I can get. Fifty. A hundred?'

'I can't believe the last lot you had are already gone.'

'Lots of chain-smoking mates, innit? And no other income at the moment.'

Dad smiled his usual smile which could mean anything at all:

that he was in a good mood or absolutely furious.

'Customs have really been going after people all autumn,' Tommy's brother continued. 'Just so you know what's going on. A few weeks back they were going over every single boat that came into Glommen harbour. I just want to be sure I can trust people.'

'It's sound. I've got other people who sell them, and I'm not so damn stupid I'd let on that I got the goods off you.'

Tommy's brother looked sceptically at him.

'Who've you got selling for you?'

'Some lads who need a bit of extra cash. Go-getter types who don't ask questions.'

'You can't have young kids working for you, Jonas, what do you think would happen if the police nabbed them?'

'They won't squeal. They'd just laugh at the rozzers. They know their rights.'

'I'll let you buy fifty cartons, no more. My stock's starting to get low and I've got too many orders. We'll have to go back out in the boat again soon.'

I now saw that the guy who came in first was Jens, the one who'd been there when they brought up the trawl net outside Anholt. At a sign from Tommy's brother, he went to fetch more cartons of cigarettes.

It was quiet again. Dad took his wallet out of his back pocket and started counting out banknotes.

'How's your brother doing?' he asked.

'No better. That fucking sea monster broke his arm. Twisted it so the bone looked like a bit of spiral pasta on the X-ray.'

'Can I have another look at him?'

'You starting to fancy animals, Jonas?'

The others laughed, but there was, like, no joy in their laughter. Or maybe that's just how it seemed to me up there, crouching on the platform above them, nearly in shock that my dad knew something about this.

'I'm just intrigued. I've never seen anything like it.'

Tommy's brother took the banknotes and put them in his inside pocket.

'Do you want to see him now?' he asked. 'I can't guarantee he'll be awake. He's ill, it seems. Refuses to eat. We don't even need to tranquillise him any more. I don't think he's got long to live.'

The double doors to the chiller room were wide open. They had switched on the lights inside. The men were standing in a semicircle around him. One of them prodded him with their foot. His tail fin moved slightly. There was some laughter. Dad's hoarse voice sort of rose above the others, like a voice in a choir. Tommy's brother, who was grinning with chewing tobacco in between his teeth. They were talking downstairs, but it was impossible to make out what they were saying. Renewed laughter blended in among the murmurs, such that you could nearly feel their excitement.

The fear had returned, like an old friend who didn't want to leave me in the lurch. I wasn't afraid for my own sake, but for the creature down there.

The men were standing close by him. Between their bodies I could see him moving, now awake, panic-stricken. There was a strange sound, panting in fear and confusion. The bloke who had come in with Jens stepped back slightly, leaving a gap where I could see the creature's face. It was like seeing my brother in the woods when they were feeding him grass and leaves. Or other times when they rubbed snow in his face or shoved his head in the toilet and flushed it. The creature's eyes were wide open, he was turning his head this way and that, opening his mouth wide as if he wanted to scream or was having trouble breathing. The men were laughing louder now; somebody prodded him with their foot again, gently at first and then a bit harder. I could see Dad down there, doing that weird thing with his mouth, the way he bared his teeth in a grimace. And then the creature on the tiled floor: the merman… twice as big as the others, but now defenceless. There was a crashing sound of something breaking. It was bleeding from fresh wounds on its body, water was mixing with blood on the floor: they'd done something bad to him but I couldn't tell what. My view was obscured all the time by bodies moving round and round in the room, like a strange dance. Then I saw Jens, who was holding a broken bottle. I realised that was the sound I'd heard: glass being shattered.

Slowly, as if everything was happening underwater, he bent over and struck with the bottle like a fencer or a villain in a movie knife fight, and stuck the shards into the creature's flesh. It flinched silently in pain. Tommy's breathing quickened next to me, and then I heard a howl. But only when I felt Tommy's hand over my mouth did I realise it had come from me – I was the one who screamed. Nobody heard anything down there; they were shouting just as loudly themselves, roaring and surging back and forth in the room as if they were a single entity. Jens had started kicking him. Like I'd seen Gerard kicking the caretaker's head in the common room. He swung with his leg and struck the creature full in the face. The wound in his mouth split open again, and more blood flowed across the floor. Then the silent screams that we could only hear inside our heads, and maybe it was those screams that were making them kick and hit even harder, all together now; their feet and fists seeming to strike him in a rhythm.

I couldn't watch any longer. I covered my eyes with my hands, the way I used to in front of the TV when I was frightened of something in a movie. And now there was a different noise. The creature filled its chest with air and let out a huge cry of agony. It was unlike any sound I'd ever heard before, a sort of bellow, like from a dying bull, I thought, and toneless, like a deaf person who can't hear their own voice. Tommy's hand ran down my back. I must have passed out, because when I came round again the men had gone.

Far away through the tunnel of sound I could hear them. The dog had started barking again. Vehicles started up and drove off. The doors to the chiller room stood open. The creature was moving slightly on the floor, its tail fin waving slowly back and forth but secured by the chain. Blood was flowing across the floor, diluted with water to a pink sap that vanished down the floor drain.

A van was badly parked on the edge of the pavement when I got home. Next to it was a motorbike I didn't recognise. The living room window was open. There was music playing at full blast – it sounded like The Rolling Stones, Dad's favourite band. I could barely remember how I'd got there or managed to pass the time after our trip to the mink farm. It was as if I'd got a puncture in my body, a tiny hole from which my strength was slowly seeping out. My thoughts kept going back to what I had seen. I couldn't comprehend where all that hate came from, the desire to harm him. He was totally defenceless. But maybe that's exactly what attracted them. The knowledge that there wouldn't be any consequences. It was like he didn't exist, a creature like him… a merman… couldn't exist.

I left my bike by the garage door and continued round to the back. The lights were on in my brother's room. I picked up a bit of gravel and chucked it at the window. He came over straight away, as if he'd been waiting for a signal.

'Where've you been?' he asked as soon as he got the window open.

'Just doing some stuff. Everything okay in there?'

'They're in the living room. I've locked myself in here. You coming in?'

'I don't fancy meeting a load of bastards. How many of them are there?'

'I dunno. Three, maybe four? Please… I don't want to be on my own here.'

I couldn't refuse him when he sounded like that. As if there was no hope, no matter how hard he searched. He waved to me as I went round the corner of the house. I saw the relief in his face, how every single muscle sort of relaxed at the thought that I was home.

Robert opened his door straight away when I knocked, and as soon as I was inside his room he locked us both in.

'It's great you're home,' he said. 'Did they notice you?'

'No. Has anything happened?'

'Nothing in particular. They've just been partying downstairs.'

'No fighting?'

'A little drunken arguing. But then they all made up again. They were even dancing. At least it sounded like it.'

As if it were normal, I thought. As if what was going on down there was what life was about.

'Is Mum there too?'

'I think so. I didn't feel like going to find out.'

As a Rolling Stones song faded out and the drunken blathering got louder in the background, I looked around the room, at the desk with schoolbooks and the jar of pens and the rubber, the wardrobe with a big hole in the door that Dad had kicked through one drunken night, the Michael Jackson posters from a music magazine I'd given him so he'd have something to put on his walls. Last summer he'd still had toys around in here, things I'd found or shoplifted for him. But they had been put away now, and the room looked bare.

'You've emptied this place out,' I said.

'I just tidied up a bit.'

'Everything you own?'

'Most of it was crap anyway. And stuff I'd outgrown. I'll be thirteen soon.'

I couldn't help smiling.

'Big lad... how long have you been sitting in here?'

'Since they started down there this afternoon. Where've you been?'

'With Tommy.'

He was scratching between his fingers. His skin had cracked again. If I didn't remind him, he would forget about his eczema.

And I'd had other things to do recently. It felt like someone was twisting a knife in me when I thought like that, that I was letting him down.

'Has something happened, Nella? You're acting really strange.'

'Do you think so?'

'And you're hardly ever home.'

That thin veil of terror in his eyes. Nothing could happen to me. Nothing about me could change; he couldn't handle it.

'And you never say what you're up to.'

'There's nothing to worry about. Relax, Robert.'

'So it's nothing to do with Gerard, then? Or has something else happened?'

Snapshots from the feed room flashed back in my mind, but I suppressed them so as not to feel nauseated.

'Nah. I swear! Everything's all right.'

He swallowed that lie with no effort at all. Because he needed it, I thought to myself. Because he wanted it. Because if I wasn't there, there was nothing at all. On the other side of me began the void.

'Let me tell you a story,' I said. 'Once upon a time there was a boy called Robert. He was growing up in Skogstorp, a little place near Falkenberg, in a street that was named after a flower, just like all the other streets in Skogstorp…'

'You don't need to. It's enough that you're here.'

He squinted a bit when he smiled at me. His glasses were dirty. He was tired. Just the tension of having Dad in the house made us all exhausted.

It took another hour or so before things quietened down downstairs. Maybe they got tired of the music, or else they started to realise there was a risk one of the neighbours might ring the police. Mick Jagger's voice was gone. Nobody was screaming or making noise. I could hear Mum laughing and unfamiliar male voices joking about something.

Against my will, my thoughts kept returning to the mink farm. After they drove off we left the building, climbed over the fence and headed down to the Mill, the pinball arcade in Olofsbo. We stayed there for several hours discussing what we should do. I was really shaky and nauseous; I couldn't make my body stop trembling. We needed a plan. We just had to help him; anything else was out of the question. We had to get him out of there, to some place where he'd be safe and could regain his strength. But no matter how hard we thought, we couldn't figure out how we could do it. Finally it started to get dark and Tommy had to cycle home.

Everything would have been so much easier, I thought now, if I just could have ignored everything, just regard everything as a weird dream, something incredible that just happened but which had nothing to do with my life. But that's not how things were now. He existed. The merman. And he needed us.

I gave a start, as if I had been daydreaming. There were footsteps on the stairs, and someone pushed on the handle of my brother's door.

'Robbie, are you in there? How come you've got the door locked?'

It was Dad. He sounded drunk.

'It was me who locked it,' I said hurriedly while the mental images were disappearing. 'I didn't know who was here.'

'Come out here. I want to talk to the both of you!'

The footsteps went downstairs again. It was no use protesting.

A minute later we were standing down in the living room. Besides Mum and Dad there were two men in the room. A tramp by the look of him, because he looked like he'd been sleeping in the same clothes for a week, and a younger bloke with a junkie's eyes. The same guy I'd seen at the mink farm, I realised, the one who had come in through the door first with Jens.

'You know why the palms of niggers' hands are so pale?' he asked in Dad's direction. 'Because they were stood on all fours when they got spray-painted. Damn, there were a lot of those jokes around for a while. I laughed my arse off when I heard 'em the first time. How come they've got such big wallets? Cos they get paid in bananas. And how come they've got such flat noses?' He made a 'halt' gesture: 'Stop. Whites only! Or such big ears?' He pretended to pick something out of his ear: 'So you got in there after all, you little rascal!'

Mum was dancing on her own over by the far wall.

She had her eyes shut and was swaying slowly in time with the music. I saw one other person bending over the record player in the corner: Leif.

'And the jokes about the Jews. D'you remember all the ones about the Jews? How do you fit a thousand Jews into a VW? Two in the back seat, two in the front seat, and the rest in the ashtray. That's fucking brilliant!'

He was definitely on something, you could see it in his pupils and his jaw, which was tense and sort of gurned when he talked.

Dad suddenly turned towards Robert and me.

'Ah, there you are! Relax, you look like you're scared shitless.'

He was wearing the same shirt he had on at the mink farm. There was a blood spot on the front pocket. I wondered what was wrong with them. What was wrong with my dad?

'I need to use your room, Nella.'

I just nodded.

'I need to store some things in there. For a few weeks maybe.'

The cigarettes, I thought. At least fifty cartons he didn't dare leave lying around. And probably other things as well that had to stay hidden for a while.

'So go and clear out what you need from your room and move in with Robbie.'

'Tonight?'

'Yes, tonight. Robbie, you can help her.'

The junkie bloke was looking at me in a way I didn't like. He was undressing me with his eyes and doing things to me in his thoughts. I took my brother by the hand and went towards the door.

'It's not so bad, Nella,' Mum slurred. 'Just for a coupla weeks… then you can move back in again. Put your mattress next to Robert's bed. You'll be cosy in there. You can help him with his homework. And Robert, Dad's got a present for you.'

I would have preferred to get out of there. But my brother stopped in his tracks, smiling reflexively as Dad took a glasses case out of his trouser pocket, opened it and ceremoniously held out a new pair of glasses.

'You know I don't like those glasses you go round in,' he said.

'But these are reading glasses…'

'So? You can't go round in a taped-up pair. Try 'em on!'

Robert was right. It was a pair of reading glasses, similar to the ones our English teacher had, but with thicker lenses. Dad removed Robert's old glasses and put the new pair on him.

'I can't see anything,' he said. 'Honest, Dad, I can't see anything.'

'No whingeing now. I know the bloke I bought them off. He said they would work. I had your prescription with me.'

'Close up yeah, but not far away, things are blurry. I'm going to feel dizzy.'

'You'll get used to them after a while. Relax now, Robbie.'

'Please, give me my old ones. I can't see with these.'

Dad gave him a chilly look. Then he took the old glasses and bent them in the middle until the frame snapped.

'You're going to wear those if I have to glue them to your face. We should've got rid of this old crap a long time ago. And I don't understand why your mum didn't do it already!'

He turned towards Mum, but she took no notice as she danced with her back against the wall, while the junkie was undressing her, one item of clothing at a time, with that empty, spaced-out expression.

'What the hell did you get up to while I was inside? Nothing but boozing… was that the only thing you did?'

But he wouldn't have been our dad if he weren't capable of turning on a sixpence.

'Come on, kids!' he said cheerfully. 'We're not going to carry on arguing in this family. I'm heading out tomorrow and I'll be away for a while. But tonight we're having a party. Now go upstairs and clear out Nella's room.'

We didn't see hide nor hair of Dad for a week. According to Mum, he was in Gothenburg. He, Leif and the junkie bloke had some business up there, she claimed, and she didn't know when they'd be back.

I had cleared out my room and moved all the stuff I needed into Robert's. Maybe it was just for a short time, or maybe I'd have to stay there all winter? Dad had demanded all the keys from me, put what he wanted to store into my room and locked the door. Mum gave us no support as usual. She was on Dad's side no matter what he did. Out of fear, I figured, or actually out of some messed-up sort of love for him.

But Robert wasn't doing very well. The whole situation with a load of criminals coming and going from the house was eating away at him. And then the new glasses. He really couldn't see anything with them. On Monday morning he declared that he was not going to school, he couldn't do it, and he was going to stay at home for the rest of the term. He still wouldn't be able to see properly, he said, couldn't keep up in lessons, and he'd rather choose to be blind than go round feeling dizzy. What I said didn't do anything to help. That his form teacher would go spare if he bunked off again. Or that the school might call in social services, with everything that entailed. Nothing had any effect on his determination. And after a while I didn't feel like nagging.

Everything that had happened recently had sapped my strength. I wanted to conserve what little energy I had left. Later, I thought, as soon as I'd finished helping the creature, I'd focus on Robert. Just a little while longer, then I'd be back to protect him.

Tommy and I spent the week trying to figure out what to do. We had some ideas, but the problem was we couldn't implement them. Work at the mink farm had started up again, the place was full of people getting ready for the next round of skinning, and at night the guard dog ran loose on the site. Tommy had gone round on a couple of evenings, and every time there were vehicles parked in the yard.

'I think they're inviting people in to look at him,' he said. 'There's loads of cars. And my brother's there every night.'

To do what they liked, I thought: mistreat him, gradually take his life. Without any particular reason at all. Because they liked doing it. Because some people were simply made that way.

Or maybe there was a reason, but we just couldn't see it? Smuggled cigarettes and the creature, Dad, Leif and the junkie guy, Tommy's brothers and a load of other dodgy blokes, maybe they were all connected in some way we didn't understand. And then it would just take a single movement at the outer edge of that fine-mesh net for things to go wrong.

Where Dad was concerned at any rate, I did find out what he was using my room for. One night that week I used the Professor's skeleton keys to unlock the door. There were cartons of cigarettes stacked up on the floor, hundreds of them, and not just the Danish brands I'd seen him buy at the mink farm. There were German fags as well, which he must have got hold of somewhere else. It seemed like he was in the process of building up a warehouse, because there were way too many cartons for him to sell himself.

There were also a dozen video recorders with labels from a video rental place in Halmstad. Strangely enough, I felt relieved. At any rate, there was nothing worse here than tobacco and stolen video recorders.

One bit of good news that week was that the caretaker was getting better. L.G. told us in our physics lesson. He'd woken up from his coma and was remaining in hospital for now, under observation.

L.G. had even been to visit him. Some of the vertebrae in his neck were damaged and he would have to wear a neck support for the rest of the autumn. But he would get well again, the doctors assured. Relief spread through the class when the information came out. It was like everybody was going round smiling for days.

Plus Gerard had been arrested, which was equally good news, at least for me. According to what I heard, they'd found him in a summer cottage that belonged to some friends of Peder's parents. They'd decided to go in heavy-handed. Because he was under age, he couldn't be convicted in adult court, so instead he would be sent to borstal after Christmas. He was still banned from the school grounds, same as the rest of the gang. I was relieved at that; I didn't have the energy to go round being scared all the time.

Maybe it was true what Jessica claimed about a whole ball of string being about to unravel, but if it was, we weren't hearing anything about it at school. People were gossiping, saying they'd broken into some houses down by the beach and set fire to a youth centre in town, but it was all just rumour.

And all the while people were distancing themselves from Gerard and the gang, it was like I was starting to be seen in a more favourable light myself. On Thursday after PE, Jessica waved to me from where she stood fussing with her hair in front of the changing room mirror.

'Are you coming on Saturday?' she asked.

'Coming where?'

'Didn't you get our invitation to the Halloween party?'

She appeared to be serious. Or else she was just seriously good at pretending.

'I thought it was meant for someone else.'

'But it's our last autumn together as a class. Just one more term then everything'll be over and people will go off in different directions. We should stick together for these last few months. It's important to share. Minus Gerard and those guys. What sickos. The caretaker actually could have died!'

She took an aerosol can out of her bag, gave it a shake and sprayed a little cloud over her hair.

'I promise, it'll be loads of fun. We've been planning it for over a month. You can wear whatever fancy dress costume you want, like in America. That's how they celebrate Halloween over there. Lovisa's sister learned about it when she was there as an exchange student.'

'Can Tommy come too?'

'Lovisa's mum said she doesn't want it to get too big, but I actually think we should invite people from the other rooms in our year as well. Not the losers, obviously.'

She had finished with her hair now and took a lip balm out of her jeans pocket and stroked the tube back and forth across her lips. Like a pro, I thought. A pro at acting like a girl.

'Want some?' she asked, holding out the tube. 'My lips get so rough this time of year. You haven't got any cold sores, have you?'

I took her lip balm, made two passes over my lips and handed it back. Like I'd seen girls in our class do all through the years, a thing that reinforced companionship and indicated that they were together. My lips felt rigid, as if I'd got candle wax on them.

'I look totally disfigured,' she said, inspecting her face half an inch away from the mirror. 'I don't understand how it's got like this. I don't even smoke. And I've stopped eating chocolate. Having spots is actually worse than cancer. You coming, then?'

'If Tommy can come along.'

'I'll have to ask Lovisa first. We're the ones organising the party.'

She stuffed the lip balm inside her bra. It felt as if I'd just been bribed.

E arly the next morning Tommy rang.

'There won't be anyone around at the mink farm today,' he said.

'How do you know?'

'Jens was here last night. I heard them talking in the kitchen. There's ammonia leaking from a tank there. There's a danger it will turn to gas. People from the council are going out to have a look at it later today. The workers have been given the day off.'

His breathing was a little quicker than usual.

'Has something else happened?'

'Yeah… Olof's coming home from hospital. My other brother spoke to him on the phone after Jens left. Down in the games room so nobody could hear. I happened to be standing right by the door and I don't know if I caught everything, but I think they're planning to move him again.'

'Where to?'

'I dunno. And they're not going to tell me, either. They're scared somebody will find him. And there will be loads of questions. There are too many people who know about him already. They're planning to move the fags at the same time. I think that's the only opportunity we're going to get.'

'So he's alive at any rate.'

'Seems that way. But we've got to act fast. Phone the school and get the day off sick. And come over here as soon as you can.'

With my brother rummaging around in his room and Mum snoring in bed, I went into the kitchen. The local news had just started on the radio, but there was nothing about any ammonia leak at a mink farm. Anyway, it couldn't be all that dangerous to be in the vicinity.

As I cycled down towards the lighthouse, Tommy waved to me from where he was sitting in an old car that had been converted into a pick-up truck. The vehicle normally sat down by the harbour with the keys in the ignition and the fishermen would use it for small errands between the docks and the town.

'Jens and my brother have gone out in the boat,' he said as I opened the door. 'I decided to borrow this for a while. If they're going to move him, they won't do it before this afternoon. Looks like we're in luck.'

'What if somebody else sees us?'

'There's nobody there. And the people from the council won't come in until Jens lets them in.'

I looked out to sea. A fishing boat was visible on the horizon, apparently heading westwards.

'So what are we going to do now?'

'Exactly what we planned.'

In the rear-view mirror I could see an inflatable dinghy and a Home Guard stretcher that were tied down in the back. Herring gulls were circling in the air above us. When I rolled down the window to get some air, I could see they were screeching, but could not hear them in the gale.

The sky seemed to be whirling; the gulls flew in ever-wider circles. And then the sea out there, like molten metal, slowly rocking in a half-mile-wide tract out near the horizon.

If I could have experienced these events from the creature's point of view, what would the world have seemed like? Sounds must have seemed very different, I thought, much harsher, filled with strange echoes as they hit walls and objects; they travelled faster on land, though not as far. In the sea, sounds could be heard from several miles away: the throb of a boat's engine or the high-pitched beeping of an echolocator, but they were never objectionable, never grated on your ears. And the light in the sea was refracted differently: green, blue and black formed the background to everything. Surroundings grew darker in the depths; ultimately all colour ceased deep down. Only near the surface were there paler gleams of white, yellow and orange.

But maybe the creature didn't know that. Maybe it only came near the surface at night. And maybe it came from a completely different part of the ocean. That's how I imagined it: that the currents had carried it from somewhere far away, here to our coast.

It must be bothered by daylight. Maybe it couldn't see at all, or maybe it saw things through a haze or fog, like my brother without his glasses. Its eyes might be unable to take in colours above the surface. Like someone who's colour-blind, I thought, where the world was just in shades of grey.

What sort of beings were approaching the place where it was, and what were those things holding it down? The doors opened, letting in more light. But doors – it didn't even understand what a door was; it only saw that the light was being refracted differently, blinding it and making it turn away purely as a reflex. Pain with every movement, from the wounds on its body… and the fear that it was those others who had come, the ones who always tortured it. The weak movements of its tail fin, and then the relief when it recognised us.

Everything was different up here, there was less pressure and gravity acted differently. The terrible force that pulled every mass towards the centre of the earth – not like in the water where it was barely noticeable, where objects took their time to sink, but where the pressure increased. You couldn't fall when you were in the sea: falling meant sinking. And if you lay against a fixed object, a flat or uneven surface, you'd hardly notice it: a rock under the surface was something completely different to a rock above the surface. He could feel that the chain was loosened from his tail, that hateful thing that had been restricting his movements suddenly gone;

there was a strange snapping sound as someone cut through the metal and the things around his arms and neck, that transparent material, the fishing line, sharp as coral, like snail shells in the mussel beds… that was gone now as well.

He could sense our presence, human beings, though there was no way he could know what a human was. Or did he know? Did he know more than we realised? Maybe we existed in his stories just like we had mermaids in ours? There must be many of his kind, I thought, a whole colony of them way down in the ocean depths… or was he the last remaining member of an extinct species? I imagined he had come from far away, from the bottom of the ocean, and one day something happened: he heard a call or just felt an unexplainable longing, just like I might feel a longing for something I couldn't even identify. That's how his quest began, slowly following along with the currents until he approached our coast.

How would they manage, those small land-based creatures who had come to help him? He could sense our intention, he knew why we were there, he could perceive our thoughts and feelings via his strange sixth sense – and the sea! He could sense the presence of the sea. Every day since they'd caught him and kept him locked up, he had sensed the closeness of the sea. The sea was not far away: its smells were everywhere, and that's where we would take him, he knew that. But how would we do it with all this gravity pulling on us, pulling on him, pressing us down to the ground all the time: what did we have to work against this terrible force that made every movement so incredibly clumsy, heavy and difficult. We, the humans, wanted him to roll onto his side, he sensed that, and we weren't going to be able to budge him from where he lay on the tiled floor. So he did it for us, rolled onto his side, up onto a softer surface, which was the stretcher, a low stretcher on wheels that belonged to Tommy's dad, who was a medical orderly in civil defence exercises. He was lying on it now and could see how the room was changing, how he was suddenly put in motion, taken to another space, like a largish underwater bay if he'd been in the sea, with walls like cliffs, with a high ceiling like the surface of the water up above… a door that opened, the feed hatch on the short side of the building, the ropes we placed under the stretcher… and how we lowered him to the ground with the old system of tackles and counterweights they used to lower the mink feed or hoist up the heavy bundles of frozen chicken. What was that sudden explosion of light: white, yellow, burning red? He understood that it was daylight, the light up there on the surface in the humans' world.

The smells hit him: the terrible stench of mink shit and piss and fetid animal carcasses – smells he did not understand and only vaguely recognised, though he knew they had something to do with death. He noticed how he was sinking, how the pressure was increasing. And what were those sounds he was noticing now… the strange noisy blasts that carried through the air? A dog's barks, if he had known what barks were, and if he'd known what a dog was. He noticed out of the corner of his eye that someone approaching him rapidly. The aggressive black creature was coming closer, mad with rage, driven by instinct, he understood; not thinking, existing solely in its senses, primed to attack any intruder who dared to encroach on its territory. What was going through his mind as he reached the ground, lying all alone on a stretcher as the dog leapt on him?

Though weakened by fever and injuries, all the sadism he had been subjected to but which could not overcome his will to live, to get back to where he belonged at any price… in spite of all that, he could sense the animal's intention to hurt him. And so, with a single lightning-quick movement, at the precise moment it leapt on him, he grabbed hold of what he assumed was its throat, lifted the dog straight up, looked at it while it desperately tried to bite him, howling with its teeth bared… and he just sort of shook it, squeezing with tremendous strength until it started to whimper and choke with its tongue lolling out. It was just hanging there, the dog, lifeless in the creature's grip until he put it down on the ground and went still again.

Everything was happening fast now: the rubber dinghy that we managed to get under the fence, which he understood he had to roll over into. All the time he kept his eyes shut; the daylight was torture for him, like sharp pins poking into his optic nerves.

We left him behind us and ran between the mink houses over to the fence. There was no one there. The site was deserted, just as Tommy had promised. He had already cut the fence open with a pair of bolt cutters. The pick-up truck was standing just outside on the overgrown road. The tow rope was fastened with a hook.

When I turned round, I saw the creature reach out to touch the dog's lifeless body. As if he wanted to make sure it really was dead.

It was several years since we'd last been in the root cellar. I wasn't even sure where the old entrance was. The mound where it was located was overgrown with brush and young birch trees.

'This'll be all right,' said Tommy, as if to reassure himself. 'Nobody ever comes here.'

'Unless somebody decides to follow the tyre tracks.'

He glanced back along the road, at the grass that had been flattened where we drove in.

'It'll rain before then. And if anybody did suspect he was somewhere nearby, where would they start looking? Not here at any rate.'

He was right. This place was almost impossible to spot from outside. Just a little mound among a clump of trees. If nobody pointed it out, you wouldn't even notice it.

The creature was lying still with its eyes shut. Maybe they'd left him alone the last few days, because his wounds seemed to have healed a bit.

His body was brownish in the daylight. The horsehairs that grew on his head and arms were black, and there was a small fin on his back that I hadn't noticed before. His chest rose slowly; it seemed like one breath every minute. His tail fin moved slightly. He seemed to have a fever again, or else he was dreaming: there were strange little twitches in his body.

I went over to the far side of the mound. The wind had subsided. I started ripping up grass, pulled out yellowed thistles by their roots and dug in the earth with my fingers until I found the old door hatch to the root cellar.

'Help me lift it,' I said.

Tommy got down beside me and grasped the metal loops, and we shifted it aside.

It was like an underwater cave down there. Over the years a round pool had formed, maybe three metres across. Perhaps that's why the cottage had been abandoned, because the groundwater rose. It was surprisingly clean. The stone walls and the roof were intact. No cobwebs. No dead frogs. The water was brackish but did not seem stagnant. It didn't even smell musty. The water must have come in from outside; there was no other explanation.

'We won't find anywhere better. We can come here in the evenings and check on him.'

Tommy was right, I thought. The root cellar was the best place we could get for now. And although he wouldn't be in the sea, at least he'd be in some water.

We could hear him again as we dragged him over to the opening, that consciousness that we could only hear in our own thoughts. He was dreaming, I realised, and we were in his dreams. We even had names, and he was repeating them deep down inside himself. But maybe I was just imagining things; maybe it was impossible to interpret his dreams that way.

It was afternoon when we left. We still had things to sort out. We needed to get hold of food for him, stocks he could eat from himself. There was fish available down at the harbour in Glommen. Nobody would notice anything if we nicked a crate from outside the wholesaler's.

I turned back towards the root cellar one last time. We had covered the door with soil and branches. The creature should be safe in there.

Once he had slipped into the water, it was like he woke up again. He opened his eyes and looked at us. His face was right beneath the surface of the water, the hairs were flowing outwards around his head like a weird aura, the colour of his eyes had changed, deeper yet clearer, almost glowing. Even though it was dark down there we saw a smile in his expression, a smile of gratitude. He was communicating to us what he was feeling, his experiences. It was so strange that I could never get used to it… He knew he would soon be back where he belonged, that we could help him get back there as soon as he was strong enough. He communicated to us that he understood he would have to stay there for a while, until he was ready to make it on his own. Strangely enough, the gash in his cheek had already begun to heal, the opening was smaller, and the same was true of the wounds on his body. Maybe water was all he needed to get better on his own?

I wondered how long it would take for someone to discover what had happened at the mink farm. The guard dog lying lifeless in the yard. The fence cut open. But I couldn't be bothered worrying about that right now.

It had started to rain. The tyre tracks would soon be gone, as would our footprints. Tommy was shivering next to me on the seat. He was nearly as short as me, and he had to stretch in order to see out through the windscreen. I bet it must look odd, I thought, if anybody is watching us. Two dwarves who'd just climbed out of the ground and were driving off in a pick-up truck in the rain.

From where Tommy and I were standing on the pavement we could see right into the kitchen. What had been planned as a class party seemed to have grown into something much bigger. Costumed figures crowded in among people in ordinary clothes. Some seemed to have come from town. There were bikes and scooters in dense clusters in the drive. The music carried all the way out to the street: *Let's Dance* by David Bowie.

I can't explain why I wanted to go there. Maybe I just wanted to be part of something. I'd borrowed some of Mum's makeup and one of her dresses that had shrunk in the wash. I had my leather boots on, which were a bit too small and had been given to me by an old lady at the charity shop when I was in there looking for clothes for my brother.

But now I was suddenly unsure. Dad had come back home that morning, and something had happened while he was away. He was like a thundercloud. He didn't even say hello to us. Without a word of explanation, he locked himself in the living room. I heard him talking on the phone in there, simultaneously whispering and agitated. Mum took some tablets and stayed in bed all day, and Robert was terrified by the atmosphere and asked me to stay at home. He sounded really desperate when I was about to leave, but for once I didn't listen to him.

'Maybe we should forget it,' I muttered. 'Maybe it's not for the likes of us...'

'Unless you regard it as a field trip.'

Tommy took a step towards the door. I really should have turned on my heel and gone home. But the temptation was too great, the temptation to try to be like everyone else.

Someone had turned the music down by the time we went in, but you could still barely hear yourself think. Some older lads staggered past with carrier bags from the off-licence. A bunch of girls in costume were crowding in front of the hall mirror. I caught a glimpse of Nicke Wester dressed as a vampire, but someone in the room behind him had switched off the light.

In the other direction, in the doorway to the kitchen, it was so crowded you couldn't make out any faces at all, just an anonymous mass of bodies. The smell of perfume and cigarettes hung everywhere.

We squeezed through the hall and went into the dining room. It was quieter there. Sandra and Lilian were standing in a corner smoking. They looked surprised to see us, but they did say hello. A group from Class 9C sat on the floor drinking beer. I felt strange; my stomach had started to hurt in a way I didn't like. I asked Tommy to wait while I went to look for the loo.

The bathroom was next to the staircase leading upstairs. A queue of desperate girls had formed outside it. Caroline Ljungman was one of them. She was holding a pocket mirror up to her face, trying to do her makeup as she waited her turn. When she saw me, she shook her head.

'Like, I'm not being funny or anything, Petronella... but who invited you?'

She was slurring her words slightly and having trouble getting her mascara brush to meet her eyelashes.

'Jessica,' I said. 'Have you seen her?'

'She's in the kitchen. Totally hysterical. Loads more people have turned up than they invited. Things are about to get out of control here. Mind where you walk – I found some broken glass on the floor earlier.'

I noticed now that she was dressed all in black: black Chinese slippers, black legwarmers over black trousers. A black top with a black brooch on the neckline. Even her nails were painted black.

'Halloween,' she said, noticing me looking at her. 'Not that I know what it's about, but it's got something to do with horror. I'm dressed as a witch. Have you got a fag?'

I shook my head.

'Lovisa's sister was here earlier. She's got her own car, a Golf Cabriolet. She told Lovisa she was going to blab to their parents if she didn't get rid of everyone within an hour. They're away and won't be back until tomorrow. But I don't think anybody's going to leave here willingly.'

We could hear a girl crying in the loo. Someone knocked on the door and asked her to hurry up.

'Who'd you come here with, by the way?'

'With Tommy.'

'Sorry to ask, but you've, like, never hung around with the rest of us, that's all I mean. You've always kept yourself to yourself… sort of off to the side. I realise you haven't had an easy time, with your parents and your brother and stuff.'

The crying continued in the loo. And Carro carried on slurring at me, something about the neighbour's car that had got scratched earlier that evening, something about people who'd come from town when they heard about the party. I wasn't listening too closely.

'Gerard and that lot aren't here, anyway,' she said suddenly. 'We should be happy about that. Have you heard about what they did?'

'Only rumours. About burglaries in houses and stuff.'

'They've been involved with stolen goods as well. And animal cruelty. There was an article about it in the paper yesterday. About all the horrible stuff they've been up to. Stabbing knives into cows' udders. Putting glass in feed troughs. And setting fire to an animal. Can you imagine? They poured petrol over a foal and set fire to her. It was last summer, but it's only just come out now. How can people do something like that?'

She stuffed her mascara into her handbag and took out a powder compact.

'I'm gonna be happy when school is out so I don't have to see them. What are you going to do when school's over?'

'I dunno. Find a job, I suppose.'

'I'm gonna go to England. On a language course. And then sixth form. I hope I get onto the science track, that gives you the most opportunities. You can do whatever you want if you do science.'

I tried to shake off the unpleasant feeling of hearing what Gerard and his gang had done. If it was true, I thought. But why wouldn't it be? It was like everything fitted together in terms of senselessness. The cat last winter, what I'd seen Dad and the others doing at the mink farm, and now the latest news about Gerard.

'You look really nice,' said Carro, and she seemed to mean it. 'Is that a new dress?'

'No, it's my mum's. It shrunk in the wash.'

'Looks cool, anyway. Is it crepe?'

She reached out her hand and touched the fabric. There was a wart on her middle finger; I'd never noticed it before. It was sort of the perfect match for her witch costume.

'Thanks,' I said. 'You know, I can't bear to wait here any longer. There must be a loo upstairs as well.'

Just as I had guessed, there was a toilet upstairs. It was like a little oasis up there. I could barely hear the noise from downstairs, and there was a faint scent of soap and hand cream. I had never seen such a nice bathroom before. Above the basin was a gold-framed mirror. The toilet was pale blue. The sunken bathtub was recessed into the floor. There were lights built into the shelves and half a dozen Jane Hellen shampoos standing in a row in the shower. There were piles of perfectly white fluffy towels on a low marble-topped bench.

I peed and wiped myself without looking at the paper. It was so typical that I'd come on now: I couldn't even trust my own body. I searched through the drawers for sanitary towels but didn't find any. Finally I folded some toilet paper and put it inside my knickers. It occurred to me that Lovisa might have some panty liners in her room. It felt like I was going to bleed through.

Lovisa's room was at the far end of the hall. At least I assumed it was hers. Everything was painted pink inside, even the bed. There were movie posters and photos of Princess Diana on the walls. In one corner was a makeup table with loads of products I'd never even heard of before.

She even had her own TV. It was behind a screen with a small leather sofa in front.

I found some panty liners in the wardrobe, took one out of the pack and went behind the screen to put it in. I could just make out the coast through the window, how the horizon sort of got darker beyond the neighbourhood of detached houses. I wondered what the creature felt like in the old root cellar. What did he think when he heard the wind in the trees up above? Did he understand anything about our world?

At least he was safe now. We'd be going there again soon. We would take care of him and make sure he got better. It was impossible to know how long it would take, but it didn't matter.

I could hear the buzz from downstairs from where I was standing. Voices carried up through the ventilation ducts. A lad's voice attempted to crack a joke: 'You might have fun without drinking, but it's stupid to take a chance.' And somebody else said: 'Are you one of those types who sit down to piss?' People were full of those lines – the annoying quips never ran out.

I thought about my brother again. It had been wrong to leave him alone at home. He was properly scared, he wasn't just pretending. I wondered what Dad had got mixed up in. I could detect his moods like a seismograph can detect the slightest movement in the earth's crust. It was something serious at any rate.

When I went back downstairs Tommy was gone. I went into the kitchen to see if he was there, but I couldn't even get through the doorway. I was pushed back with the flow, past people who were bellowing into each other's ears to make themselves heard.

In the lounge downstairs, people had started dancing. One guy with deck shoes and a Young Conservatives lapel badge was DJing. In one corner I could see Petter Bengtsson snogging a girl from Year 7. He had her up against the wall with one knee between her thighs. Just the idea of someone sticking their tongue in my mouth made me feel sick. I imagined them going at it for hours until they got cramp in their tongues and their breath started to feel sour and strange. It seemed so boring, all that pawing of bodies, and the girl who kept pushing his hand away when she thought he'd gone too far.

I went upstairs again, squeezing past the bathroom where the door stood open and someone was crouching down and being sick over the side of the bath, made a wide arc around some lads who seemed involved in an argument and ran straight into Tommy.

'Where've you been?' he asked worriedly. 'I've been looking for you.'

'I've been looking for you, too.'

He took hold of my arm and started to lead me away.

'Gerard's here... I've just seen him. I put our jackets by the back door. Lovisa's upset. She doesn't want him here.'

I don't know why, but I suddenly felt terrified that he was in the house. We turned left and continued down a hall. Tommy opened a door and suddenly we were in the conservatory. I stopped dead in my tracks. There, sitting in a chair with my jacket on his lap, was Gerard.

I hadn't seen him since the morning he beat up the caretaker. He'd just got a haircut. His hair was spiky on the top of his head, but long at the back. He looked tired, as if he hadn't slept in a long time.

'I found this jacket on the floor,' he said. 'Is it okay if I borrow it for a while? It's cold in here.'

'We were just about to leave,' said Tommy.

'Isn't the party any good? I haven't had a chance to check out the atmosphere yet. Loads of drinking, of course. People trying to act grown up. I've always thought that was ridiculous.'

He took a soft drink bottle out of his lap. Orange pop.

'I don't drink alcohol,' he said. 'Don't like it. Never have done, actually. To be honest, I don't see the point in getting drunk. What good is it if you lose control? If anybody knows about that, it's you, Ironing Board, with your parents.'

'What do you want from me?' I asked.

'I dunno. Maybe just to tell you you're no longer a suspect?'

He turned his head to the side and peered out into the garden.

'Man, they've got a nice place here,' he said. 'Lovisa's family. Almost looks like Dallas. Like Sue Ellen might turn up at any moment with a drink in her hand. Dentists, is that what they are – her parents? I don't remember.'

He turned to look at me again.

'The cat was Peder's, but maybe you already worked that out? Or more accurately, his little sister's. She was really sad when it disappeared. Despondent, in fact. Peder says he didn't tell anyone what we did, but that was where everything started, it was like a path leading on to loads of other stuff. And then, after that business with the caretaker, it was Peder who suggested I should hide out in the summer cottage. We'd been in there before. It belongs to some mates of his parents, from Borås. A little shack down by the beach at Stafsinge. They're hardly ever there, only for a week in the summer. There are no neighbours, the place is completely deserted, and yet the police found me after two days. You've got to wonder how that happened.'

It was like he was recounting the plot of a book, but couldn't really remember the order things had happened in. Maybe he noticed that himself, because he sort of pulled himself together.

'Besides, Peder is the only one who emerged from this situation unscathed. All he's gonna get is a little fine. Whereas I am getting sent away next term. And all the stuff that came up in questioning, even though he swears he didn't squeal to anybody. Don't you think that seems odd, Ironing Board?'

I didn't want to know any more details. I didn't want to get involved in anything else that had anything to do with Gerard.

'Why aren't you telling him this? That you've figured out it's him.'

He drained the last from the bottle and took out a new one. He seemed to have a whole stash in his lap.

'Why should I do that? I might be mistaken. Besides, it's not interesting.'

He was keeping him on tenterhooks, I thought, expertly leaving Peder in a state of uncertainty. In the space of a second he went from letting him think he knew everything, to making it seem that everything was normal.

'I don't know if you think about this stuff, Ironing Board, but when people are uncertain you can get them to do almost anything. Some really sick stuff, in fact. Because they have to prove they're – what's the word – loyal?'

'Can I have my jacket now?' I said. 'We've got to go.'

'You'll get it, don't worry. Let me finish first. Have you managed to get my money?'

'What?'

'Come on, you still owe me a grand. Regardless of who snitched about the cat.'

He was smiling the whole time. As if this was all a game.

'I'm not giving you any more money. You got that Walkman and five hundred kronor. That's plenty.'

'Come on, Nella, let's go.' Tommy took the jacket out of his lap and handed it to me. Gerard let it happen, even extending his arms to the sides in a gesture possibly meant to show we could have taken it long ago.

'Only it's more than a grand now. I should've had it two weeks ago, that was what we agreed. Twenty per cent weekly interest is not unreasonable in this situation – you can ask your dad about that. Let's make it fifteen hundred.'

I didn't understand what Dad had to do with this. Nor did I understand what he expected me to say. So I said nothing, just took my jacket from Tommy and checked that everything was still in the pockets.

'You look really fit in that dress,' Gerard said. 'It suits you. You're even fitter than average. On a scale of one to ten I'd give you a seven… or maybe even an eight. I see now you've got some makeup on. That lipstick colour looks good on you.'

I felt like I was going to be sick when he said that. He might as well have groped me.

'And here come my footsoldiers,' he said, turning towards the door where Ola and Peder had turned up. 'Is there anything going out there?'

'Lovisa wants us to clear off,' Peder said. 'It wouldn't surprise me if she called the cops.'

'Your problem, Peder, is that you get stressed out over nothing. And Lovisa is not the one who decides when it's time for us to go.'

He turned back towards me.

'I want it by Monday at the latest. I'm serious this time. No more haggling, no more lame excuses. Otherwise something's gonna happen…'

Gerard's deadline expired on Monday, but I didn't hear anything from him. Because I still didn't have any money, I let the matter rest. I'd had enough fear, I thought. After Christmas he was going to be sent to borstal in another town. I just had to hold out until then.

Besides, I had other things to think about. The day after Lovisa's part, Olof came home from hospital. Tommy listened in as he was brought up to date on the situation downstairs in their games room. The creature was gone… the sea monster, as they called him… and there was no trace of him. The brothers didn't know what to think. It seemed completely implausible that anybody had managed to get into the mink farm and release him. The fact that the guard dog lay dead in the yard but nothing else had been touched or stolen just made it more mysterious. Jens and Olof had looked through every single room in search of something that might solve the riddle. But the rain had helped us: that night over an inch had fallen, and all traces were gone, except for the hole we cut in the fence. Neither of the brothers had any suspicions about us.

But they seemed concerned because it had some connection with their business dealings. Tommy didn't understand exactly what, but something seemed to have happened on that front as well. Something that made them cautious.

All that meant we couldn't let our guard down. If we were going to check on the creature, we'd have to wait. It was crucial that we didn't go near the abandoned cottage, at least not for a while.

Instead, I was pleased my brother had decided to go to back to school. At lunchtime he turned up by my locker, looking the same as usual, minus his glasses.

'My stomach won,' he said with a smirk. 'I can't go round being hungry any longer.'

Nobody bothered to go food shopping at home any more. And at school at least he'd get one hot meal in his belly every day.

'I just won't be able to see a thing in lessons,' he said. 'I'm more or less blind without my glasses.'

'We can go to the school nurse and see if she can sort out some new ones. Or the school welfare officer. I can help you if you want.'

Robert shook his head.

'Later,' he said. 'For now, I'm just here to eat. And to explain why I've been off. And this is a good day, because we've got home economics.'

'What are you making?'

'Pancakes with cream.'

That's the kind of thing people couldn't understand, I thought as I watched him head off towards the Year 7 cloakroom with his uncertain gait and his back slightly stooped: that some kids went to school only so they wouldn't go hungry. It suddenly seemed so messed up, with all the kids who hid the fish they didn't like under a mountain of napkins so the dinner ladies wouldn't see how much they were throwing out. But those glasses needed sorting out. I put it on my mental to-do list.

If Mum had a list like that, it didn't show. It seemed like she'd gone to bed and was never going to get up again. Everything was going downhill at home. Every room was a pigsty. She stayed in her bedroom with the curtains drawn, sleeping the days away. We didn't see hide nor hair of Dad, either. He would head out every afternoon and not come back until late at night. Since his return from Gothenburg, he was barely contactable. I was becoming increasingly convinced that something had happened during that trip that terrified him. Leif and the other dodgy blokes seemed to be out of the picture. Or maybe not, because one afternoon when I came home, Dad was sitting on the sofa waiting for me.

'We need to talk,' he said.

I stood in the doorway, and he seemed to be all right with that.

'I've got to get away from here. And it might be a while before I get back. I mean, I'm not going back inside… not doing more time. I just need to stay away.'

'From what?'

'From certain people. I plan to clear out your room beforehand so you can move back in there.'

'Can I go now?'

He looked at me, almost in surprise.

'Sure. Just look after Robbie, there's a good girl. He won't make it on his own.' He made a significant gesture in the direction of upstairs. 'And Mum… well, you can see what shape she's in.'

'Don't worry.'

'I want you to know I appreciate it. That you keep things ticking along here at home. I'm sorry, Nella, really, for everything. I know how it feels. I didn't have any adults I could count on either when I was fifteen. I was homeless.'

He went silent and looked down at his hands. As if he didn't really understand what he should do with them, I thought.

'You're strong, Nella. You'll get through this. I trust you.'

He winked at me.

'Tell Robert I'm sorry about that business with his glasses. I didn't mean anything bad, I just wanted him to have a new pair.'

He got up from the sofa, as awkwardly as an old man.

'I saw something strange the other week,' he said in a quiet voice. 'Something I never thought I'd get to see. There are things in this world that are completely incomprehensible.'

The creature, I thought, it was the creature he was talking about. He felt guilty about what they'd done to him.

'And people react bloody strangely to strange things. Isn't that right?'

Maybe he was just babbling. I didn't want to know. I didn't want to think about who he was, what he had done or what he was going to do.

'I'm clearing off the day after tomorrow,' he said. 'If nothing else comes up in the meantime. Then we'll see when I come back.'

The next day in the lunch break, Mum was waiting for me in the common room. It felt surreal to see her standing there, confused among a mob of students who'd just come out of their lessons. She was dressed up, had put on some makeup and was carrying her bag on her shoulder. As I got closer, I noticed a bruise above her left eye.

'I need to speak to you, Nella,' she said. 'Come on, let's go outside.'

I took my jacket and followed her out. Without saying a word, we went over to the smoking area. She took a packet of fags out of her bag, tapped out two and held one out to me.

'It's funny,' she said. 'I don't know anything about you, really. Not even whether you smoke.'

She'd been drinking; I could smell it on her breath even though she'd been sucking on a Fisherman's Friend to cover it up. I shook my head.

'Good. And don't start, either. Don't start doing anything else. You can see what shit you've got in your genes if you look at me.'

She lit her cigarette and blew smoke out of the side of her mouth.

'I don't actually know what happened. With this, with life or whatever you want to call it. You reach out to take hold of something... and then you realise it's nothing but air. You basically can't count on anything, not even yourself.'

It was Dad who'd walloped her, I thought. Even so, it wouldn't be enough of a reason for her to leave him. And as if she could read my thoughts, she said:

'It's not because of... He just feels under pressure. A load of crap has happened, and the situation has got threatening. He's clearing off soon and doesn't know when he's coming back. And when I told him I've had enough, that I'm thinking of leaving him, then it boiled over.'

She was looking past me, out over the schoolyard where the pupils had started to stream out for recess. Normal kids, I thought, with normal parents. Not kids who stood in the smoking area with their mum and worried about her black eye.

'So what are you going to do?' I asked.

'What needs to be done.'

Maybe she was feeling sorry for herself, because her uninjured eye suddenly filled with tears.

And somehow, strangely, I felt tenderness towards her as she stood there in her best discount-store coat, smoking and feeling sorry for herself. She had nothing. She'd lost everything long ago and didn't even know what she'd lost.

'Somebody else can take over here,' she mumbled. 'Somebody will have to look after you two if neither Dad nor I can.'

'What do you mean?'

'I'm going up to the headmaster's office now. There are a load of meetings I have to attend. With you and Robert's form teachers. With the child psychologists and social services.'

It was only then that I understood what she was really talking about.

'So you're just going to leave?'

'Same as your dad. And you're not accusing him…'

She dropped her fag on the ground and stubbed it out with the toe of her worn-out shoe.

'And what's going to happen to us?'

'I don't actually know. I'll try to sort this out as best as possible.'

'What if they split us up? If we end up with different families.'

But she didn't reply. Just straightened her coat and walked off, without turning back.

O ver to the left I could see all the way down to the sea. There was no one in sight. Just the vacant fields, heather moors and the sun breaking up more and more clouds. I shouldn't have been there, in plain sight if anyone should happen to turn up. But why would anyone? The abandoned cottage was in an out-of-the-way place; people steered clear of it.

That stuff Mum said made me really confused. She was going to walk away of her own free will, but before then she was going to hand over responsibility for us to somebody else. I couldn't bear the thought that Robert and I might get split up. That simply couldn't happen. I wouldn't be able to cope.

But who said that was going to happen? I bet they wouldn't split up siblings. Where had I got that idea from?

I felt like I was going to be sick. The sensation of a chasm opening up inside me was nothing new – I'd grown up with it; that's how my life was. And yet I never got used to it …

The mink farm could not be seen from where I stood. The only spot I could be seen from was on the opposite side, the small road leading off towards the lighthouse. I was alone. Out of danger. Everything was all right. Those were the sort of thoughts going through me, like little reassuring telegrams.

The entrance looked exactly the same as we had left it: the soil and branches we had covered the door with were still there. Nobody had been there. Or left any tracks, anyway.

I wondered what Mum was doing just then. Sitting in the head-master's office, trying to explain the situation? That she intended to abandon us. That neither she nor Dad was capable of looking

after us any longer. That she hoped they'd be able to find suitable
foster families for us. I'd cleared out of school before the bell rang
again, without even saying anything to Tommy, just cycled down
to the abandoned cottage as fast as I could.

I took off my gloves and dug out the door. There was no noise
from inside. For a moment, I imagined he was gone. That somebody
had found him after all and taken him away. Otherwise I would
have heard him, I thought, that silent language he transmitted
to us in his inexplicable way. Or maybe he was dead? Maybe he
couldn't handle it any more, the shock, the injuries… everything
humans had done to him. Just men, I thought, always just men.

'Are you there?'

But there was no reply. Only silence within me. As if I were
empty, devoid of all feeling.

The hatch door was exposed now. There was a gap up at the top.
I stuck my fingers into it, braced myself with my feet and pulled
until it fell aside.

He was lying on his back with his face just under the surface of
the water. His eyes seemed brighter now, clearer, sharper as he
observed me. But his expression was terrified. He'd been silent
because he didn't know who was coming, because I was completely
lacking in feelings, which is why he couldn't recognise me. Because
he was afraid they'd found him again.

There were a few stone steps leading down into the root cellar.
I sat down on the step closest to the water's surface. If I'd wanted
to, I could have reached out and touched him.

I thought of that painting by John Bauer that was in our Swedish
textbook, of a girl sitting by a small lake in a forest and looking
at her reflection in the water. I'd always wondered what she was
looking at. Because it wasn't her reflection she was interested in, it
was what was underneath. That's how I thought of myself sitting
there, like the girl in that picture.

The creature asked if something had happened. He sensed it,
that I was worried and sad. He wished he could help me, he said,

but he understood nothing about our world, our rules. The best thing was if I just sat there and calmed down.

He was happy to see me, he explained; he hadn't recognised me at first and had thought it was the others, the ones who wanted to harm him, but now he knew that wasn't the case. He felt better now, stronger. He could tell because his hunger was back. Soon he would need to eat again. For the first time in a long time he had an appetite. And there was nothing left of the fish we'd left for him; he'd eaten everything.

'I'll come back soon. With Tommy, if you remember. We'll bring some more food for you. As much as you want.'

He said he understood. And oddly enough, that reassured me. The creature reassured me, without my noticing. As if he were singing an inaudible song for me, a lullaby or comforting song that went straight into my nervous system and put everything right. As if he could dry my tears on the inside and fix what was broken just by being himself.

He asked if he could help me. If I came with him out to sea, he said, he could help me there. But he understood that wouldn't work. We were different creatures, not from his species; we were here on the surface, in our world, which was completely different from his. He wondered why my friend wasn't with me. Had something happened to him as well? Had the others taken my friend, the same ones who had harmed him? I calmed him down, explained to him that there was nothing to worry about, everything was fine, Tommy was safe and we hadn't forgotten our promise to take him back to where he belonged.

His mouth sort of pressed together into a grimace which I knew was a smile. Soon, he said, soon he would be ready to return.

His gills were moving, like soft valves underwater. The gash in his cheek had almost completely healed. It was the water that healed it, I thought, the same as it was healing the other wounds on his body.

Then I saw another remarkable thing: he suddenly did a trick for me. As if he wanted to show he was on the road to recovery by twirling around. He rolled over two or three times in the water before coming to a rest again, on his back, just under the surface and looked at me with those almost glowing eyes. *Do you understand?* he said. *I'm better now. Soon I'll be ready…*

It was getting dark outside. I thought about Mum and my brother, and that the worst possible thing might happen: they might split us up… And the creature sort of followed my thoughts, comforted me from where he was down there in the water – not that he understood what it was about, but he understood I was afraid. *Everything will be all right,* he whispered inside my head. *Don't be sad, everything will work out.* As if he knew more than I did. As if he had a premonition of everything that was going to happen.

I was awoken in the middle of the night by the phone ringing. At first I didn't know where I was. I'd gone straight from dreaming to reality. Then I noticed my brother next to me. He was lying on his side, holding my hand and snoring almost imperceptibly, and had stolen the whole duvet.

I got up. It was pitch-black outside. I had fallen asleep beside him with my clothes on.

The phone was ringing ageing downstairs, irascible, insistent that someone should answer. I crept past my parents' bedroom. The door was open.

The room was empty. The wardrobe doors were wide open, as if they'd left in a mad panic.

The phone kept ringing as if it was possessed. It was on the hall table underneath the cracked mirror. I picked up the receiver and heard the Professor's voice.

'Nella, is that you?'

'Yes.'

'You've got to come here. The place is on fire. Can you bring some clothes? It's below zero and I'm standing outside, naked.'

'Are you okay?'

'A bit underdressed for the conditions is all. I suppose I could warm up if I went closer to the house. But I don't fancy it. It's blazing.'

'Where are you ringing from?'

'There's a phone point in the garage. But it's going to die at any moment …'

I grabbed a few clothes from Dad's wardrobe upstairs. He was obviously travelling light, because his winter coat and boots were still there. I could hear my brother snoring through the wall. Did he know where Mum was? Had she told him about her plans?

Then I remembered I had a job to do. The Professor hadn't sounded scared, but maybe he was just in shock. I stuffed the clothes into a plastic carrier bag and went out to my bike.

I saw the fire from several hundred metres away. The sky was lit up above. I could also smell the burning because the wind was coming in off the sea. It was freezing cold. The puddles had frozen over, and I nearly wiped out when I turned off onto the track leading up to the house.

The windows were illuminated from inside, as if the fire was living its own life in there, moving back and forth in a sort of dance across the floor. I could hear sirens far off in the distance.

The heat became almost unbearable the closer I got. And the noise… I'd never heard anything like it. Like a single uninterrupted crash, a fire machine that was running and making an infernal racket. There were strange hissing sounds when the flames found fresh wood to bite into, and explosion-like blasts when ceiling panels came crashing down.

The Professor was standing a hundred feet from the house by the old barn. As I made a loop around the yard to avoid the heat, I could see him as clearly as if it had been the middle of the day. The fire was illuminating everything in the vicinity. He was naked except for a pair of long johns and a scarf draped over his shoulders. He had a pair of wooden clogs on his feet. His face was sooty and he looked immensely sorrowful. He didn't even seem to notice me until I was standing right in front of him and handed him the bag of clothes.

'How nice you could come,' he said. 'I didn't know who to call.'

He mumbled something inaudible while I helped him into the coat. That was his life that was going up in flames in there, I thought, his books, all his strange collections. The keys were probably melting in the heat up in the attic. The taxidermy animals, postage stamps, collections of coins, beer mats, books, reference books, piles of newspaper clipping – everything was on fire. He hadn't even got his crutches out.

'It's arson,' he said as he pulled on Dad's trousers.

'How do you know?'

'I just know… somebody who didn't give a damn whether I was at home or not.'

The sirens were getting closer. The fire brigade were on their way.

'I was lucky enough to wake up in time. The cat woke me. Or maybe I just dreamt she was sitting by the bed howling at full volume. The room was filled with smoke by that point. But I haven't seen her since then. Do you think she's still in there?'

He was in shock, I now realised. Underneath the soot his face was as white as a sheet. His eyes darted around, and he didn't seem to be taking in that I was there.

'I'm sure she made it out.'

'I jumped from the window up there. Don't ask me how, and don't ask me how I'm still standing up.'

Some people had started to gather further down the drive. Neighbours, I guessed, from the nearby farms. They seemed completely immobile, or else the heat was so fierce they didn't dare to come any closer.

'But you didn't hear anything?' I asked. 'No voices or anything like that?'

'Scooters,' he said. 'Leaving the road. I saw them, too. When I jumped. They stood still. Their lights were on. Then they just rode off, into town.'

'Maybe to ring for help,' I said. 'Can't you hear? The fire brigade are on their way.'

We could see the fire engines over on the main road now. Soon they would turn onto the gravel track leading up to the house.

'What the hell am I going to do now?' He sounded desperate. 'Where am I even going to live?'

I didn't have a clue what to say to him. I didn't have a clue

how I was going to come up with anything that even approached
reassurance.

The vehicles were getting closer. They took a detour across the
field to avoid the flames. Then they turned ninety degrees and
drove straight through the wooden fence up into the farmyard.
I put my arm around the Professor's waist. This was my fate, I
thought, to comfort people who were even sadder than I was. Not
because I had it better than others, but because it always just fell
to me.

'We need to try to get hold of your mum,' I said. 'And you've got
to sit down somewhere. Can you walk if I hold you up?'

He didn't answer. Just stared wild-eyed towards the house. The
flames were reflected in his eyes. It looked horrible, like a scene
from a nightmare.

'Let's go over to the neighbours. Do you see… they're standing
over there by the road. They'll help us.'

But we didn't need to go anywhere. Suddenly there were lots of
people all round us. Firemen checking the outbuildings, the shed
and the woodshed. Others had started fighting the blaze. Maybe
I was also kind of in shock, because I could hear people speaking
quite clearly even though the noise of the fire was deafening and
some of them were standing over a hundred feet away.

Two paramedics came over to us, but the Professor took no
notice of them.

'How did it go with your essay, by the way?' he said absently. 'I'd
like to read it when you've finished.'

'Of course you can. And I'm glad you helped me. Thanks.'

'It wasn't easy. There's not much that's been written about
mermaids, you see. Mainly fairy tales with tragic endings.'

The paramedics also seemed to realise he was in shock. Without
saying a word, they wrapped him in a blanket and helped him over
to the ambulance.

Three days later I met Gerard at the pinball arcade in Olofsbo. The meeting had been arranged. He'd rung the doorbell that morning, and when I opened the door he was just standing there holding his crash helmet, a roll-up in the corner of his mouth, looking straight at me.

'I want you to come to the Mill tonight,' he said. 'Eight o'clock. We need to have a chat.'

He peered over my shoulder into the house.

'Is this how you live, Ironing Board? All on your own. Like Pippi Longstocking. Bloody hell, look at the state of the place!'

He knew Mum and Dad had left, I thought. He knew what was going on. He'd been keeping us under surveillance.

'And both you and your brother are holed up at home. You haven't been at school this week.'

He was right on that count as well. But that was information that was easier to come by. Gradually, it dawned on me that he was actually there on our front step at nine in the morning.

'You can say whatever you've got to say to me now,' I said. 'I don't need to meet with you somewhere else to do that.'

'The Mill is a better place. I haven't got time right now.'

He turned and picked up something he'd placed behind him on the step. I saw what it was even before he handed it to me: a taxidermy hare in its winter coat. From the Professor's collection.

'I thought you might like to have this. Or maybe your mate would want it back. It was a shame it nearly got ruined. It almost looks like it's alive.'

I peered down to the street. Just his motorbike was there, a blue Puch Dakota with Esso stickers on the petrol tank. No sign of Ola or Peder.

'What do you want from me?'

'Just to talk a little about the future. But first you get this hare. As a reminder that I keep my promises.'

The phone started ringing. It had been ringing constantly the past few days, but we hadn't bothered answering.

'I won't keep you,' he said. 'That might be important, somebody who needs to get hold of you. Come to the arcade at eight. And bring my money.'

He's sick, I thought as I watched him walk over to his bike and kick-start it. He just wasn't right in the head. He even waved to me as he rode off, down towards Solrosvägen, and finally the phone stopped ringing.

'Who was it?' asked my brother when I closed the door. He'd just got up and hadn't even put any clothes on.

'Nobody you know.'

'He was riding a motorbike anyway. Is there any breakfast?'

'Only crispbread. But I'll go shopping today.'

I didn't want to make him more worried than he was already. So Mum and Dad had finally cleared off, just as they'd warned me they would; they left two hundred kronor in an envelope on the hall table and disappeared out of the picture. That sort of thing just didn't happen, but it did happen to us.

Mum hadn't even said anything to Robert. That job had fallen to me.

'What's going to happen now?' he asked when I explained the situation to him. And I answered quite honestly that I didn't know.

That was three days ago, on the morning after the fire at the Professor's place. We hadn't been to school since then. There was no point. The women from social services would still turn up. Attendance and compulsory education were irrelevant. There was no chance they would let us stay here together.

The phone started ringing again when I went into the kitchen to sort out my brother.

'Aren't you going to answer it?' he asked.

'If it's L.G. or the school welfare officer, I still don't feel like talking. Much less so if it's some concerned woman from the council.'

'What if it's Mum or Dad, though?'

'It's not, so you might as well not get your hopes up.'

The Mill was a combined arcade and café on the edge of Olofsbo. Kids from Glommen and Skogstorp often hung out there at weekends. In the summer there was a miniature golf course too, and an outdoor dining area. During the tourist season it was usually rammed with people, but in the autumn it was quieter.

Gerard was sitting at a table down at the far end with a cup of coffee. My school bag bounced against my hip as I walked over to him between the rows of pinball machines. I'd brought along four cartons of cigarettes. Just as he'd promised, Dad had cleared out my room before he left, but he was obviously in a hurry because he didn't manage to take everything. I found them under the bed. Hopefully they would work as a down payment.

'You're on time,' Gerard said. 'I appreciate that. How's your friend doing, by the way – the Hungarian?'

'He's at his mum's place.'

I sat down on the chair opposite him. He took a drink from his cup, put it down again and wiped his mouth with the back of his hand.

'He was lucky. He could just as well have ended up in hospital with smoke inhalation. Or with burns in the worst-case scenario. There's not much left of the house.'

'You're gonna do time for that.'

'For what? I have no idea what you're talking about. I just want my money. And yet you still haven't come up with it.'

I took the cartons of cigarettes out of my bag and put them on the table. 'They're worth two hundred,' I said. 'And they're easy to sell. I need more time to come up with cash.'

Gerard looked at me with a concerned expression, as if he was sad about something, but I knew he wasn't, I knew that nothing was right behind those placid brown eyes; everything was, like, short-circuited in him. Then he bent down under the table and took something out of a duffle bag.

'You can keep those,' he said. 'I've got more than enough myself.'

He was holding a carton of his own – the same German brand that had been stacked up in my room. I felt a shudder run down my spine. What was it Tommy's brother had said to Dad at the mink farm: *You can't have young kids working for you, Jonas.*

'I want cash, Ironing Board. I've already got loads of fags. By the way, where's your old man keeping himself?'

It was Gerard who'd caused him to leave, I thought. It was Gerard he was terrified of. I wasn't sure how, but they were connected in some way.

'People are ending up in a bad way because of you. Even made homeless, and you don't want anything like that to happen again, do you?'

'You'll get the money next week. I promise.'

That's how it was. Even adults were scared of him. Because he had no boundaries. Because he was capable of anything. I mean, I'd seen it myself, by the kiosk last winter, in the common room when he'd nearly killed the caretaker. And then the Professor's house that he burnt to the ground, even though he must have known he was asleep inside. And something had happened to make Dad realise as well.

'Let's say the day after tomorrow instead. At the latest. Eight o'clock. Remember, I warned you, Ironing Board, but you didn't listen.'

He finished the rest of his coffee, peered out of the window down to where you could just make out the sea beyond the rows of summer cottages.

'By the way, d'you know anything about something going missing from a mink farm?'

I made every effort to appear relaxed. Relaxed and surprised at the same time.

'Huh?'

'Just wondering. I know Tommy's brothers found this thing, or rather caught it, and now it's disappeared. So I thought you might know something about it. You and Tommy are best mates, so maybe you've talked about it?'

'Like I said, you'll get your money.'

'It was at a mink farm near Olofsbo, a living creature. I saw it once myself, really fascinating, I wouldn't have thought a thing like that actually existed. But somebody cut a hole in the fence and went in and took it.'

He saw the creature, I thought. Tommy's brothers showed it to him. So he knows them, he buys fags off them, and maybe other stuff as well. He's taken over loads of business from Dad, joined forces with other criminals, maybe with that junkie guy who was at our place? But he's lying about the other stuff. He's not even guessing, he's just plucking it out of thin air to see how I react.

'I haven't got a clue what you're talking about,' I said.

'Okay. Just wanted to check.'

I was just as good a liar as him. Maybe even better. His expression revealed that he believed me.

As I was sitting in my room that evening, it struck me how hopeless everything was, that my circumstances basically consisted of a dwindling number of choices.

Gerard wanted cash and I had absolutely no idea where I was going to get any. From a shop, I thought, if I could get to an unmanned till. Or the teachers' lounge at school. The bags and jackets hanging outside the office would have money in them, but how much would that net, a hundred kronor at most?

But there was another possibility if nothing else worked. People were prepared to pay to have young girls take their clothes off or to touch them. In Year 7 I briefly knew a girl who got money that way. She had a hard time at home just like me, hung around in the town centre because she had no other choice, and went round with a load of dodgy people. She had lived in various foster homes in the area but was actually from an entirely different part of the country. All you have to do is stand around long enough outside the Klitterbadet pool, she'd told me once, or in the town square in the evenings.

Sooner or later some bloke would always come up and make a sleazy proposal. And then she'd accompany him into the Kronan multi-storey car park or the public toilets by the Domus department store.

She disappeared from town soon after that, and I couldn't even remember her name. But I did remember being frightened by the idea. But desperate times call for desperate measures. If you're really up against it, everything has its price.

The phone rang again. It was past ten o'clock so it couldn't be from school or social services. Maybe it was the Professor who needed to talk about what had happened. Or Mum calling from a phone box, wanting to explain what she'd done. Come up with an excuse that didn't ring true, so she wouldn't be plagued by a guilty conscience.

I waited for the phone to stop ringing before going into my brother's room. He'd fallen asleep with the light on. I tucked him in and switched off the light. Then I went downstairs and got the torch out of the cleaning cupboard.

I could hardly see my hand in front of my face as I cycled down towards the sea. A new low-pressure system had moved in. If there were any stars up in the sky, I couldn't see them. I pulled up the hood on my raincoat. It was bucketing down, and the rain was falling diagonally in the wind.

I left my bike behind a bus shelter down by the coastal road and took a shortcut across a field until I came to the path that led to the abandoned cottage. I couldn't see the house, and could just make out a structure between the fields. The rain ran down my hood in little streams, meandering before the edge, and then dripped onto my eyebrows and cheeks.

It felt as if the world was getting darker the further away I got from the main road. At one point I trod awkwardly in a rut and nearly sprained my ankle. I didn't dare turn on the torch yet; it would be visible from far away.

I passed the north face of the house. It looked creepy standing there abandoned with broken windows and a collapsed roof. Other eras brushed against me as I went by, past times that had nothing to do with me. I forced myself to look the other way, into the darkness, towards the root cellar on the other side of the yard.

I didn't turn on the torch until I was shielded by the trees. As I pushed the branches away from the door I could hear the creature inside. He was awake. And he knew that it was me who had come.

I felt sort of dizzy when I opened the door. He was luminescent in the dark. It was like sea-fire, I thought, only much brighter.

His scales were phosphorescent, and so were his eyes. The whole pool was illuminated; the bluish-green light shone on the walls, ceiling and the water around him. Maybe that's how he could see so far down there in the ocean depths: his body functioned like a sort of lamp.

He remained still a few inches below the surface of the water and looked at me. I was welcome there, he said, he'd been waiting for me. Where'd I been all this time? And I told him that some things had been going on that prevented me from coming.

I sat down on the bottom step. His smell hit me; of sea and seaweed, and other things I couldn't describe. I just sat there thinking about what had gone on over the last few days, sort of got it all out, went over everything that had happened while the creature asked questions, questions that went beyond themselves, or were hidden in themselves, were both questions and answers, as if they were inextricably linked like pearls inside oysters.

At one point he reached his hand out to me, brought it out of the water and put it in mine. I felt the claws tentatively close around my palm, how the webbing between his fingers clung to my skin. His hand was warm, much warmer than mine. Then he closed his gills, floated up to the surface, breached it with his face, opened his mouth… the mouth that was both human and a sea creature's… and drew in air through his throat before slowly sinking back into the water.

Strangely, I didn't feel cold. The water had been warmed by his body and served as a heater. I noticed that I was getting warm, so I undid my raincoat. The sound of the zip made me aware of the silence outside. It had stopped raining. There were footsteps coming across the yard, shoes or boots squelching through the mud.

The creature looked calm: if he could hear anything, he was definitely not afraid.

'Wait,' I said. 'I'll come back.'

I went up the steps. Squatting down, I replaced the door over the opening. Darkness again. The wind had died down. But the creature was still talking to me: *Don't be afraid*, he said, *it's not anyone who's going to harm us, you're safe, everything will be all right...*

Tommy was standing six feet away from me with his back to the farmhouse.

'Is that you, Nella?'

'Who else would it be?'

'I don't know. You can barely see your hand in front of your face.'

He put something down on the ground.

'Fish,' he said. 'A whole crate, straight off the boat. He must be hungry.'

His teeth glinted in the dark when he smiled.

'I've been worried about you. You haven't been in school all week. And nobody answers your phone.'

'A load of stuff has happened. How did you know I was here?'

'I went round to your house. Just now. I had to check if everything was okay. Nobody opened the door when I knocked, but you'd forgotten to lock the door so I went in. Robert was in bed asleep. Nobody else was there, and I could only think of one place where you might be.'

He pushed the crate aside with his foot.

'So I went back home and got some food for him. As long as we're here, I mean.'

He came over and put his arm around me.

'What's happened?' he asked. 'Tell me.'

And so I told him, about Mum and Dad who'd cleared off, about my fear that Robert and I would get split up, about the fire at the Professor's place which he already knew about, about Gerard who was behind everything, who was now making deals with his brothers, and about how he wanted his money in less than forty-eight hours' time. I told him about my plans for the next few days, how I was going to come up with the amount he claimed I owed him and how I was terrified it wouldn't work out. I started to cry as I told him all this, and I hated myself for it, because I was taking a liberty, because the worst might not have even happened, and so I was not entitled to be sad yet.

'I'll speak to my brothers,' said Tommy. 'They might be able to get him to calm down. And by the way, I've got money. You can borrow some off me if the worst comes to the worst.'

I got to the Mill at the agreed time. Gerard was on his own this time as well. He was standing at a pinball machine, feeding coins into the slot. He nodded to me when I came in the door, pressed the start button and started playing. I sat down at the table and waited, the same table where we'd sat the last time, listened to the clatter of the pinball flippers, the sound the machine made for every bonus, and the rattle when he finally got a free play. He glanced at the counter to remember his score before leaving to sit down.

'Have you got the money?' he asked.

I counted it out onto the table, fourteen hundred-kronor notes and the rest in tens.

The arcade was just as empty as last time, just one girl who was standing by the till counter drying cutlery. Gerard gathered up the banknotes and counted them one more time.

'That's right,' he said. 'Did you rob a newsagent's or something?'

'It's a loan.'

'From Tommy, I suppose? He spoke to his brothers about us, I heard. Makes no difference, Ironing Board. Business is business…'

He put the money back down on the table and looked over at the pinball game that stood flashing with a new ball in play.

'If I'm honest, it makes me bloody furious that you're trying to get Tommy's brothers involved in this. Just like it makes me furious when somebody snitches to the cops or L.G. about something I've done. This is between me and you.'

He gave me a glassy look.

'I've got two free plays,' he said. 'You can have one if you like.

Double or quits. Then the matter will be settled and Tommy won't need to go and squeal about things that have got nothing to do with him. If you win, the matter will vanish.'

'I've got to get home.'

'To Robert?'

I didn't like it when he called him by his name, as if he knew him. It felt more natural to hear 'retard' or 'pissypants' coming from his mouth.

'Don't forget to take the money with you,' he said.

'Huh?'

'I don't need it. I mean, you've changed the rules of the game.'

I didn't know what to say. Everything depended on what he meant, but I didn't get it.

'I'm going to play my free plays,' he said, 'and then I'm out of here. The next guy who sits down at that table is definitely gonna put it in his pocket, so think carefully.'

It wasn't even my money. Tommy had taken it out of his savings account that day. He'd got his mum to sign a document saying it was okay. And he'd also spoken to his brothers about me. I hadn't a clue what they said to Gerard. I didn't even want to know; I just wanted this to be over once and for all.

'One more thing, Ironing Board: just because I'm not taking the money, that doesn't mean we're quits.'

'So what does that mean, then?'

'You can figure it out yourself. You're good at maths.'

He didn't want it to be over, I thought. He didn't want to lose the upper hand. He tried to get another free play with the last ball every time. And he was going to carry on as long as he could. I took the bundle of banknotes and put them in my jacket pocket.

'So we're agreed?' said Gerard.

'About what?'

'That you still owe me. Because you're keeping the money and I don't want it.'

He gave me a searching look, then looked out of the window.

'You lied the last time we met, didn't you? When you said you didn't know what was at the mink farm. I realised after you left. I saw it in the way you walked towards the door… people notice that sort of thing. Or I do, anyway. Intuition, it's called. When you just know.'

He couldn't be serious, I thought. He was just testing me again.

'I'm positive, Ironing Board. I could see it in your walk. A satisfied walk. Like you thought you'd managed to fool me. You know where he is, don't you – the sea monster? You went there and took him away. But there must have been several of you. That's obvious. He weighs a couple of hundred kilos at least.'

He was just rambling. He was making wild guesses. There was no other explanation.

'I don't know what you're talking about.'

'I'm sure you do know. Very well.'

He glanced over towards the pinball machine again. The design on the playing surface featured a mermaid, oddly enough. A woman with long black hair, breasts and a fishtail. I wondered why I hadn't noticed it before.

'I really don't know what I'm going to do with you, Ironing Board. I just don't get you. Have you got any suggestions? How the hell are we going to sort out this situation?'

But I didn't reply. It wouldn't have mattered what I said.

A few uneventful days passed. I stuck around at home with Robert, going out only to shop with our dwindling household budget, and not answering the phone. Time was slowly running out, and it was as if we couldn't bring ourselves to worry about it.

Post came as well, reminders about phone bills and electricity bills Mum hadn't paid, and letters from social services and the headmaster's office. We didn't open them: neither of us fancied taking a peek into the future.

One morning there was a postcard from L.G. in the letterbox. He'd written that he was worried about me and wanted me to get in touch with the school. It was only a matter of time, I thought, until people from social services came round.

I stayed away from the abandoned cottage. The creature was getting on well anyway. He had food and water, and he was getting stronger with every passing day. Soon, I thought, very soon we would take him back to the sea...

I only made one phone call during that time, and it was to the Professor. He still seemed to be in shock. His voice was hoarse and thick. He spent his days lying on the sofa at his mum's, he told me, and took tranquilliser tablets. The police had sent forensic people out to the scene of the fire, and everything indicated that it was arson. He was terrified, he said: somebody had tried to kill him. I was just on the verge of telling him about Gerard, but I could tell from his voice that it wasn't the right time yet. He needed to recover first. Later, I thought, I would explain everything. I would return the stuffed hare to him and suggest contacting the police. But it was as if I was waiting for things to clear up before then. For time to start moving forward again, for something to happen... For the story to come to an end so that a new, better one could begin.

I didn't think about anything in particular that morning. Well, except Mum, I have to admit. Mum. I dreamt about her in the night, that she came back home... In my dream I was happy about it. I loved her in the dream, almost as much as I love my brother. I dreamt she came home to take care of us. She was sober. I thought she was pretty, standing there in her red discount-store coat with her keys in her hand, just inside the door. Where was Dad? I didn't know. It was like he wasn't part of the story. Only Mum was back, and she wasn't going to betray us. It wasn't right, she said, for Robert and me to be split up and end up in different families.

I was awoken by noise from Robert's room. He was sitting in there, drawing. I knew he was because he always sings when he's sitting down with his drawing pad, the same tune over and over again. And then he suddenly stopped. He's out of drawing paper, I thought. That's why.

I went down to the kitchen. The fridge was empty. There wasn't even a carton of milk in there. We needed breakfast.

Robert hadn't eaten yet. But he didn't want to bother me about it.

We needed bread, butter and something to put on it, as well as more drawing paper if they had any in the shop. Robert is good at drawing, a lot better than I am. I often told him that – that he might become an artist some day. And then he wouldn't have to deal with any letters or numbers.

I opened the envelope out in the hall. Twenty kronor was all we had left, which would be just enough. I thought I'd nick a few other things while I was in the shop, so we could make dinner that evening too. But then… what would happen then? This couldn't continue forever.

We'd had a visit the previous day. The doorbell rang early in the morning. We listened to them standing on the front steps talking to each other: a man and a woman, judging by their voices. When nobody opened the door, they went round and tried the garage door and tapped on the windows. They called our names a few times just to make sure. Finally they gave up, got in a car and drove off. The next time they came back they would be accompanied by the police.

I put on my jacket and went out. It was a cold autumn day in mid-November. Unusually, the sun was shining. The streets were empty. All of Skogtorp's kids were at school. The housewives were pottering around their detached houses; the dads were at work. I thought about the dream I'd woken from. Mum in her red coat. Her being home again. And that made me happy.

Everything went smoothly at the supermarket. A packet of spaghetti fitted perfectly into the lining of my jacket. A little bottle of ketchup was stuffed down the side of my boot. Breakfast in the shopping basket.

I paid and left the store. A row of flags flapped in the wind outside the store. I could smell the sea. Some gulls were screeching from a wheelie bin a little way off.

I followed the asphalt path over to the maisonettes. Jerry-built places with junk cars standing in front of the garages. Paint that had already started peeling from the façades. Graffiti on the fence outside. The playground with its broken swings.

The door was wide open when I turned into our street. I wonder if it was me who'd forgotten to shut it. I went in and called to my brother, but got no reply.

He wasn't in his room, either. The bed was unmade. There were some dirty socks lying on the floor. The drawing pad was open on the last page, a drawing of a smiling space alien. It looked like E.T. I went back downstairs. No Robert there either. I called out again, even though I knew I'd get no answer. His shoes were still in the hall and his jacket was hanging on its hook. I didn't understand what was going on.

I went out on the front steps and looked down the street. No sign of movement. Silence. Other than the buzz of some scooters in the distance. I started to alternate between sweating and freezing. When I called out again, there was panic in my voice.

I searched for over an hour on my bike, rode into every street named after a flower, checked the community hall and the playing field and asked about him at the newsagent's and in the shop. Nobody had seen him.

I cycled over to the school. The schoolyard was deserted. Lessons were in session. I went over to the Year 7 wing, peered into a couple of classrooms through the windows until I found his class. Nine special-needs lads sat hunched over their books while a teacher wrote something on the blackboard. But Robert wasn't there. I didn't think he would be.

Finally I headed home again. I switched the radio on. Michael Jackson was singing *Billie Jean*.

My brother's smell was still in the air, from his hair and his clothes – everywhere, it seemed like. I started to cry, completely unrestrained.

The phone rang early in the morning. It was still dark outside. I knew it was Robert before I even answered.

'You've got to help me,' he said. 'Do as they say, Nella.'

His voice was muffled, as if he had gravel in his mouth. I could hear him making an effort to keep his breathing under control.

'Try not to panic, Robert. Try to stay calm. Things will work out, do you hear me?'

'I'm freezing,' he said. 'It's cold. I haven't got any shoes or a jacket. Not even socks.'

There were voices in the background. It sounded like they were ringing from a phone box; I could hear the wind outside.

'Where are you?'

'I don't know. I can't see anything. They put something over my eyes… I'm sorry, Nella.'

'I want to speak to them. Give them the phone.'

Peder's voice came on the other end of the line.

'You should see your idiot of a brother, Ironing Board, totally pissed himself and covered in shit. Bloody hell, the state of him.'

He hadn't dared to do anything other than tag along, I thought.

They had come over to our place, got him in his room where he sat drawing, didn't even let him put his shoes on, just set him on the pillion seat of one of the scooters and rode off with him.

'Okay,' I said. 'Just tell me what you want me to do. I'm listening.'

'Wait…'

Peder was talking to someone, but I couldn't hear what it was about. My brother was sobbing in the background until somebody said 'shut up'.

'Ironing Board, are you there?' It was a new voice now: Gerard's.

'I'm listening.'

'We've got to sort out your debt to me. This can't go on any longer.'

There were some beeps on the line. The money for the call was about to run out.

'I'll do exactly as you say. Just put some more coins in. I don't want to get cut off.'

'Please don't natter on so fucking much. Listen instead. Have you got anything to swap for your brother? Money won't cut it any longer.'

'The merman…' I said.

'Huh?'

'I know what you want. You'll get him. Just don't hurt Robert.'

'Great. And how are we going to arrange it?'

'I can't explain. I have to show you.'

'Don't you trust me?' He started to laugh, a cheerful snorting laugh, as if I'd just cracked a joke. 'D'you know he gobbed on me, your brother. Right in my face. I got spit in my mouth. Is that contagious? 'Cos he looks right bloody sick, your brother.'

'Can I speak to him?' I asked. 'Let me talk to him, please.'

His voice turned ice-cold again.

'You have no damned rights in this situation. You're not going to ask me for another bloody thing. The only thing you're going to do now is to say where we're going to meet.'

'By the old abandoned cottage,' I said. 'Behind the mink farm near Olofsbo. But you won't find him no matter how hard you look. I have to show you where it is.'

The sky had started to brighten. It took on a different hue down by the coast. The light was refracted in the sea, bounced back and coloured the sky a pale pink. I felt cold, even though I was dressed warmly. I had some extra clothes for my brother in a carrier bag at my feet.

Starlings were stirring in the old fruit trees. I'd just seen a fox bounding away over the field. I could sense the creature over in the root cellar. He was asleep.

Water dripped from a hole in the roof, striking the dirt floor of the cottage at intervals a few seconds apart. There were wisps of fog on the field, like eerie, hovering bushes.

I was listening to something without knowing what it was. Time, perhaps, a long-ago time that existed alongside mine, but was seeping into my time by accident.

I peered over towards the overgrown track. That's where they should come from, unless they cut across the fields. I wonder where they'd been with him overnight? Maybe they had secret hiding places, just like Tommy and I did? Their own abandoned cottage with a long-forgotten root cellar…

A tractor chugged somewhere in the distance. Puffy clouds sailed sedately across the sky.

'Here he is, Ironing Board!'

A voice came from a spot behind me. I turned round, but could see no one. Only the house with its yawning window-holes and lopsided door.

'Stay where you are.'

They were somewhere inside. They'd got there before me – and waited.

The door opened and Peder stepped out. He was holding my brother by a noose tied round his neck. They'd pulled a woolly hat down over his face so he couldn't see. Peder dragged Robert after him as if he were an animal; my brother was taking careful steps so as not to stumble. He was barefoot. His trousers were wet through. His clothes caked with mud. They had bound his hands behind his back with a hanky.

'I'm here now, Robert,' I said. 'Just stay calm. I'm going to get you away from here.'

A movement in the corner of my vision made me turn round. It was Gerard coming out of the cottage with a wooden chair under his arm, followed closely by Ola.

'Can you hear me, Robert? Everything's going to be all right. I promise.'

'He's not going to answer, Ironing Board. He hasn't said a peep since last night. I think he's been struck dumb by fear.'

Gerard didn't even look at me while he spoke; he was just feeling the chair, tugging its legs as if he wanted to check what condition it was in.

'Robert, can you hear me?'

No reaction. His head just lolled.

'You see? He doesn't even know where he is. And the way I see it, this never needed to happen.'

Peder had started tying a loop in the free end of the rope, tugged at it to test how firm it was, and looked over towards the shed as if he were searching for something. I wanted to say something again, but it was like I'd lost the ability to speak.

'Okay, Ironing Board. I'm gonna do something really fucking nasty to your brother now so you understand that this is serious.'

I realised the rules of the game had been changed again as Peder started to pull him over towards the shed.

'Down on your knees!' he roared. 'Come on now, you fucking spacker!'

Robert sank down into the mud. He looked like a condemned prisoner there, with his hands bound behind him and his face covered by the hat. He was directly underneath the opening to the old hay loft. A beam that was part of a lifting device extended several metres above his head.

My voice sounded strange and shrill when I turned to face Gerard.

'You wanted me to show you where he is… the creature. That's what we agreed.'

'I don't remember that.'

'You were going to let him go in exchange – that's what we said.'

'Unfortunately there's nothing I can do now. It's in Peder's hands.'

The water was still dripping from the roof of the cottage in a steady rhythm like a clock. My brother was turning his head in every direction, as if trying to identify the location of the sound. Peder stood behind him with one foot on his shoulder. He was holding the rope, but suddenly seemed unsure what to do.

It was only then I realised what they were going to use the chair for.

When Ola went to fetch it, placed it underneath the beam and looked up to assess its position.

'You can tie him to the hook there,' he said. 'The one that's sticking out.'

'I need to cut the rope if it's gonna work. Otherwise he'll hit the ground.'

'The rope will give way anyway after a while. It's gonna burn like hell.'

My brother was whimpering and panting at the same time. His whole body was shaking.

'Are you joking?' I tried to sound as calm as possible. 'Peder, stop it now!'

'Shut it, Ironing Board! You were the one who blabbed about the cat… and that was where it all started. You've got to pay the price for that.'

'You know it wasn't me. It was you. It was your sister's cat.' I turned to Gerard: 'Why aren't you telling the truth? That you figured it out a long time ago.'

But Gerard just nodded over to him, started him up with a single glance, got him to fasten the loop around the hook and pull on it.

It was like I was suffering from paralysis. This stuff that was happening wasn't really happening. The petrol can Peder got from the shed... they must have brought it with them and hidden it there... the total insanity of seeing him empty it over my brother, several litres on his head, on the cap, as if it were water, as if he really just wanted to wash him clean of all the dirt.

Over in the root cellar the creature had woken up. I could hear him. And he could hear me. Somehow he knew what was happening; he understood everything. So he tried to calm me down, get me to focus my concentration. That was the only way, he said: I had to think clearly; they hadn't decided yet, and I had the power to change the course of events.

I took a step closer to my brother, but Ola held me back.

'I don't know what's left to negotiate,' Gerard said. 'Sooner or later you reach a point where there's no use talking any more – when you've got to do something. And that's where we are now. Unfortunately.'

'Get up,' Peder said as he poured petrol out to make a fuse between my brother and the shed. 'And now lift your foot. Get up, I said. This is a chair, understand, and when it gets knocked over it's goodbye for you.'

The petrol was making him cough and gag. He was drenched in it; there were fumes rising rom him. He got up. His legs were shaking. Peder took his right foot, placed it on the chair and sort of lifted him up. The chair legs sank down into the mud.

Then I heard the creature again. It was too late, he said, we wouldn't be able to do anything now, he realised; he understood where these actions were leading.

I could hear him more clearly than ever before. As if he was vibrating within me, like he was making my whole body shake with that voice that was not a voice, which did not consist of sound or words.

And the others could hear him as well. I only realised then...
that he had taken them into his range, although I didn't understand why.

Gerard stood stock-still.

'What is that?' he asked, turning to Peder.

'Dunno.'

'Can't you hear it? What the hell is it?'

But the voice was not coming from outside; it was coming from
themselves, from within their bodies, as if they had hollow spaces
in there, large chambers that suddenly started to resonate. He was
speaking to them. And he was letting me listen in on everything, letting
me step into Gerard's consciousness so I could hear through him.

Come! he said. *I want to show you something. I want to challenge you, little
person... come to me... what have you got to lose?*

But without words, just as pure feelings, something far more easily
comprehensible and clearer than language, and impossible to resist.

'What is that?' asked Gerard again. 'What the hell is going on?'

Peder and Ola heard it as well. He was luring them to him.
They could not defend themselves. They didn't stand a chance,
and as if following a command, they started walking towards the
root cellar.

That's how I interpreted it, because he let me understand
everything. How he was basically leading them away from the
yard, all three of them, away from my brother who was standing
there on the rickety chair with a noose round his neck, drenched
in petrol; how he was luring them, calling to them, alternately
screaming and whispering inside them with his inaudible voice,
making them forget about Robert and me and go towards the
place where he was.

They walked slowly over towards the root cellar. Peder first, as if
he still wanted to prove his loyalty to the boss. The door was open.
He must have worked it loose somehow, maybe kicked it out with
his tail fin.

Ten metres from the opening, they stopped. Peder put down the petrol can. Gerard took something out of his jacket, a metal object of some kind.

'Who's going first?'

The others looked down at the ground.

'Is it going to be me as usual, then?'

He looked ruefully at them as the sound of the water got louder and louder inside, as if heavy waves were striking a pier. And even though I was standing on the other side of the yard, I could see it splashing, how water was sort of being cast out from the opening, as if somebody was in there with a bucket or bailer. I heard him again. He told me to hurry, to get out of there as fast as I could.

My brother was still on the rickety chair in front of me. He hadn't moved since Peder secured the rope on the beam. And I hadn't moved either. Time had put us onto a side track, and in a parallel world Gerard and the others were still going closer to the root cellar. *Go*, I heard the creature saying. *Hurry!*

My paralysis vanished. I was up with my brother in an instant, removing the noose from round his neck and helping him down to the ground.

'Come on, Robert!'

He didn't seem to understand anything. Like he wasn't there, just staring uncomprehendingly into space.

'We've got to get out of here. Here, hold onto me!'

I took him by the hand and ran like I'd never run before in my life, away from the abandoned cottage, away from what I saw out of the corner of my eye or maybe with an eye that had suddenly sprung up in the back of my head. As if I was seeing events through the creature's eyes, I thought, through his consciousness, as if he was letting me peek into himself and witness what was happening. How the petrol they'd poured over him suddenly caught fire, how the root cellar was shaking, how he got hold of Gerard even though he was on fire, knocked the slaughterman's bolt gun out of his hand and pulled him in through the opening. How earth and stones started to come crashing down when he beat his tail fin against the roof and walls: the mound that collapsed under its own weight, cubic metres of rock and earth over flames and water, as if we'd ended up in a mudslide or a minor earthquake. And Gerard's terrified screams went silent as if someone had pulled the plug, while my brother and I sprinted down towards the sea.

BORÅS,
MAY 1984

Five months later I got a letter from Robert, the first sign of life since we'd been split up just before Christmas. He ended up with a family down in Skåne. The couple he was placed with were teachers and had two children of their own. They were nice to him, he wrote, but in a slightly chilly way. It was not the first time they'd fostered a child. Before Robert they'd had a girl from northern Sweden, and before that a disabled guy whose parents needed some respite. To me, they sounded like pros, adults who take in foster kids for the money.

My brother wrote that they had a big house and two cars; maybe it was a matter of big loans that their salaries didn't cover, so they took in problem children in order to make ends meet. At any rate, I could tell that not a lot had happened with his schoolwork. His handwriting was more spidery than ever, and his letter was full of spelling mistakes. For example, he spelled my nickname *Nela* instead of *Nella*.

His letter was six pages long, and it took me at least an hour to decipher it. He wrote like Dad: under great resistance, as if he had to struggle with every single character.

He was doing well in spite of everything, he assured me. It was the dad in that family who had taken him under his wing. He was keen on shooting air rifles, and in his first week my brother got to go along to a shooting range. Even with his glasses, he proved to be good at it, and now he'd begun to train with a club. His foster brother Erik was also keen, so they spent quite a bit of free time together. It felt weird to read the expression 'foster brother', as if he were being pulled even further away from me by those words.

Erik was the same age as Robert. He was spoilt rotten and had loads of nice brand-name clothes, which Robert got as hand-me-downs because he was smaller. There was a foster sister as well, Elinor, who was in Year Eight and liked horses. At first she had barely spoken to him. Perhaps she thought he'd soon get swapped for someone else and didn't really think it was worth the effort to get to know him, but things had got better over time.

The first month he'd spent most of his time pining for me. It had been hard, especially at Christmas, even though a support person from the children's mental health service had been there. Our own Christmases in Skogstorp would usually descend into chaos, and yet it felt much worse to him to be sitting there in the midst of someone else's happiness and watch strangers hand out presents to each other. He had been given a model building set and a hand-me-down Lacoste shirt from Erik.

Gradually he had grown accustomed to his new environment. It got easier week by week, both at school and with the family. He had his own room and put up the old Michael Jackson posters he'd got off me. His room was much bigger than the one in Skogstorp; it was located away from the other bedrooms and even had its own en-suite.

The mum in the family was the one he had the hardest time with. She wasn't unkind to him, more like uninterested. And she always took her own children's side. Especially the first time there had been some conflict. His foster siblings thought it was unfair he got the room with the en-suite, and there were some rows about the shower, who got to shower first and that kind of thing, and sometimes about what there was to put on their bread at breakfast. His sister Elinor thought he ate too much. The mother would usually side with her. But it didn't matter, he wrote, he could understand it; after all, he would always take my side against everyone else on earth, no matter what it was about.

As I stood there by the window in my room in a terraced house on the outskirts of Borås and read his letter, I couldn't believe five months had passed. It felt like a lifetime. And I had no idea when I'd get to see him again, whether it would take months or years.

At school he'd been put into a remedial class, he wrote, and some of the pupils had violent tendencies. He was frightened of several of them. A big lad who went by the name of Hosepipe was particularly dangerous. He could fly into a rage at any moment, and my brother had borne the brunt on several occasions. The other pupils didn't pay much attention to him. But they might be nastier to him than he realised, because he couldn't understand everything they said. The Skåne dialect, he wrote, was like a whole different language.

One bit of good news was that he'd got new glasses, with thinner lenses. His foster parents bought them for him in Denmark. Everything was cheaper in Denmark – even glasses, he explained. They usually went to Helsingør once a month to go shopping, and sometimes he got to go along. So now at least he'd been abroad, and it wasn't such a big deal that he'd missed out on the class trip in Year Six.

I could see him before me as I read his letter, among those strangers, certainly a little taller now as he was growing, in hand-me-down brand-name clothes from his foster brother and a pair of stylish glasses from Denmark. I knew how much that meant to him, and yet it felt painful, as if being split up was the price we'd had to pay.

He'd got my address a week before when Mum went to visit. It was during the Easter break, and she only stayed for an afternoon before she got the train back to Linköping. It was like she was ashamed, he wrote. Not because she smelled of alcohol, because she did, but because she was such a failure she couldn't look after her own children. Robert asked after me, where I was living and how I was doing, and when we would see each other again. She gave a vague answer, there was a load of secrecy around everything, a custody case that was still under way, but finally – in secret –

she gave him my address. I found it completely incomprehensible, not only that they split us up, but that they were also keeping our locations secret from one another.

I had already known Mum was in Linköping. She'd phoned a few times, but didn't say what she was doing there or whether she was in contact with Dad. My new family didn't seem to know either, or else they weren't allowed to say.

The last time I'd heard from her she said she would try to regain custody of us, but it might take a while. Once you'd signed a document giving away your children, it could take several years of investigations before you got them back.

I folded up the letter and looked out at the garden patch. Robert hadn't mentioned any of the events at the abandoned cottage or with the merman, which I finally told him about, but maybe it was too painful for him to remember? We'd agreed not to tell anyone what Gerard and the others had done to him that day or how everything turned out. Not because we thought justice had been done, but to avoid a load of new investigations and being treated like victims in need of help. Of course, it hadn't helped: they still split us up.

Spring was approaching outdoors. Tulip stems were poking up through the flowerbeds. Gunnar was going round with a strimmer to tidy up the lawn. Unlike my little brother, I would never bring myself to use the term 'foster dad' about him. Nor was it my 'foster mum' who stood in the living room sorting laundry with an easy-listening radio station on. That was Annie, Gunnar's wife and the mother of Lars-Inge who was three years older than me and lived in a room in the basement.

I went to Lars-Inge's old school in the centre of town. I even had his old form teacher, a science teacher called Sonja. The pupils in the class came from the same neighbourhood of detached houses where we lived, and many of the boys knew Gunnar because he'd been their football coach in primary school. So that lent me a certain social status. Nobody was nasty to me, but they all stuck with their own kind, especially the girls in their usual cliques.

Within the family, Gunnar was the one I liked best. He wasn't talkative, worked at a factory in town and dedicated his free time to his car, a Mercedes he'd gone over and brought back himself from Germany. Occasionally he would give me strange looks, sort of as if he wanted to ask me something but couldn't quite figure out what. Annie was the one who decided I would live with them. She volunteered with the Red Cross, and suddenly one day she decided it was time to contribute to the welfare of society by taking in a girl from a problem family. Once I was there, she seemed to think it wasn't as exciting any longer; she was polite but avoided contact with me.

Instead it was Gunnar who tried to be helpful, with school and everyday problems and what I should do with my future. The day before my brother's letter arrived he told me they were looking for summer interns at his workplace, and if I was interested he would make sure my name was near the top of the list. I said yes. A summer job was a start, at any rate.

I lay down on the bed again, the place where I spent most of my time since I'd come to stay with this family. On the bedside table was my old school yearbook from Skogstorp, open to the page for Robert's class. I couldn't look at it without starting to blub. Other than an old passport photo from the booth at the Domus department store, that was the only photo I had of him. Kneeling in the front row in those incredibly ugly glasses with sellotaped arms and a plaster over one lens, surrounded by classmates who the other kids at school called idiots or retards. But still with a smile on his lips, as if he still had hope for this life in spite of everything, that things would get better sometime in the future.

Oddly enough, Ola was one of the last people I'd spoken to in Falkenberg. It was about a month after the events at the abandoned cottage, just before Robert and I were going to leave our temporary accommodation and each be sent to our new families. He was standing there waiting for someone at the Kronan shopping centre, and he said hello as I happened to walk past.

Gerard's death had already been written about in the paper —
several articles, in fact, about the tragic accident in which a young
boy suffocated when a root cellar collapsed. According to Ola, he
and Peder had been so terrified they initially didn't tell anyone
what had happened. For over a week people were asking about
Gerard, his parents and the police, their own parents, but they
didn't say a word, not until people started to direct suspicions
towards them — thinking they had something to do with his
disappearance. Then they decided to talk, but they would only
tell a simplified story about an accident. They told the police it
was a game that had got out of hand, that Gerard decided to set
fire to the root cellar, and for some reason the roof fell in on him.
They were scared they would get blamed for it, and that was why
they hadn't said anything.

Soon after that, the fire brigade dug out Gerard's body. Maybe
they came across the merman's corpse in there as well. In my
mind's eye I could see some firemen discovering the remains of
something that appeared to be a small whale, half-charred at the
bottom of a flooded root cellar, with the body of a fifteen-year-old
boy on top of it; they wouldn't have had a clue.

Neither the paper nor the local radio station mentioned anything
about it. But maybe there wasn't enough of him left for them even
to guess what it was? That's how I imagined it: his body must
have been bloated with water in there, or charred. Or his remains
ended up buried further down underneath the stuff that had caved
in and so were not discovered.

Ola told me what happened during the last few moments while
my brother and I were running for our lives. How Gerard poured
petrol over the creature, and the creature yanked him quick as a
flash into the cellar as it burned. Everything was ablaze, and finally
the cellar collapsed.

Presumably they were in a state of shock, I thought. They didn't
even try to dig Gerard out, just ran off.

It was strange to be standing there with him in the shopping centre, listening to his story. I should have hated him, I thought, for everything they'd done to me and my brother. But I did not feel any hatred. Just a sort of resignation, a sense that we were born to become who we are and never had any real choice. In the end there was something that linked us: the merman. There were only a few of us who knew of his existence. Ola was one of them, and in some strange way it tied us together.

Later that spring I found out what had happened to Dad. It was via Tommy. I hadn't had any contact with him since I left Falkenberg. I wasn't up to it. But finally I rang him up.

It was in mid-May and he sounded overjoyed to hear my voice again. He asked me a million questions about how I was doing and when we would see each other again, and I couldn't answer any of them. We were heading in different directions, I thought, and maybe we would never see each other again.

Tommy told me what he was up to, about life in Glommen, how things were at school and that he could hardly wait until school was over. He was going to get a permanent job on a boat that summer, he said, not his brothers' – he didn't want that – but on a neighbour's. He told L.G., who seemed sad I had moved away, about Jessica and Carro who had been shocked about Gerard's death for several months, about Ola and Peder who got sent to borstal in Växjö after New Year. He said he'd bumped into the Professor in town. He'd got a new temporary job at the library and was still living with his mum.

It was towards the end of our conversation that he suddenly mentioned Dad. My suspicions about that junkie guy who was at our place one evening turned out to be right. It was him and Gerard who had forced Dad to leave town. According to what Tommy had heard from his brothers, they had taken him up to Gothenburg. In the car, Gerard suddenly held a slaughterman's bolt gun up to Dad's head and pulled a woolly hat over his face, and they drove off with him to a flat somewhere. Tommy didn't know what they did to him there, but at any rate it was nasty enough to make Dad realise Gerard was capable of doing absolutely anything. Soon afterwards he cleared off. Gerard and the junkie guy took over some of his business dealings, including a whole distribution network for black-market cigarettes.

I was only half-listening to what Tommy was saying. I couldn't take in any more pain. And Dad was basically already gone from my life. Maybe he was in Gothenburg, where he knew loads of people, or maybe he was back in Falkenberg now that Gerard was gone, or maybe he was in prison? I hoped he was all right wherever he was – he was still my dad.

'Don't you want to know what happened at the abandoned cottage?' I asked when Tommy stopped talking. 'With the merman?'

Tommy hadn't said a single word about the creature, and that seemed strange after everything we'd been through.

'I don't know,' he said, 'but I figured you were there when I heard about Gerard.'

'He died saving Robert's life.'

Tommy was silent, and I realised he didn't want to talk about it any more. Maybe he was scared; maybe it had something to do with his brothers. I didn't know. But that's how it was, I thought: we would never mention what happened again. He wanted to move on with his life there in Glommen. So one story had come to an end and a new one had begun – one that no longer included Tommy.

The sounds from the house were growing stronger as his voice faded out, as if he was gradually fading and disappearing from my life. Lars-Inge calling to Gunnar from the basement. Annie rattling around in the kitchen. I had no idea how long I'd be staying here. There was just over a month until school would be out, and after that everything was up in the air.

There was only one thing I was afraid of, I thought as I sat there with the phone pressed to my ear, and that was that I might not get to see Robert again. It was so typical of my brother to forget to write his return address on the letter or to enclose a phone number where I could reach him. I was afraid that little mistakes like those could have huge consequences. That life would lead us so far apart that we'd never find our way back again. That was what terrified me. That there was no real beginning, and no real ending either.

I dreamt about my brother every night that spring, and whatever I did reminded me of him. He was the one I would choose before anyone else in any situation; he was like the whole meaning of my life. At the abandoned cottage I wouldn't have wavered for a second if I really had been faced with a choice. I would have given up the creature for Robert without batting an eyelid.

But I didn't have a chance. The creature did it for me. The merman made the choice. He was the one who got them to let Robert go; he was the one who lured them to him, even though he must have known how things would turn out.

Sometimes it was as if I didn't trust my own memories. As if I'd just imagined everything. But of course that wasn't true. The merman had existed; I'd met him and got to know him, and I was thankful. He had taught me something that could not be put into words, and I would never be able to explain that to anyone in an ordinary language.

As I lay on my bed in my room I could hear him within me. The voice that flowed through me and comforted me. And when I closed my eyes I could see him, luminescent in the water in the old root cellar... how he did tricks for me, reached out his arm and touched my hand. I could feel the warmth from his body as he floated a few inches below the surface, the warmth that filled the space, spreading into me like an ancient force. I saw the smile in his eyes, his big dark eyes, his gills, claws and that powerful tail fin... and I knew those images would be imprinted in me for the rest of my life.

The Hundred-Year-Old Man
Who Climbed Out of the Window and Disappeared
by Jonas Jonasson

Sitting quietly in his room in an old people's home, Allan Karlsson is waiting for a party he doesn't want to begin. His one-hundredth birthday party to be precise. The Mayor will be there. The press will be there. But, as it turns out, Allan will not …

Escaping (in his slippers) through his bedroom window, into the flowerbed, Allan makes his getaway. And so begins his picaresque and unlikely journey involving criminals, several murders, a suitcase full of cash, and incompetent police. As his escapades unfold, Allan's earlier life is revealed. A life in which – remarkably – he played a key role behind the scenes in some of the momentous events of the twentieth century.

'Arguably the biggest word-of-mouth literary sensation of the decade' *The Independent*

'A mordantly funny and loopily freewheeling debut novel about ageing disgracefully' *The Sunday Times*

'Imaginative, laugh-out-loud bestseller' *Daily Telegraph*

'Fast-moving and relentlessly sunny' *The Guardian*

'It should carry a health warning for spouses or partners who are easily irritated by the sounds of helpless chortling' *The Irish Times*

'First-rate' *Der Spiegel*, Germany

'Completely crazy, an incredibly funny story' *Aftonbladet*, Sweden

NOW AVAILABLE IN
PAPERBACK, EBOOK AND AUDIOBOOK

The Best Book in the World
by Peter Sternström

Two authors. One idea. Who will be the first to write the best book in the world?

Titus Jensen is waiting for his big break. But he's middle-aged, has a fondness for alcohol and never gets taken seriously.

Eddie X is cool. Eddie X is a hit with the ladies and loves being the centre of attention. A radical poet and regular on the festival circuit, he is looking for his next big project to gain more adoring fans.

One night, after a successful literary event at which Titus reads from The Diseases of Swedish Monarchs and Eddie X waxes lyrical to the thrashing tones of metal band The Tourettes, the unlikely pair get horribly drunk together and hatch a plan. There's only one thing for a budding writer to do to get worldwide recognition: write the best book in the world – a book so amazing that it will end up on all the bestseller lists in every category imaginable, thriller, self-help, cookery, business, dieting… a book that combines everything in one!

But there is only room for one such amazing book and as the alcohol-induced haze clears Titus and Eddie X both realise they are not willing to share the limelight. Who will win the race to write the best book in the world, and to what unimaginable lengths will they go to get there first…?

'Well written and enjoyable' *Aftonbladbet*

'Spot on satire' *Stockholms Fria Tidning*

'Funny, original and lovingly disrespectful' *Tidningen Kulturen*

**NOW AVAILABLE IN
HARDBACK, EBOOK AND AUDIOBOOK**

Cold Courage
by Pekka Hiltunen

When Lia witnesses a disturbing scene on the way to work, she, like the rest of the city of London, is captivated and horrified. As details unfurl in the media the brutal truth transpires – a Latvian prostitute has been killed, her body run over by a steamroller and then placed in the boot of a car to be found.

As the weeks pass and no leads are found, the story quickly disintegrates but Lia can't easily forget. So when she meets Mari in a late night bar one night she feels fate might have brought them together. Like her, Mari is a Finnish woman in London finding her way, something of an outsider, very independent. But there is much more to Mari than meets the eye: she is a psychologist who possesses an unnatural way of being able to 'read' people, see into their inner most thoughts and pre-empt their actions. She uses her 'gift' to try to help people and has formed a close unit she calls the Studio, a kind of team of investigators, who are not beyond breaking the law to put the world to rights.

Mari and Lia strike up a firm friendship and when Lia shares her plaguing thoughts about the murder, Mari thinks she and the members of the Studio can help where the police have failed. But Mari and Lia are about to set foot into extremely dangerous territory, especially as Mari has a will to control others, take vengeance on those she deems deserve it and use the Studio to unscrupulous ends.

'Rich in details, sure in its descriptions of London and smoothly written, this novel is a stylish debut.' *Turun Sanomat*, Finland

'Confident, unique and captivating thriller.' *Kaleva*, Finland

'Pekka Hiltunen hooks the reader of his new thriller from the very first page.' *Apu*, Finland

NOW AVAILABLE IN HARDBACK AND AUDIOBOOK